AN ABANDONED CHURCH . . .
A CACHE OF MISSING WEAPONS . . .
AND A WOMAN WHO WAITED IN FEAR . . .

Two small windows let in enough moonlight for Brad Spear to make out the sacristy, the room where the long-gone priests had put on their robes and where the various sacred vessels had been stored.

Nita came in and quietly shut the door after her. "I was right," she whispered, nodding across the dirty floor.

Stacked against the far wall were four cases of Springfield rifles.

Something moved in the deep blackness beside the altar.

Spear's hand swung down to his holster.

"Not smart, señor."

A gun barrel pressed into the back of Spear's neck. Nita made a move, but the voice from the darkness stopped her. "I kill him, señorita, unless you remain still."

It was Paloma. He moved around in front of them with his gun still in his hand. "I'm disappointed. I hoped for more of a struggle." He shrugged, laughing. With his gun aimed at Spear, he reached out with his free hand and pulled at the edge of Nita's blouse.

"Damn you," said Spear, "don't touch her."

"Ah, such small breasts." Paloma let go of Nita's blouse and thrust his hand into the waist of her skirt.

"Maybe her——"

"Leave her alone!" Spear lunged, reaching for the Mexican's gun hand. . . .

The Lady
RUSTLER

The Lady RUSTLER

BY CHAD CALHOUN

A Dell/Banbury Book

Published by
Banbury Books, Inc.
37 West Avenue
Wayne, Pennsylvania 19087

Dell ® TM 681510, Dell Publishing Co., Inc.

ISBN: 0-440-04628-9

Printed in the United States of America

First printing—August 1982

Chapter 1

The Texas Panhandle

Actually his troubles started in Kansas, about twenty-five miles short of Dodge City.

Brad Spear was aboard a Kansas Pacific train that was chuffing across the yellow autumn plains. It was a hot, hazy afternoon and he was being helped out of his trousers by a beautiful blonde soprano.

The young lady was kneeling in front of Spear, who sat on the edge of the satin sofa in the center of her opulent private car. She was a shade on the plump side and the frilly dressing gown that was her sole garment could not quite contain her full pink-tipped breasts.

"Whatever must you think of me, Bradley," she said as she slid one dark trouser-leg free. "To enter into carnality with such wild abandon." She paused to sigh before tugging the other pants-leg off. "What would my myriad admirers across the length and breadth of America think of me were they to learn I am but a slave of passion?"

"No need to tell 'em," Spear replied, standing and pulling the lovely blonde up to face him.

Breathing anxiously, her blue eyes half shut, she worked on the pearl buttons of his long johns. "I care not what the world thinks, I must follow the dictates of my heart. Mustn't you?"

"Not exactly my heart that's guiding me at the moment."

"Ah, yes, so I perceive." Her smooth, warm fingers closed gently around his erection as she let it free from his underwear.

Over her shoulder Spear could see a bright poster tacked up over the ornate, flowered wallpaper of the private train car. It depicted the blonde somewhat more thoroughly clothed than she was presently, with a diamond tiara sparkling in her golden hair. *Nelly Quill*, large crimson letters proclaimed, *The Girl With The Golden Throat*.

Next to the poster was a window which gave a view of the dry yellow prairie they were rolling across. The flatlands were blotched with tumbles of white bones, the remains of the buffalo slaughtered here a few years back.

"Oh, Bradley, I know full well that this time it will be even more . . . What are you gazing at, dearest?"

Spear was frowning at the trio of mounted men he'd spotted riding hard across the yellow plains toward their train. "Looks like we got company."

There came a sudden and enormous squealing, a huge clattering of metal on metal and the hissing of steam. Air brakes wheezed, the walls of Nelly Quill's private car rattled, the crystal pendants of the wall lamps tangled and tingled.

"My God!" exclaimed Nelly as she was thrown against the Pinkerton agent.

"No, but prayin' won't hurt." He took hold of her, deposited her on the sofa and sprinted toward the chair over which he'd hung his gunbelt.

The lovely singer's face was flushed, and one handsome breast had escaped completely from her gown. "What on earth is happening?"

"I hope to be back to tell you," he said, taking a step toward the rear door, his hand closed over the butt of his Colt .45.

Suddenly the rear door of the car came smashing open and a man with a double-barreled shotgun stepped across the carpeted threshold. He wore a full-length grey duster and a dented derby. His face was puffy, decorated with a week's collection of stubble and the scabs of a recent brawl.

"Well now, looks like we interrupted some mighty friendly doin's," he observed in his gravelly voice. "Get your goddamn mitt away from that shootin' iron, dude."

"Oh, Bradley, who is this dreadful man?"

"Ain't you never heard of the Walden brothers, ma'am?"

"Who?" Nelly asked. Her wide eyes fixed on him, she tucked her wayward breast back behind the lace of her dressing gown. "I know about the James boys and—"

"Naw, we're *real* train robbers." He struggled to keep his eyes on Spear and off her front. "Not a bunch of pantywaists like Frank and Jesse and those boys."

"You can still end up the way a lot of the James gang did up in Norfield," mentioned Spear, who was still standing near his dangling six-gun.

"I ain't got no more time for jawin'. Pile all your

valuables and money on that there fancy little table yonder, folks."

"Which Walden are you?" Spear asked. "Ben or Bob?"

"Neither one. I'm Scalper Bates." With his free hand he lifted his dusty derby. The top of his head was covered with a red bandana. "Run into some mean Comanches about ten years back. They took my scalp, but I lived. 'Fore I was through I got me one dozen of their scalps. Used to wear 'em in my belt till they got too gamy. Well sir, this ain't fillin' the collection plate, now is it, folks?"

Spear gave a sigh. "Reckon you'll have to give him the diamond tiara, Nelly."

She frowned. "But I—"

"What you gabbin' about, hombre?" Scalper swung the shotgun to aim right at the detective's midsection.

Spear nodded at the wall poster. "The diamond headpiece, thing she's wearing in the picture there. Made out of silver, crusted all over with big, fat diamonds."

Scalper gave the poster a quick glance. "Jesus, that looks to be worth one hell of a lot of money."

"It is," Spear assured him with a thin grin. "But we'll give it over to you if you promise not to hurt either one of us."

Scalper laughed. "Listen, I can take it even if I kick you around a few times, dude."

Shrugging, Spear said, "We'll have to trust in your honor. Nelly, fetch the tiara."

"But Bradley, I—"

"It's in the drawer of that little low table over there. Don't you remember?" He pointed at the small marble-topped table near the sofa. With emphasis he said, "Just bend over and get it."

"Oh yes, of course." Smiling nervously, she walked to the low table. Letting go of the front of her dressing gown, she leaned over and reached for the brass handle of the little drawer.

Both of her impressive bare breasts came cascading free and into view.

"Holy Christ!" exclaimed Scalper, making his first major mistake of the day. He couldn't resist staring at the singer's lovely chest. He only gazed for ten seconds or so. But that was more than enough time for Spear to whip his long-barreled .45 from his holster and fire.

The train robber yowled as the slug tore into his right arm. He cursed, tried to get off a shotgun blast at Spear.

Spear was moving. He dodged to his left, dived at the outlaw and slammed the butt of his gun into the man's temple.

Scalper groaned, swayed, dropped to one knee.

Spear brought up a knee and it crunched into the falling man's stubbled face. Smashing into the carpeting, Scalper passed into temporary oblivion.

Spear scooped the shotgun out of the man's slack fingers. "Do you have a pistol, Nell?"

"A teeny one, a derringer I carry in my muff." She was still standing at the table, one hand pressed to the gully between her breasts. "I feel so tawdry, using my bosom to distract this man."

"Get the damn pistol and stay here," he ordered as he strapped his gunbelt on over his long johns. "Shoot anybody who moves."

"Do you intend to venture into public so sparsely clad, Bradley?"

"Yep. Even though it may ruin my social standing

hereabouts." He dropped his .45 into the holster and, shotgun clutched in both hands, moved to the open back door of the private car.

The sound of gunshots came from the passenger cars at the front end of the halted train. As Spear stepped out into the yellow afternoon, he saw no one around the caboose of this Kansas Pacific. All of the activity was taking place up at the front of the train.

Nodding to himself, he tucked the shotgun under his left arm and dropped to the space between Nelly's car and the red caboose. Slowly he eased around for a look at what was occurring up ahead.

There were five horses standing beside the tracks near the engine. Four were riderless, but in the saddle of the fifth sat a lean-faced young man in buckskins. He held a Springfield rifle at the ready, his attention on the activity in the front passenger car.

Spear dodged quickly to the other side of the private car and chanced another reconnoitering glance.

A lone horseman, bearded and armed with a six-gun, was stationed four cars ahead, watching this side.

Crossing back to the other side again and making sure the buckskin lad wasn't looking his way, Spear went up the metal ladder on the side of Nelly's private car.

Don't cut a very dignified figure, he admitted to himself as he barefooted his way along the roof of the car. He jumped to the roof of the next car, flattened out and crept along on his belly.

The bearded train robber didn't notice Spear until the Pinkerton agent had leapt onto the curving top of the car he was halted beside. Quickly he swung his .44 up. "What the hell you—"

That was all he got to say. Spear had triggered off both barrels of his borrowed shotgun.

The bearded man's chest turned to a red tattered mess as he rose out of the saddle of his rearing horse. The snorting animal tripped and fell on its side. The outlaw landed on top of it, slid across its flank and crumpled into the grit and grass at the rail edge.

Spear scooted down the ladder on the dead man's side of the car. This particular car was the one the railroad set aside for low-paying customers, and it was called a Zulu car. It was packed with westbound emigrants, cooking equipment and makeshift beds. Dozens of the emigrants, including wide-eyed kids with ragged haircuts, were staring out the windows at him when he landed on the dry grass.

Spear avoided the kicking horse and took the dead man's six-gun out of his hand. Grimacing at the blood-spattered gun, he flung the weapon off into the grass.

Still five of 'em to account for, he thought, hunching over and moving forward.

While he was moving along, a series of unusual sounds reached him. First was the splintering of wood and then the deadly chatter of a machine gun. It banged away, firing several rapid bursts for a few moments. Then there was silence.

By that time Spear had reached the vicinity of the baggage car, where the noise had been coming from. He hesitated for a moment before crossing the tracks between cars.

Four of the five horses, still riderless, were galloping away across the hazy plains. The fifth horse and the youth who'd been in the saddle were sprawled beside the tracks, bloody and torn, looking as though they'd been stitched by some enormous sewing machine.

"Bit of a good show, eh?" inquired a delighted voice from within the baggage car.

The sliding side doors had been pried open, and in the opening Spear saw the tall, ruddy and blond Englishman who was his client.

"Get 'em all, Mr. Ramsey?" Spear asked flatly.

"Every bloody one," announced Peter Ramsey, patting the Gardner quick-firing gun he'd set up. "Damn clever the way I routed these churls, if I do say so myself."

"Clever," said Spear.

Ramsey stepped over a dead body, then dropped gracefully out of the car. "I surmised the ruddy beggars would eventually smash into the baggage car, don't you see?" he explained with a broad smile. "Decided to try a bit of a stratagem. Did a bunk, sneaked in here, broke out one of the Gardners and arranged a jolly good little surprise for the blighters." He noticed Spear's attire at last. "I say, Brad, old boy, you're running around in your underwear and are dappled with blood. Did you also tangle with some of these churlish desperadoes?"

"A couple," he answered. "But look, Ramsey, I was hired to protect you. If you're going to risk your damn neck every—"

"Don't be a spoilsport, Bradley lad!" Ramsey chuckled, giving him a resounding pat on the back. "I'm having a whizzer of a time and, by Jove, we're not even in Texas yet!"

"I was just thinking about that," said Spear.

Chapter 2

They'd stuck him with the Englishman nearly two weeks ago.

That had happened in New York City on a crisp, clear fall evening. Spear, a tall, wide-shouldered man in his middle thirties, had paid off his hansom cab in front of the glittering façade of Orlando's Restaurant on Fifth Avenue. As the cab went clattering away into the night, the detective took a final puff on his thin cigar before flinging it into the gutter. Even though he didn't usually deck himself out in white tie and tails as he had done tonight, Spear could've passed for one of Orlando's upper-class patrons. His clothes fit him well. His close-cropped beard added distinction to his tanned face. And yet there was something about his eyes and the outdoor look of his face that hinted he was from elsewhere and had spent a good part of his life in wilder places west of here.

The foyer was dazzling, a carnival of glass and gems. It was a large octagonal room, walled with mirrors. From its domed ceiling hung a crystal chandelier dripping with multifaceted prisms. The women waiting for tables, both the slender beautiful ones and the squat ugly ones, were frosted with jewels. Diamonds, rubies and emeralds flashed and flickered in the gaslight. Many of the tuxedo-clad gentlemen sported sedate, diamond stickpins and gleaming gold watch chains.

The two people in the foyer who noticed Spear first gave him different looks. The young, slightly plump blonde woman in the white satin gown who was waiting behind the rope barrier to be admitted noticed him and smiled. It was not a smile of recognition but of appreciation, and once she'd bestowed it, she returned her attention to the cadaverous millionaire at her side. From the headwaiter, who somehow sensed that Spear was not the heir to a fortune or even a wealthy business mogul, he got a sneer.

Spear, countering with one of his thin grins, kept on walking toward the fat little man.

The headwaiter started to turn away, busy with a note in his gloved hand.

"Beg pardon," Spear said to him.

Barely angling his head, the fat man answered, "I am afraid, sir, we have absolutely no table available this evening."

"Just point out Mr. Pinkerton's table," requested Spear, "and we can both get on with our business."

The disdain fell from the fat pink face. A smile appeared, dimpling the pudgy cheeks. Even the marcelled mustache perked up. "Ah, it is Mr. Spear, is it not?"

"It is."

"But of course, sir." He unfastened the velvet rope holding back the dozen other patrons. "Please come with me. Mr. Pinkerton has been anxiously awaiting your arrival."

Spear paused to gaze at the very pretty blonde who'd smiled his way a few minutes ago. He was close enough to admire the ample breasts swelling against the low-cut satin bodice and to inhale the sandalwood perfume she used.

A faint flush came to her cheeks, signaling that she knew she was being scrutinized. But she did not turn.

"This way, sir," repeated the headwaiter, a trace of impatience showing through.

Spear obliged.

The dining room was vast, carpeted in rich maroon. Its walls were covered with wine-colored velvet. The white tablecloths glowed, the silver settings sparkled. And on a velvet-covered dais a discreet string quartet played Mozart. There were beautiful women and portly men all around, animated chatter and laughter of varying degrees of sincerity.

"Mr. Pinkerton," announced the fat headwaiter beside a small table in midroom, "your distinguished guest has arrived."

"So he has, Maurice." William Pinkerton half rose, held out his hand to Spear. "As always, Brad, it's a pleasure to see you." He was a plump man with thick, dark hair and a substantial mustache.

Shaking hands, Spear inquired, "Your father doing well?"

"Getting crustier every year. Sure to outlive us all."

Spear sat opposite him and after the headwaiter had gone bustling off, said, "Glad to learn I'm distinguished. Did you tell him that?"

The associate director of the Pinkerton National Detective Agency laughed. "Anyone who can afford to dine at Orlando's is automatically distinguished."

Spear glanced around. "Didn't know you thought this much of me."

"Actually," said Pinkerton in a lowered voice, "I'd much prefer to dine at Hoffman House. Our new client, however, insisted on this place."

"He's joining us here?"

"After dinner for a brandy," replied Pinkerton. "Our whole dinner goes on his tab, by the way."

"Then I won't have to order à la carte," Spear grinned. "Who is our client?"

Pinkerton paused, then said, "Brad, is that striking young woman being seated yonder a friend of yours?"

Without turning, Spear responded, "Nope."

"She's certainly been eyeing you in a . . . well, cordial way. Any notion who she is?"

"According to a poster I saw up on Broadway this afternoon, she is none other than Nelly Quill, noted soprano."

"Imagine being that beautiful and having a golden voice as well."

"In a few years she'll be chubby," Spear returned. "Now, about our new client—"

"Every time we dine, women make sheep's eyes at you."

"This is the first time we've had dinner together in months."

Pinkerton said, "I remember when we lunched at the Palace out in Frisco, just before you went into the Black Hills after Judge Dalrymple. By the way, both my father and my brother Robert were quite impressed with the way you handled that case."

"I know. I was impressed with the bonus you sent."

Pinkerton smiled. "I was happy to learn you were

in the East, because this new assignment is ideally suited to you."

"Where do I have to go?"

Pinkerton cleared his throat. "Texas."

"Oh."

"You don't like Texas?"

"It's a great place, if you're a cow."

"As a matter of fact, this job involves cattle."

"It'd have to, since cows and outlaws are all they have in Texas. Who's our client?"

Folding his hands, Pinkerton said, "This isn't exactly an investigation. There is a sort of mystery to solve, but our client feels he can deal with that aspect. He wants you to serve as . . . an escort."

"A bodyguard, you mean? Or just a social companion, because that—"

"Let me explain a bit more about the situation. Our client . . . Yes, Alexis?"

A tall, thin waiter had materialized. "The gentlemen are, perhaps, ready to begin their dining experience?"

"I believe we'd like a bottle of wine first," Pinkerton told him. "How's a pinot noir sound to you, Brad?"

"Like it'll be overpriced."

Alexis said, "Ha ha," politely.

"We'll have a Chateau Perdu '73, Alexis, if you have one in your cellars."

"I believe so, Mr. Pinkerton." He bowed and vanished.

"Tell me about our client," Spear said with a hint of exasperation.

"His name is Peter Ramsey," Pinkerton imparted. "He's a Britisher, arrived in New York City from London only last week."

"First trip over?"

"I believe so, yes."

"Probably wants me to protect him from wild buffalo and savage redskins," said Spear. "No doubt all his notions about America come from dime novels such as Thomas Alexander Stormfield grinds out."

"You're jumping to conclusions, Brad. That's not smart detective work."

Spear grinned, straightening in his chair. "You're right," he admitted. "Who's financing Ramsey?"

"He represents an English outfit called Horesham Cattle Estates. Some three and a half years ago, Horesham invested three million dollars in the cattle ranch of one James Phillips in—"

"That'd be Big Jim Phillips?"

"It would. Heard of him?"

Spear nodded. "He's supposed to be tough and shrewd."

"And honest?"

"Far as I know. Ramsey and his associates have reason to suspect otherwise?"

Pinkerton coughed into his hand and looked up. "Yes, that looks fine, Alexis."

Their waiter, displaying a bottle of pinot noir, proceeded to uncork the wine and pour a splash into Pinkerton's wineglass. "Our last bottle of Chateau Perdu, sir."

Pinkerton tasted the wine, sluiced it around in his mouth, swallowed. "Yes, excellent."

Alexis filled their glasses, delicately placed the bottle upon the table and took his leave.

After sipping his wine, Spear reminded Pinkerton, "You were telling me about what's worrying the Horesham folks."

"It boils down, Brad, to the fact they've made ab-

solutely nothing back on their quite substantial investment thus far. Concern has been growing over the past
few months, and now Ramsey is here."

"What's Big Jim's story? How does he account for
the absence of profits?"

"Phillips maintains that operating expenses have
been much larger than anticipated, mainly because of
cattle rustling."

Spear rubbed at his bearded cheek. "Where's his
spread? Around Austin, isn't it?"

"Yes, just outside Tascosa, Texas."

"There is one hell of a lot of cattle borrowing going on down there," said Spear. "Local outlaws are
thriving, along with considerable gents from south of
the border."

"That's one of the things Ramsey intends to look
into."

"I'm supposed to get him there safely."

"He's unfamiliar with the country, the customs
and the dangers. The Horesham organization contacted
our New York office. I happened to be in town and I
knew you were passing through. So I got in touch with
you."

"Sort of a nursemaid chore." Spear tapped his
forefinger against the stem of his wineglass with a hint
of annoyance.

"I think the job'll prove quite lively."

"Oh, so?"

"Ramsey intends to bring a good deal of arms and
ammunition to Tascosa with him," said the agency
man. "He wants to be prepared in case there's any rus-
tler-chasing to be done."

"How much is a good deal?"

"He's been talking about at least two wagonloads." Pinkerton leaned back in his chair. "I'll let him give you the details."

"Yep," said Spear, "I'd be much obliged if he would."

Peter Ramsey kept one step ahead of Spear as they strolled along under the streetlights of Fifth Avenue. "Fascinating, city, this," he remarked, gesturing at the marbled mansions they were passing. "Nobs live like blooming kings, don't you know, while the poor huddle in tenements."

"Unlike London," said Spear.

It was a few minutes beyond midnight and a faint mist was settling over the city. Carriages were still rolling along the night streets, trailing laughter and glitter.

"Ah, Spear, you mustn't believe everything you read in the pages of our late Mr. Dickens," said the tall blond Englishman. "Why, the poor of my homeland live, when compared to those of the United States of America, in a veritable paradise."

Spear grinned thinly. "Suppose, Mr. Ramsey, you explain to me what you plan to do in Texas."

Ramsey slowed, took hold of Spear's arm. "Are we likely to see Indians?"

"On Fifth Avenue? Not likely."

"No, old man, I mean when we reach your Wild West," explained Ramsey impatiently. "I've read a good deal, you know, and I'm quite anxious to encounter Comanches and Apaches and the like."

"Few years too late," Spear told him. "Most of the Indians've cleared out, settled on reservations. After the buffalo were slaughtered, eating became a problem."

The Englishman said, "It's a bloody shame, the way you've treated your aborigines. Herding them like cattle, exterminating the poor beggars as though they weren't fit to live on this earth."

"Yep, we should've handled things the way Great Britain did with those other Indians, ones who live in India."

"See here, old chap, there is absolutely no comparison between the policies of the U.K. and those of the U.S. of A."

"Suppose," suggested Spear, "we drop the international debate and talk about your problems in Texas."

Ramsey, after a few seconds, nodded. "Horesham Cattle Estates, Ltd. is quite unhappy, as I mentioned at Orlando's, about the way things have been going in Texas. A good deal of money has been poured into the Phillips cattle empire and as yet we have seen not one bloody farthing in return on our investment."

"Big Jim has given you explanations for that."

"Oh, to be sure, the chap is quite eloquent when it comes to telling us why there's no blooming cash coming into the Horesham coffers."

"But you don't believe him?"

"The man has an excellent reputation. Naturally his background was thoroughly looked into before a single pound was invested," the Englishman said. "I don't want anyone to get the notion we've lost faith in him. My trip is simply for the purpose of determining what *is* going on. Quite possibly the situation will be exactly as Phillips has painted it."

"Which is that rustlers have hit him hard?"

"Yes, old man, that seems to be the chief cause of our lack of profits. Phillips has spun some fascinating yarns around the operations of these cow thieves. One gang of them is allegedly led by a *woman*. Fancy that, will you. A blinking lady rustler, who, judging from

Big Jim's accounts, is a combination of Robin Hood, Joan of Arc and Medusa." He laughed, rubbing his big hands together. "I'm quite keen on the idea of meeting up with the wench."

"She's probably, if she exists at all, some dumpy ex-hooker who smells like bear grease."

"Ah, Spear, I fear you have no sense of romance, old boy."

"Very little, nope," the Pinkerton agent admitted. "Why are you taking so much ammunition and so many weapons?"

Chuckling, rubbing his hands together, Ramsey replied, "If we have to go hunting for those blooming rustlers, Spear, I want to be well prepared."

"The bills of lading you showed us at dinner," said Spear as they continued along the street, "indicate you're planning to haul out enough hardware to equip a middle-sized army. Rifles, machine guns and so on."

"Yes, we'll be prepared for some lovely little battles."

"You and me? Against hard-bitten owlhoots who chew buckshot instead of tobacco?"

"I am intending, don't you know, to recruit a bit of help." Ramsey grew more enthusiastic. "From Phillips' own ranch crew to begin, and then—"

"A private army?"

Ramsey laughed. "Call it that, if you will, old boy. We're going to have a smashing time of it."

"Provided you live long enough to play general."

"Don't be such a pessimist. If you must know, I've handled chores of a similar nature before. I—"

"Where?"

"Eh?"

"Where did you run a homemade army?"

"Well, it was in India," answered the Englishman.

"I was fresh out of Cambridge, you know, and I lent an uncle of mine a hand in putting down a bit of a revolt."

"This is going to be a hell of a lot different," said Spear evenly. "Over in India you belonged to the ruling class. Down in Texas, you can bet, they aren't going to concede anything like that. Any cattle thief knows that the best he can expect when he's caught is a rope. So he's going to be damn anxious about not getting himself caught."

"I'm aware of all that, old man, which is precisely why—"

"We're going to be going up against not only local outlaws," Spear continued, "but also gents from across the border in Mexico. They don't have very much respect for *gringos* at all."

"All the more reason to carry plenty of—"

"My notion is, Mr. Ramsey, that if you go barging into Texas like a Fourth of July picnic, you're going to stir up one hell of a lot of trouble."

Ramsey halted beneath a street lamp. "Then what are you advising?"

"Leave the hardware behind. We'll go in quiet-like, take a look around."

"No, no, Spear. That simply is not my style."

"Your style is likely to get you killed," Spear countered. "Since I'm supposed to be escorting you, I wouldn't like to see that happen."

Ramsey chuckled. "Have no fear, old man. If I'm killed, no one will blame you. I'll see to that."

"Somehow," said Spear, "that doesn't cheer me up much."

Chapter 3

Spear crossed the threshold of his New York hotel room and reached for his six-gun. Then he remembered that because he was allegedly in a more civilized patch of the country and duded up as well, he'd left his Colt .45 home tonight. In another few seconds he relaxed, realizing that the figure sitting just beyond the circle of lamplight didn't pose a threat.

"Evening, Miss Quill," he said, bowing slightly in her direction and then shutting the door of his room.

"What ever must you think of me, Mr. Spear?" inquired the blonde soprano, rising gracefully up from the tufted chair. "Intruding upon you in this manner."

He grinned. "How'd you manage it? The lock hasn't been fooled with."

She reached into her satin gown and from between her handsome breasts drew out a brass key. "I, forgive me, borrowed this from the desk."

"Didn't know they made a practice of handing 'em out." He took a few steps in her direction.

"I have a certain celebrity in the East," the beautiful singer explained, dropping the key onto the claw-

foot table beside her. "People enjoy doing favors for
me."

Spear shrugged out of his fancy coat. "Excuse me,
Miss Quill, but I'm not used to being dressed up." After draping the coat over a chair back, he undid his tie
and unfastened the collar stud. "To what, as a gent
said in a play I saw the other evening, do I owe this
unexpected visit?"

She laughed, softly and a little nervously. "You
must think I'm dreadfully forward," she murmured,
watching him. "I assure you, however, Mr. Spear, that
I seldom intrude into the hotel chambers of men I do
not know. Most especially at such a late hour as this."

Spear sat in a wing chair and began tugging off
his shoes. "Might help the situation some if you were
to explain about why you're here."

"I don't know if you happened to notice, but I
was dining this evening at Orlando's with——"

"I noticed."

She took an impressive deep breath. "Forgive me,
but I couldn't help overhearing some of your conversation with the illustrious Mr. Pinkerton." Her eyes went
wide. "Is he indeed the founder of the famous detec-
tion agency?"

"Son of the founder. One of two." He dropped his
shoes on the thick Persian carpet.

Nodding, she sat again. "Let me come to the
point. I gathered, especially after that exuberant young
British gentleman joined you, that you are about to
embark on a journey westward."

"I am, yep."

"In a very short time?"

Spear paused for a moment, then told her,
"Maybe you better tell me, Miss Quill, how come my
comings and goings interest you."

"Yes, I had better." She folded her hands on her satin lap. "I am, as you possibly are aware, a professional singer of some renown."

" 'The Girl With the Golden Throat.' "

She smiled, blushing faintly. "Exactly. In a few days, you see, I am to depart from New York City to begin a tour through, you'll forgive my saying, the less civilized parts of this great Nation of ours." A look of distress touched her pretty face. "This will be my first tour of the wilder portions of America and I am . . . well, I must admit to a certain feeling of trepidation."

"Understandable. What's the first stop on your tour?"

She swallowed. "Dodge City, Kansas."

"Dodge City's one of the most wide-open, hell-raising towns west of the Mississippi."

"Yes, I am fully aware of that," said the soprano. "My manager, however, has been able to arrange financial guarantees of a most impressive kind. The journey, should I survive it, will greatly enrich me. And him."

"Were you thinking of offering me a job to look after you?"

She nodded her head vigorously. "That, indeed, is the sole purpose of my nocturnal intrusion," she confessed. "I was, let me quite candidly confess, greatly impressed with your general appearance and demeanor. Since you're going to be journeying in the same general direction as I am, it occurred to me that—"

"I am going to Dodge by train," he explained. "After that I'll be traveling by wagon over into Texas, since the rails don't run into the Panhandle yet. But I already have a client."

"I was aware of that, Mr. Spear, yet I hoped

against hope you might be persuaded to add me as a sort of, shall we say, subsidiary client."

"Afraid not," he said, standing. "One client at a time is what I can safely handle."

She stood, too, sighing. "I am greatly disappointed."

"There are plenty of detectives in New York. Some of 'em are even reliable. Have your manager hire one."

"I couldn't travel with just *anyone*."

"Then how about your manager himself? Isn't he going along?"

Her nose wrinkled. "You've never met Otto. He'd be no help at all. And he intends to remain here in New York, toiling for his other clients. I'll be venturing forth with only my maid for company and protection."

"A good hefty maid can provide a considerable amount of protection."

"If I were to travel to Dodge City on the same train as you, you'd have no objection to that, would you?"

"You'd make an interesting traveling companion, but—"

"I have my own private car and I'm certain it can be hooked up to just about any train."

"Long as I don't have to do anything official for you."

She gave a pleased laugh and threw her arms around him. "Oh, thank you, Mr. Spear." Rising on tiptoe, she kissed him on the mouth. Her warm, eager tongue parted his lips and darted inside.

Spear responded, sliding one hand down her smooth back to rest on her satin-covered buttocks. He pulled her close against him, his loins rubbing hers.

Nelly kissed his cheek, his ear, his forehead.

"What ever must you think of me, behaving in such an abandoned fashion?" she said breathlessly, her eager fingers unfastening his shirt studs.

"My opinion of you is rising," he assured her.

"So I noticed." She stopped working on the shirt to begin plucking open two sets of buttons at his crotch. In less than a minute his member was free, and she was stroking and caressing it appreciatively. She licked and teased him with her tongue as she helped him shed his trousers.

Spear got free of his shirt unaided. Then he lifted her up off the floor and carried her over to his wide four-poster bed. The window showed him the misty street far below and a lone carriage drifting by and vanishing.

"Haven't seen a man in a union suit in quite a while," she said, panting as Spear aided her out of her dress.

Spear glanced down at himself, his throbbing flesh jutting through the white cotton. "Whole lot of men don't go in for underwear at all." He quickly divested himself of the garb as Nelly removed her lacy underthings.

Her breasts were large and the nipples were already erect. When he bent and licked at them with his tongue, the young woman moaned contentedly.

She reached out, caught his head and guided him down to the center of her, warm and sweet-smelling.

Spear parted the curly blonde hair with knowing fingers, then began to use his tongue. She was already moist and soft inside, and each probe of his tongue made her shiver with expectation. And each time he thrust his tongue, he probed deeper and deeper, lingering a bit longer. Her hips rolled, and rose and fell as Spear drove her ecstasy higher and higher, until finally her fingers pulled at his hair. "I want you *now*!" she said with desperation.

He rose up and straddled her body. Nelly took hold of his erection with both hands and smoothly guided him inside her.

She surrounded his staff with a welcoming warmth. Her arms locked around him and she kissed at his face and chest.

Spear moved slowly at first, prolonging each thrust and each partial withdrawal. Slowly, gradually, he increased the tempo and the force.

Nelly groaned with pleasure, "Don't stop, don't stop!" She matched his thrusts with her own give and take.

Spear stroked even faster, in and out with a driving intensity, bringing Nelly to the brink of climax. After a seeming infinity of anticipation, he exploded within her, pumping into the center of her.

"Oh, God," she murmured, biting at his beard. "Oh, God." Her whole naked body grew taut and quivered, and at his final release she gave several spasmodic jerks and cried out with joy.

He slowed the pace of his thrusting and finally ceased, but remained inside her.

She was breathing hard and perspiration dotted her flushed face. "Going to bed with you after such a short acquaintance," Nelly said. "What ever must you think of me?"

"Nothing but the best," he replied.

Chapter 4

There was no doubt Dodge was a cow town. The smell of them was strong in the night air of Front Street. The sound of them, lowing and complaining, drifted up from the pens south of the railroad tracks.

Dodge was also a loud, glowing town, and noise and brightness came spilling out of the saloons, dance halls and gambling joints that lined the main street.

Brad Spear halted on the wooden sidewalk, leaned against a candy-stripe pole in front of a darkened tonsorial parlor and relit his cigar. He was dressed in dark trousers, shirt and vest and his holster was out in the open.

He'd been a detective for the Pinkerton Agency quite a few years and he didn't spook easily. Tonight, though, he had the notion he was being watched. So far he hadn't spotted the watcher in the crowded streets of Dodge City. He simply had a hunch there was one. As he tossed a second match into the dry, dusty street, he took a careful, narrow-eyed look back the way he'd come.

Three bowlegged cowboys came tottering out

through the swinging doors of the Long Branch Saloon, the one in the middle laughing uncontrollably and hugging his middle. The other men, in dusty cowhand clothes, went ambling off toward the Dodge Theatrical Palace. A dance hall girl, hands on plump hips, was arguing with a red-headed muleskinner in front of a place that was spewing brassy music out into the warm night. None of them seemed to be paying any attention to Spear.

But ever since the train had pulled into Dodge, close to sundown, Spear'd been feeling uneasy. Leaving Peter Ramsey to supervise the unloading of the Englishman's portable arsenal, he'd escorted Nelly Quill to her suite at the Imperial Plaza Hotel, which was nowhere near as elegant as its name.

He'd had dinner, alone, at a small restaurant named simply Mom's. If Mom had served her own kin many meals like the one he had tried to down tonight, they must all long since be under the sod, Spear thought.

Tapping his chest as he recalled the longhorn steak, Spear moved on.

Hardly anybody knew I was coming here, he reminded himself. So it's unlikely they could've rigged up any sort of reception committee.

They did know Ramsey was due, however. It was just possible there were folks down in Texas who'd be mighty pleased if nobody connected with the Horesham Cattle Estates, Ltd. ever reached there. Their feelings would no doubt be extended to any Pinkerton agent who was accompanying Ramsey.

And don't forget Nelly, he thought to himself.

The golden-haired soprano had pushed right into things. She arranged circumstances so she'd travel to Dodge on the same train as Spear. She knew a hell of a lot about what he and the Englishman were up to. Spear had a pretty realistic notion of himself; he knew that most women, a satisfactory number anyway, found him attractive. Nelly's interest in him might well be, as she'd assured him several times since they'd met in New York, a purely physical one.

"Or she could be conning me," he said softly to himself.

He pushed up the brim of his Stetson with his thumb, shaking his head. Maybe he just needed a dose of tonic.

He came to the cross street he was seeking and turned to the left. Light was slanting out of the open doorways of the Meech Brothers Livery Stables & Wagoners. There was wheezy concertina music coming from in there, too.

Glancing once around, Spear entered.

A small, wiry man with a grizzled set of whiskers was perched atop a bale of straw, squeezing a tune out of a battered and faded concertina. "Oh, I am a lonesome cowboy, bound for the Western plains," he sang in a rapsy voice. "Oh, I am . . . Evenin', pilgrim." He winked at Spear. "Ain't this the awfullest singin' you've ever heard in all your born days?"

"Comes pretty near to being," nodded Spear, crossing the straw-strewn dirt floor toward the older man. "Why do you do it?"

"His Lordship out back claims to like it." He jerked a stained thumb in the direction of the rear door. "Says as how it's right authentic."

"That'd be Mr. Ramsey?"

"*Mister?* Heck, I figured he was a Lord Ramsey or a Sir Ramsey at the very least."

"Are you one of the Meech brothers?"

"Hell, no." The bewhiskered man jumped off the

bale, his squeeze-box gurgling. "Name of Seamus Tuck, best damn bullwhacker in these parts." He spat on the floor. "Or any other parts, for that matter. You the Pink?"

"Yep. Name of Brad Spear."

Tuck's left eye came near to closing. "Don't go funnin' an old-timer," he warned, holding out his hand. "Well sir, even if you is a smart aleck, I'm pleased to meet up with you."

Spear shook hands. "You'll be driving a wagon, huh?"

"Hell, I'm the head man," explained Tuck. "I drive the head wagon, look after the horses, get you dudes to Tascosa safe and sound, palaver with wild Injuns should we meet any, sew your scalp back on for you should they get rough, skin any buffalo as needs it, and sing you several dozen authentic little ditties."

"Sure sounds like you'll be worth whatever it is Ramsey's paying you." Spear crossed the building toward the corral area out back.

"Not enough, is what he's paying me," said Tuck.

Two covered wagons stood out in the fenced area. Beneath a kerosene lantern that dangled from a high fence pole stood the blond Englishman. His hair was disheveled, his face flushed. "Jolly good," he was saying, mostly to himself and not to the two men who were finishing up the loading. "Jolly good indeed. Ah, hello there, Spear old fellow."

Spear joined him. "Who're the gents doing the work?"

"Couple of industrious blokes recommended by the stablemen."

"Not part of the crew going with us?"

"No, old man. Only Tuck and an associate of his will be making the journey to Texas."

Spear nodded. "Meaning these fellows'll be staying in Dodge and talking about what an impressive collection of guns and ammunition we're hauling."

The Englishman blinked. "Well, a good many of the town's people know that already, since just about everyone saw the goods being drayed from the depot here."

"True." Spear leaned against the fence. "We're pulling out at dawn, aren't we?"

"Bright and early," answered Ramsey. "I must say, you know, I'm deucedly excited about this whole venture. In fact, I'm hoping we get a chance to do battle with some blooming rustlers."

"And a chance to get our heads blown off?"

"No venture of this sort is without hazard, Spear," Ramsey declared. "One must be prepared to take risks."

"Just so you don't go charging into anything until you're sure of the setup," advised Spear, dropping his cigar to the ground and grinding it under the heel of his boot.

"I say, Spear," said Ramsey, "I know you poohpoohed the stories of a mysterious and beautiful lady outlaw who rustles cattle, but I've been hearing tales again here in Dodge."

"Suppose we wait and see," he replied. "Might be we're going to tangle with a whole regiment of beautiful lady crooks, or it might be we'll only be up against the usual ugly men."

"I suppose that's sound advice. Yet I can't help speculating about this lady, wondering what she's like."

"Think I'll bunk down here tonight."

Ramsey glanced around the corral. "Here, old man? Is there something wrong with your room at the Dodge House? If it is lacking in any way—"

"Room's fine. Even the cockroaches are the handsomest I've seen in many a day," Spear assured him. "I want to keep an eye on our hardware."

Ramsey rubbed the side of his nose with a forefinger. "I've already arranged for Tuck to spend the night on guard."

"Good. We can while away the time singing the old songs."

The Englishman chuckled. "You're rather a stubborn chap. Remind me of a colonel I knew in India. . . . Ah, but I see the lads have finished their labors."

While Ramsey paid off the two men, Spear remained leaning against the fence. The sounds of merriment drifted through the night from Front Street, mixed with an occasional scream and an occasional burst of gunfire.

It happened a few minutes shy of three a.m. What saved Spear was the fact he wasn't where he was supposed to be.

The buzz-saw sounds of Seamus Tuck's snoring inside the dark stable hadn't kept Spear from dozing off. What awakened him on his bedroll bunk inside one of the loaded wagons was the single nervous whinny of one of the horses in the stalls—the whinny and a faint scraping sound. The sound a boot sole makes on hard earth.

He eased out of his makeshift bed, plumped it up to look like he was still in it, and dropped his nearby Stetson over the place where his head was supposed to be. He backed out of the rear of the wagon and into the darkness.

The wagon barely creaked a moment later when a slim dark figure climbed up over the tailboard.

Spear couldn't make out much about the slender, boyish figure that was looming over the place where he was supposed to be sleeping. As he'd anticipated, his nocturnal visitor mistook the blankets and hat for him. He couldn't make out the flash of the knife in the darkness, but he saw the slender arm rise and fall.

"Those blankets aren't in need of ventilation," he said aloud, drawing his .45.

There was a surprised gasp, and something came whizzing by Spear's head. The dark silhouette quickly fell away from the rear of the covered wagon.

Spear had dodged, banging into one of the fence posts. He untangled himself and dove at the wagon.

The slender, dark figure was running back into the stable.

"Hold on," warned Spear, sprinting in pursuit, "or I'll drop you!"

Five long strides into the dark cavern of the building and he collided with something. He stumbled to his knees.

"Hell's fire! What's goin' on?"

Tuck had come running for the corral from his bed of straw and put himself smack in Spear's path.

"Move!" Spear ordered, getting to his feet and skirting the wagon driver. He ran for the front door.

There was no sign of his assailant outside, only darkness and stillness. A quarter of a mile or so away a dog barked unenthusiastically a few times.

Holstering his gun, Spear went back inside. He grabbed a lantern off the wall and lit it.

Tuck was brushing straw from his bedraggled suit of red flannel long johns. "Am I havin' a nightmare or did a herd of folks go barrelin' through here?" he asked, his bloodshot eyes blinking rapidly.

"Herd consisted of two," Spear said. "Me and somebody who tried to knife me."

"Knife you? What the devil for? I thought we was guardin' against thieves, not murderers."

Carrying the lantern, Spear returned to the corral. "Wanted to kill me, then you. After that, haul our guns and ammunition off."

The older man shivered as he came barefooting out into the night chill. "Kind of excessive, ain't it? Slicin' both of us up," he observed. "A couple conks on the noggin'd put us out of the way just as good."

"Some folks don't mind killing." He explored the area he'd been standing on when the knife was thrown at him.

"How many of 'em was they?"

"One."

"Just one, and he was fixin' to knock us both off and steal the limey's fireworks?"

Spear found the knife in the dirt near a fence post. "Looks like an old buffalo skinner's knife," he said, examining the long, sharp weapon.

"That's what she is, sure enough," confirmed Tuck, teeth chattering. "I got a glimpse of that feller you was chasin'. Now that I think of it, he wasn't husky enough to've been in the skinnin' trade. Matter of fact . . ."

"What?"

"Well sir, I didn't get a real good look." Tuck scratched his whiskers. "But that feller was built mighty slight, slight as a gal. Sound too loco for you?"

"Nope," said Spear. "Nothin' sounds too loco in this town."

Chapter 5

Ramsey, smiling broadly, brought her in out of the morning.

She was a good-looking woman of twenty-eight, tall and red-haired. Even though she was wearing a man's checkered shirt and a simple tan riding skirt, her femininity showed through. She carried a small suitcase.

Spear had just finished saddling the sorrel mare he was going to be riding. He slid his rifle into the saddle boot and came walking across the stable to the new arrivals. "Who's the lady?" he asked the Englishman.

"Allow me, old man, to introduce Mrs. Molly Cartland," Ramsey said. "Mrs. Cartland, this is Brad Spear."

She held out her hand.

Spear ignored it. He took hold of Ramsey's shoulder and urged him out into the corral yard, past Seamus Tuck and his long, lanky associate hitching up the last team of horses.

"I say, Spear, you're behaving like a ruddy boor," the Englishman informed him, "being rude to the charming Mrs. Cartland."

"Who is she?"

"I just introduced you—"

"I mean, why the hell did you bring her here?"

Ramsey took a step away from him. "See here, old boy, the lady happens to be in need of transportation to Tascosa." He squared his shoulders. "I encountered her last evening at the hotel restaurant after leaving you here. When I heard of her sad plight, I quite naturally offered—"

"Where's Mr. Cartland?"

"That's part of the problem. Her spouse journeyed out to Texas over three months ago. Seems the loving couple have the title to some fifty thousand acres of free government land. At any rate, her husband went on ahead to look the spread over and make arrangements for them to take up residence." Ramsey shrugged. "She's had no word of the chap since."

"All of which has nothing to do with us."

"I know that, old man, but she's all alone. I hate to see a charming lady put up with the rigors of stagecoach travel when I can provide—"

"This isn't exactly a church picnic we're going on."

"She's fully aware of that," Ramsey responded with a frown. "I must say, old man, you seem quite on edge this morning. Perhaps sleeping in this blooming stable's made you a bit jumpy."

"Quite early this morning," said Spear, "someone snuck in here and tried to kill me."

"Eh?" Ramsey's hand came up to his mouth. "Are you jesting?"

"Not a joke, nope. Somebody was aiming to sink a knife in me. And maybe in Seamus Tuck as well."

"In order to steal the weapons?"

"I didn't get much chance to discuss motives."

After a few seconds the Englishman smiled. "Well, old man, you've quite obviously survived. Annoying to be attacked in the wee small hours, I admit, yet you've come smiling through. Did you manage to apprehend your attackers?"

Spear held up a forefinger. "Just one attacker, who got clean away."

Ramsey glanced toward the attractive woman in the stable doorway. "Now surely you don't think Mrs. Cartland is in any way connected with what happened?" he asked. "I mean to say, the lady is quite obviously exactly what she says. A woman most anxious to locate her husband. I fear, though I didn't voice my suspicions to her, that her husband may have long since been dry-gulched or bushwhacked. Such things do go on with some frequency in these parts, do they not?"

"Yep," Spear answered. "Now look, Ramsey, I'd feel a whole lot easier in mind if you'd tell the lady she better go by stage."

"Can't, old man." Ramsey gave a stubborn shake of his head. "She has my word. The word of a Ramsey is unimpeachable."

"Okay," Spear agreed. "Let her come along, then."

"I'm glad you're being sensible at last."

"Sensible may not be quite the right word."

Seamus Tuck spat to his left, then flicked his twelve-foot leather whip with his left hand, producing a loud snap. "Goddamn your miserable hides! Get movin'!" he shouted. He was in the lead wagon, urging the three teams of sturdy horses to move faster through the dusty early morning street of Dodge City. The whip cracked twice again, never quite hitting any of the broad flanks.

"You flea-bitten bastards! Move!"

In the second wagon, huddled behind the lanky young man who was handling this team, sat Ramsey and Molly Cartland.

"Jolly, isn't it?" beamed Ramsey. "So blooming colorful?"

"It is," said Molly, shifting slightly on the bedroll that served as a seat for her. "Colorful, though not especially comfortable."

"Eh? Let me fetch you a quilt out of the trunk."

"No, thanks. I don't want to make any more trouble."

"No trouble, dear lady." Moving on hands and knees, Ramsey worked his way deeper into the tightly loaded canvas-topped wagon. "We've a long trek ahead of us and you might as well be comfortable," he called.

"I'm afraid your Mr. Spear already thinks I'm too much trouble."

"He's rather a dour chap." He managed to reach a hump-backed trunk. "Highly efficient at his work, of course, but a bit on the gloomy side, don't you know."

"Perhaps he's right and I'm simply in your way."

"Not at all, not at all," Ramsey assured her while struggling with the lock. "You are, quite frankly, a welcome addition to our little caravan." With a grunt he got the trunk lid lifted. "Spear is, after all, considerably jaded. He can't appreciate the grandeurs of this marvelous country as you and I can."

Molly laughed softly. "I don't know if I'm in an appreciative mood any longer myself. When Sam and I first came westward, I—"

"Sam's your wayward husband?"

"Samuel Edward Cartland," she said, nodding. "We were married in Philadelphia three years ago. I grew up there, but Sam had been living and working in Texas and Kansas ever since he was twenty or so."

Tugging out a padded, tufted quilt, Ramsey said, "How old is the gentleman at the moment?"

"Forty-six," she answered, touching her knuckle to the corner of her eye. "In fact, his birthday fell just a week back. It's the first one since we were married that we didn't spend together." She sniffed, rubbing more vigorously at her eye.

"Here, here. I'm sure we'll run into the blighter ... I mean, the chap, once we reach Texas." With the quilt clutched against his chest, Ramsey started making his way back through the cases of shells, guns and explosives. "Ruddy shame your railroad trains don't run any farther than Dodge City. This final leg of the journey shan't be too rapid."

She extracted a lace-trimmed handkerchief from the pocket of her riding skirt. "I'd been looking forward to settling down on a spread of our own." She dabbed at her eyes.

Ramsey settled in beside her in the cramped wagon. "Forty-six, did you say the fellow is?" He fashioned the quilt into an improvised bolster.

"Yes, Sam is nearly twenty years my senior." She tilted forward so he could fit the folded quilt between her and the nearest crate. "I seem to be drawn to mature men."

"Only twenty-nine, myself," he revealed. "Must strike you as a babblin' infant."

"Not at all, Mr. Ramsey." She smiled and tucked the damp handkerchief away. "You're a gentleman who is obviously wise beyond his years."

"Really? Yes, well, nothing like a spell in India to mature a chap. Friend of mine, chap by the name of Guthrie, had his hair turn white overnight after a bit of a row with some of the Thugs. He was barely twenty-four at the time."

"Your maturity is more of the interior sort," Molly told him.

He nodded in agreement. "This is going to be a jolly trip," he sighed. "Jolly."

Spear was riding alongside the first of the two wagons. He scanned the false-front buildings on either side of Front Street as they rolled toward the edge of town.

Up on the balcony of a bright yellow bordello a young lady with shiny blonde hair was hanging some very frilly black lingerie over the wooden railing to dry. She noticed Spear and waved, her silken kimono parting to reveal a small pert breast.

He tipped his hat.

"Sodom and Gomorrah," observed Seamus Tuck.

"Not quite that bad," Spear said to the wagon driver.

"Worse," said Tuck, spitting through his whiskers. "They didn't have whores washin' their underwear in public in Sodom. Leastwise, if they did, the Bible don't say a dang word about it. And that lass ain't no more than sixteen. Shameful. Gal ought to be least eighteen before she starts sellin' herself professional."

"Speaking of ladies, what do you know about Mrs. Cartland?" Spear asked.

"I probably know more than I'll tell ya."

Spear grinned. "She's been staying in Dodge, according to her, for a spell. Heard anything about her?"

Tuck said, "She ain't been walkin' the streets or robbin' the poor box at the Union Church."

"That's comforting news. Who's she been friendly with?"

"Nobody, far as I know." He eyed Spear. "It sure wasn't her as tried to skin you last evenin'."

"Apparently not."

Spear drew away from the lumbering wagon and rode along parallel to it at a distance of a dozen feet.

On the rickety side of a livery barn at the edge of town, a skinny youth was slapping up a big new poster.

See Nelly Quill! it urged.

"Not bad advice," Spear said to himself. "But I won't be able to follow it right yet."

Chapter 6

Thomas Alexander Stormfield removed his high hat, wiped at his prodigious forehead with his handkerchief and sighed warmly. "This part of Texas," he observed as the buckboard bounced along, "is not noted for its variety, I imagine."

"Nope," agreed the leathery little cowhand who was driving the two-horse team.

Stormfield returned his hat to his perspiring head, tugged at his mutton chop whiskers and gazed around him forlornly. They were surrounded by a never-ending expanse, an endless, hazy yellow flatness that quivered in the hot morning sun. "A forestation project would work wonders in these parts," he declared. "'Twould provide shade for one thing and give the weary sojourner something besides grass to contemplate while wandering across this monotonous inferno. The trees might even attract birds, whose songs would cheer—"

"Already got birds." The driver jerked a thumb up at the vast, glaring blue sky.

Squinting, Stormfield looked upward. "Vultures,"

he noted, recognizing the distant circling creatures. "I had more in mind songbirds, their lilting songs to lift the jaded traveler's heavy heart."

"Had a canary once."

"Indeed?"

"Died."

"A pity." Stormfield shifted on the uncomfortable seat, wiped his face again with his wrinkled linen handkerchief. "Looking on the bright side, I suppose this is all grist for the mill. Yes, I can use this bleak countryside in my new series of dime novels."

"Read at one of them books of yours once."

"Ah?" The portly author smoothed at his candy-stripe vest. "Did you enjoy the experience?"

"Some."

"I see." He coughed. "Which of my myriad titles did you peruse?"

"Hum?"

"Which book did you read at?"

"Can't remember exactly. 'Cept it had 'Masked' in the title."

"Could it have been, perhaps, *Fearless Phil, the Masked Revenger of the Wild West; or, The Code of the Plains*?"

New wrinkles appeared on the driver's wrinkled face. "Nope."

"Then it might have been *Bison Billy, the Masked Swordsman of South Dakota; or, Nearly Scalped by Red Men*?"

"Nope."

"Can you, perchance, have read the initial novel in my latest series of epics? It is entitled, simply, *Sweetwater Sid, the Masked Texas Avenger; or, Trapped Among the Long Horns*."

"That's it, sure enough."

Stormfield absently reached back to pat the topmost of his suitcases. "Did you enjoy the tome?"

"Hum?"

"Like the book?"

"Some," the driver admitted. "But I can tell you where you went wrong."

Rubbing at his plump midsection, the novelist invited, "By all means, do, sir."

"You made the print too little," replied the cowhand. "Give me a headache readin' it. Had to hold the goddamn book up next to my nose and scrunch my eyes all up."

"Yes, I see." Stormfield sighed. "Unfortunately, I have no control over the makeup or typography . . . over the size of the print."

"What I could make out wasn't all that bad."

"Thank you." Stormfield locked his hands around one knee. "How much longer before we reach the Tumbling W Ranch?"

"We reached it more than an hour ago, when we passed through that gate in the barbed-wire fence." He indicated the surrounding landscape. "Mr. Wilbur Rudd owns everything you can see. Over one hundred thousand acres."

"A substantial domain."

"Ain't bad for a small spread."

"Where exactly does Mr. Rudd's domicile lie?" Stormfield inquired.

"Hum?"

"The ranch house. How far are we from it?"

"Ain't far."

"In miles?"

" 'Bout twenty."

The portly novelist sighed once again.

* * *

The ranch house was a sprawling one, made of adobe and timber. There was a lone tree standing in the front yard. Reclining under the tree in a very small patch of afternoon shade was an ancient brown dog. He opened blurry eyes and barked feebly when Stormfield disembarked from the buckboard.

"Be silent, noble animal," advised the author, stretching and then wincing at the resultant creaks his body produced. "Ah, I fear I am nearly too old for endless traveling on a hard plank. And you, sir, must be my host."

From the shade of the wide veranda a tall, rawboned man of sixty-one had emerged. He was dressed in faded blue jeans and wore a grey high-crown Stetson. "I'm Wilbur Rudd." He came down the wooden steps holding out his hand. "Mighty pleased to have an author of your reputation as our house guest for a spell."

"I truly appreciate your allowing me to abide with you while gathering material for my latest series of epic novels." He shook the rancher's worn hand, bowing slightly. " 'Tis most gratifying that a mutual friend of ours was able to arrange all this."

"That's so," agreed Rudd. He leaned close to Stormfield and whispered, "We can talk over our real business inside."

"To be sure," smiled Stormfield.

"Want I should bring them suitcases inside, Mr. Rudd?" The driver was squatting beside the ancient dog and patting its neck fondly.

"When you get a chance, Piet. Bring 'em to Aunt Kate's room."

"I hope I'm not forcing one of your family members to decamp in order to accommodate me."

"Aunt Kate ran off with a snake oil salesman

three years ago," explained his host. "We still call that bedroom after her, though. C'mon in."

Once inside the cool breezeway Stormfield became aware of the tinkling—slightly off-key—of a piano in some distant room. "One of your offsprings is a musician?"

"That's Maude, my oldest daughter." Rudd beckoned Stormfield to follow him. "You can meet her later. She's back with us for a spell. Keeps getting widowed."

"An unfortunate tendency."

"Her last husband, name of Rusty Baumhofer, got himself trampled to death in just about the last buffalo stampede in these parts." Rudd shook his head. "Always was an unlucky cuss."

He opened a door and stood aside so the author could enter a spacious bedroom. The bed was sturdy, wooden-framed. There were three wood-and-leather chairs and a hefty bureau in the room as well. The high, narrow windows showed an endless vista of prairie.

"Much better accommodations than I could have procured in Tascosa," observed Stormfield while glancing around the room approvingly.

"You can't live well in Tascosa unless you're a whore," said Rudd, shutting the door. "Do you have some sort of official identification with you, Mr. Stormfield?"

Stormfield placed his high hat atop the bureau. "I would prefer you did not inform your family of my other calling." He reached into a breast pocket of his coat.

"Haven't told a soul, don't intend to. Only Maude and my boy, Leon, live here now anyway. Mrs. Rudd's in St. Louis seeing to the burying of an uncle."

"Sad."

"Not especially, since he was a certified son of a bitch and he looks to've left the missus around one hundred thousand dollars."

"We often find a little ray of sunshine in even the darkest of tragedies," Stormfield said with a restrained smile. "Here you are, sir." He passed the ranch owner a wallet packed with an impressive array of official documents.

Rudd studied them. "Yep, you're sure enough with the United States Secret Service." He handed the papers back. "You can keep pretending to be a writer as long as you're here, though."

"Sir, I *am* a writer," corrected Stormfield, drawing himself up straight. "Novel upon novel has sprung from my fertile pen. Indeed, even while I am under your hospitable roof and investigating the matter you and our government wish to have investigated, I shall be producing reams of prose for my next opus. It is to be entitled *Sweetwater Sid's Lucky Draw; or, The Bandit Queen of Texas*."

Rudd sat down in one of the chairs. "You're like to get some firsthand stuff around here. We got us a lady rustler who's been playing hell with the herds."

Rubbing his hands together, Stormfield began to pace the floor. "Yet you don't believe, according to what you wrote to Washington, sir, that this reckless young woman is involved in the disappearance of Elisha Klein."

"Nope, I don't," Rudd replied. "Fact is, your Mr. Klein was sort of friendly with this Anita Torquay."

"Friendly with an outlaw?"

"I believe she was passing him information."

"You mean this distaff bandit queen knew Klein was a U.S. government agent?"

"I'm not sure about that," the rancher confessed. "See, Klein was posing as the representative of an Eastern banking concern. He was staying at a boarding house in Tascosa and riding out into the countryside to talk to various cattlemen. Idea being he was looking for sound investments for some back East dudes."

"A plausible subterfuge."

"Maybe yes, maybe no. My guess is somebody tumbled he was a Secret Service man."

"Meaning he is no longer among the living?"

Resting a palm on his knee, Rudd leaned forward. "You'll be one hell of a lot safer around here, Mr. Stormfield, if you figure he's dead," he advised. "Figure that whoever did him in will want to do the same damn thing to you, if they get wise to what you're really up to."

Nodding, Stormfield sat on the edge of his bed. "We know that someone, over the past year and more, has been highjacking ammunition and weapons intended for the various military outposts in the Panhandle. Those same weapons often end up in the hands of Mexican bandits and cattle rustlers who strike into Texas from south of the border. The Secret Service is most anxious to have this unsavory trade curtailed and ceased. Acting on information that some of this highjacking and smuggling of weapons may be centered in the Tascosa area, Elisha Klein, a personable young man with a knack for handling himself well in rough spots and tight corners, was dispatched here. You, because of certain connections with officials in Washington, were the only person who knew the real nature of Mr. Klein's business."

"I didn't tell anyone, if that's what you're implying!"

"Tut tut, sir, I am merely reviewing the facts,"

Stormfield assured him. "You are above reproach." He steepled his fingers against his chest. "Had Klein, before he disappeared two months ago, confided in you? Did he give any indication of who it was he suspected?"

The rancher gave a sad shrug of his wide shoulders. "He played things close to the vest. Leastways, when it came to sharing any of his suspicions with me."

"What do you think? On your own?"

"Well sir, I've never liked Big Jim Phillips," said Rudd, mouth tightening. "Although most everybody else in these parts thinks he's foursquare and as honest as they come." He shrugged again. "There's just something about the man I don't cotton to. That isn't proof of anything. And Klein never mentioned having any doubts about Big Jim."

"You also don't think this lady rustler did away with Klein?"

Rudd shook his head. "Nope. Tell you something. Could be she isn't anywhere near as black as she's been painted."

"I intend to find out," said Stormfield.

Chapter 7

Spear sat up, wide awake. He shed his blankets, rolled them up neatly, and then picked up his Stetson from where he'd deposited it when he'd turned in three hours before. The sky was a deep, clear black, heavy with glittering stars and a thin crescent moon gleaming silver. It ought to be about midnight, he thought.

Standing, Spear fished out his pocket watch. "Yep, five past twelve." He stretched, yawned and went walking toward the campfire. He'd awakened right on time for his shift.

The two big wagons rose up beside the fire like a pair of dark, slumbering monsters.

Seated on a log near the small fire was Molly Cartland. She smiled tentatively when she noticed his approach. "Midnight already?"

"Little past." He squatted down a few feet away from the red-haired woman. "Your watch's over, ma'am."

"I'm not especially tired. Would you mind if I sat up with you on your shift for a bit?"

Spear shrugged.

Molly folded her hands in her lap. "We've been traveling together for weeks now," she remarked, "and in another day or so we'll reach Tascosa."

"True," he agreed, arranging himself on the ground and glancing out at the surrounding darkness.

A hunk of firewood suddenly sputtered and crackled.

Molly paused for a moment, listening to the sound of the flames, then said, "I haven't been any trouble, I've pulled my own weight. I've done my share of cooking, taken my turn at watching."

"Maybe when we hit town we can have 'em strike off a medal for you."

She made an angry snorting sound, rose to stand over him. "You're the most exasperating son of a bitch I've run into in six states."

"Thank you, ma'am." He grinned up at her, pushing the brim of his hat back with his thumb.

Giving a frustrated sigh, she slapped her palms against her thighs and walked a few paces away. Turning around, with the firelight reflected in her red hair, she said, "Why is it you don't like me, Spear?"

"I don't dislike you, Mrs. Cartland," he told her amiably.

"Then why can't we at least carry on a civilized conversation?"

"I was hired to look after Ramsey," he answered in a quiet voice. "See to it he gets to Tascosa safely, along with all this damn artillery of his. It's a twenty-four hour a day job."

"I'm certainly not keeping you from doing your duty."

"I don't just worry about trouble coming at us from outside sources."

"Oh, I see," she said in a sarcastic tone. She came

close to him once more, knelt on the ground. "You've got me tagged as a spy or some such thing, someone who's along to do Peter harm."

"That possibility has occurred to me," admitted Spear. "Until it gets proved true or false, well, I intend to keep an eye on you. While keeping my distance."

"You're being ridiculous," she said angrily. "What about that old goat Seamus Tuck and his half-wit partner, Wally Anderson? How do you know they aren't spies?"

"I don't."

She shook her head, red hair brushing her shoulders. "Your work has ruined you. You go through life suspecting every living creature, not trusting a single soul. That's an awful way to live."

Spear said nothing.

"You remind me of my husband, you're just like him," she said.

"Only a mite younger."

"Every woman doesn't want to marry a boy with peach fuzz on his cheeks. An older man has many things a young man can't offer. Anyway, you're not all that young yourself. In your middle thirties at least."

"Be sprouting a long grey set of chin whiskers before I know it."

"Having a conversation with you is just about impossible," she complained.

"That being the case, Mrs. Cartland, why don't you turn in for the night?"

"You seem to delight in calling me missus all the time."

"That's why you horned in on this jaunt, isn't it? Because you're Mrs. Cartland and you're anxious to run down Mr. Cartland?"

"You could still call me Molly."

"Okay, Molly, suppose you head for your bunk."

She laughed. "You seem to have been telling Peter some tall tales. He has the ridiculous notion you're quite the lady's man. I find you quite the opposite."

"Only works with certain ladies."

Molly leaned toward him. "I suppose, then, I'm not the sort of woman you waste your time on? No, I imagine you prefer the sort you can buy at the nearest brothel. That way—"

"Ma'am," he said, taking hold of her wrist because he had a hunch she was working up to slap him. "I'm not the kind of gent you can argue and squabble into bed. Not that I don't enjoy trading nasty remarks with you, but I have to warn you it won't lead any place."

"Why, you arrogant son of a bitch! If you think I'd ever so much as . . ." She swung her free hand hard, intending to smack him across the cheek.

Ducking, Spear caught that hand, too.

Molly stayed taut and angry for several silent seconds, then leaned and pressed her lips against his. After a long, thorough kiss, she moved her mouth from his lips to his ear and whispered, "We don't have to quarrel, Brad."

He used his left hand to push aside her jacket and undo the buttons of her checkered shirt. She was, as he'd realized a few moments earlier, wearing nothing beneath the shirt. Her breasts were small and dusted with freckles. The sharp, upright nipples were dusky.

Spear closed a rough hand over her right breast, squeezing at it. The nipple grew firmer as he stroked it between his fingers. Doffing his hat, he bent and took the nipple deftly between his teeth. He slid his hand down her warm, smooth skin toward her stomach, around her waist, and down to the soft, naked flesh of her full buttocks.

Molly sighed, tangling both her hands into his dark hair as he moved his hand around to probe her triangle, forcing his middle finger into the moist, soft center of her.

"Don't wait, don't wait," she pleaded. "Take me now. Now, please!"

Lifting up the red-haired woman, Spear carried her away from the glow of the fire. He placed her gently on the ground near his bedroll. Spreading out the blankets swiftly, he set her upon them.

Molly got quickly out of her shirt and skirt, already half removed. And when his staff emerged from his trousers, she fondled it with both hands and took it into her mouth. After wetting it completely, she settled back on the blanket. "Now," she begged softly.

Spear entered her easily. She murmured and locked her long, smooth legs around him. He went in deep and hard, thrusting into her vigorously.

"Don't stop. Don't stop ever . . ." she said through gasps of pleasure.

They climaxed together and the intensity of it shook her body from head to toe.

Spear slowed, but didn't withdraw. He pulled the tangle of blankets around them.

Molly smiled against his chest. "You're not such a son of a bitch after all," she said, breathless.

About a half-hour before dawn, Spear was sitting alone and fully dressed near the campfire. There was a chill stillness all around him and he had the collar of his sheepskin coat turned up.

Maybe Molly Cartland was right about one thing.

He was getting along in years. Not old or even middle-aged, but just not young anymore.

Could be it was time he settled down. Hell, when his dad was the age Spear was now, he'd been married for years and had three sons. Thing was, Dad wasn't a footloose man. Nope, he was content to work the lumber camps of Oregon year after year, build a house and raise a family. He'd died fairly young, in a stupid lumber camp accident, and that was that. Being steady and honest hadn't brought him much.

Spear adjusted his collar, watching the fire.

There was something about being awake during the darkest hours of the night that got you to thinking on the gloomy side. You thought about people you'd loved who were dead and gone, about women you hadn't seen in years. Even about what the hell your life was all about and what it added up to. If anything.

Spear had been a Pinkerton agent a good many years now. Started when he was hardly out of his teens. Sometimes he did think about getting into some other line of work, but nothing ever came along that interested him as much. He didn't have too many illusions about what he was doing. He wasn't burning up with faith in his mission the way some preachers claimed to be. He simply did what he had to do, pretty certain he was on the right side of things most times.

A few months back, while working on a case in the Dakota Territory, he'd met a young woman who'd hit him somewhat differently than most of them usually did. She'd seemed important, almost essential to him. Yet when the job was finished, he'd let her go away, back to Boston to build a new kind of life for herself. He could've gone up to Boston from New York City, taken a train and been there in a matter of hours.

Maybe the trouble was that he really yearned to see her again—and this had scared him some.

Spear shook his head and got to his feet. Better make another circuit of the campsite. There hadn't been any trouble so far and they were nearly to Tascosa.

He stopped, his eyes narrowing. He'd been facing the fire for a spell and now that he gazed out into the dark he couldn't see a damn thing.

He'd heard something, though. The faint sound of a shod hoof scraping across pebbles. A horse waiting out beyond the camp, to the south somewhere and not more than a couple hundred yards off, Spear judged. Restless and shifting its hooves.

Spear walked casually over toward the head wagon. Ramsey slept inside that one, in a hammock he'd rigged up for himself above the cases of rifles and ammunition.

Seamus Tuck, preferring to sleep under the wagon, lay wrapped up in a buffalo robe.

"Don't make another move, you dadburned . . . Oh, it's you, Spear." The bearded driver, six-gun in hand, crawled out from under the covered wagon to squint up at him. "How come you ain't over by the fire?"

"Hush," advised Spear, squatting. "We got visitors out in the dark yonder."

"Visitors? Injuns, you mean? Don't tell me the damn Comanches have broken the damn treaty."

"Don't know who or how many it is," Spear told him. "Hustle on up into the wagon and tell Ramsey to break out one of his machine guns. We may need it again."

"Sure, I'll sneak up slick as . . ."

A rifle shot came whistling out of the blackness

and hit a cooking pot hanging some three feet or so above Tuck's grey head.

Throwing himself flat, he scooted back under the wagon.

Spear had gone rolling across the ground the instant he'd heard the shot. The three shots that followed missed him, too. He sprinted to the second wagon and climbed in. "Grab a rifle," he told Molly, who was kneeling in the midst of a makeshift bed, wearing a cambric nightdress.

"What's wrong, what's going on?"

"Somebody's shooting at us."

The whooping and hollering started now as a group of men came riding down toward the camp, their six-guns and rifles blazing away.

"Keep low," Spear urged as a shot came ripping through the canvas of the wagon. He helped himself to one of the Winchester rifles in the nearest crate. "They all seem to be coming from the same direction, so face that way and start shooting."

Molly was loading a rifle for herself while he loaded his.

Three more shots shredded the canvas, another thudded into the wooden frame.

Down under the wagon Wally Anderson complained, "They're tryin' to kill me dead!"

Spear worked his way through the cases toward the rear of the wagon. "Stay in here and keep shooting, Molly." He dove out over the tailboard.

A bullet thunked into the grease bucket as he ducked behind a wheel of the wagon.

The night was ending and a thin grey light was showing across the level line of the horizon, revealing seven men riding a jagged circle around their two wagons and tethered horses. They were dressed in jeans and chaps and Stetsons, a couple with dirty bandanas pulled up to mask their faces. Keeping up a steady fire, they laughed, shouted and whooped.

Spear aimed the rifle and fired.

The bandana that was hiding his target's face suddenly flew away. The man dropped his Navy Colt and jerked both hands up to his face to press at the bloody wound and somehow stop his life from gushing out of him. He went snapping free of his saddle and fell into the campfire. His sheepskin vest began to smolder, but he was beyond caring.

"Blooming churls!" Ramsey had lifted away part of the canvas covering of his wagon and had one of his Gardner quick-fire guns working.

The machine gun chattered and a rider rose up on his mount, a great red line ripping across his chest. Blood came sputtering out of his open mouth as he rode right into the side of the wagon.

The five surviving raiders saw the work the machine gun had wrought and pulled back some, but still they sent shots at the wagons.

"I'm dead! I'm surely and completely defunct!" insisted Wally Anderson under the wagon.

Spear scowled, listening. Gunfire was commencing farther off. Then he saw five new riders galloping across the brightening horizon. The one in the lead was a girl, a raven-haired girl, wearing dark-colored men's clothes.

"Hold your fire!" Spear shouted at Ramsey.

The girl's party was shooting not at their wagons but at the raiders.

Caught between two lines of fire, the marauders decided to hightail it away.

Spear got off a shot at a youth who was bringing up the rear of the departing raiding party. He winged him and the young man left his horse and came crashing to the earth.

The dark girl and her four riders didn't stop, but went riding off after the dawn raiders. When Spear went out to gather up the youth he'd potted, both groups were riding hell-bent in the general direction of Tascosa.

The young man, a pug-nosed fellow with a low forehead and straw-colored hair, was alive but out cold.

Spear stood over him for a moment, then knelt to treat the arm wound. "I want you to survive, to tell me who the hell you're working for."

"Brad," a voice came from behind him.

It was Molly, a blanket over her shoulders, walking barefooted toward him. There was an odd, almost dazed, look in her eyes.

"Better get some clothes on," he advised her, taking out his hunting knife and cutting away the bloody cloth of the sprawled youth's sleeve.

"They meant to kill us," she said in a faraway voice.

"That they did. I'm hoping we can find out from this young gent who they are."

"I recognized one of them."

"Oh, so?"

"It was my husband, Sam Cartland," she said.

Chapter 8

Spear walked over to the place where the wounded young man was sitting, his arm in a bandana sling. He nodded at Tuck, who'd been watching over the captured gunman. "I'll take over."

Tuck lowered his shotgun. "Be a lot simpler to just plug him here and now. Save us all a little trouble in the end."

"Why don't you shut up!" the young man exclaimed.

"What's your name?" Spear asked him.

Muttering, Tuck shuffled back toward the wagons some fifty feet off.

Spear repeated, "Name?"

"You shut up, too!"

Spear grinned and pushed his hat brim up with his thumb. "Maybe I better explain that I'm the only cool-headed one hereabouts. All the other folks on this expedition are in favor of stringing you up as soon as we come to a suitable tree."

"That don't scare me none."

"Who you working for?" Spear moved nearer the seated youth, his eyes narrowing.

"He'll fix you for what you done to me," the young man promised. "Come back and get me and kill every damn one of you."

"Sure," said Spear. "Soon as he gets through running scared."

"Steve Janson ain't afraid of some jackass like you."

"His name is Steve Janson, huh? Seems to me I've heard tell of him."

"He'll fix you good, Spear."

Spear nodded. "And you know who I am."

"Sure, you're a Pinkerton bastard."

"Seems to me I read about Janson before heading this way. He heads up a sizable gang of rustlers."

"So what if he does?"

"Shooting up a wagon train doesn't fit that pattern."

"This was a special deal, to wipe you jackasses out and take . . ."

"Take what?"

"I don't know. Nothin', really."

"The guns and ammunition," Spear concluded, taking hold of the gunman's good arm. "You fellows knew what we were carrying."

"Maybe we did. So what?"

"I want to know who told you. I want to know who put you up to this little raid of yours."

"Go take a flyin' leap at—"

"How far from Tascosa you figure we are?"

"I don't know."

"Twenty miles at least," Spear speculated. "In your shape, take you maybe a full day to walk that. Maybe you know this country well enough to find water. Thing is, if that wound busts open again and you start to bleeding, well . . ."

"What the hell you talkin' about?"

"Leaving you here when we move on."

"I'm hurt. I can't go walkin' nowhere."

Spear shrugged. "Stay here then, sit until you get better."

"I could die."

"Yep, that's possible sure enough."

The boy licked his dry lips. "Suppose I was to tell you a few things? What'd that get me? You turn me over to the marshal in Tascosa and I'll be danglin' from a rope in a few days anyhow."

"I saved your horse," reminded Spear. "I'll give him back to you and let you ride off."

"No kiddin'?" He eyed Spear. "How do I know I can trust you or not?"

"You don't."

He scratched at his pug nose. "I'll take a chance," he decided. "It ain't much, what I know. This here raid wasn't Steve's idea, though. I do know that. Somebody else put him up to it."

"Who?"

"Don't know that. He got a letter, come to his camp."

"And where's that camp?"

"Don't know that neither," he insisted. "They always pick me up at a friend of mine's, little spread about thirty miles south of Tascosa."

"Suppose you want to get in touch with them?"

"Can't. No way to do that." He studied his boots.

"Sure?"

"Well, you could maybe leave a message with the baldheaded bartender at the Golden Door Saloon in Tascosa. His name's Curly."

"Usually is," said Spear. "What were your orders on this raid this morning?"

"Kill everybody, take the guns."

"Kill everybody including the lady?"

"Nobody told me who was with you. All they said was kill whoever showed."

Spear frowned. "Know a gent named Sam Cartland?"

"Nope."

"He was riding with your bunch this morning."

"What's he look like?" the youth asked.

"Not sure, but he's an older fellow, in his forties."

"Oh, sure, that's Doc probably."

"How long he been part of your outfit?"

"Couple months only. Comes from San Antonio, I think."

"What else do you know about him?"

"Nothin'."

"You gents've been rustling cattle from the big spreads," said Spear.

The young man licked his lips again. "Well, some."

"Including Big Jim's place?"

He shook his head. "Not since I signed on almost six months ago."

"Why not?"

"Don't know. See, I ain't in on the plannin' and such," he explained. "Steve don't figure as how I'm ready yet."

"What about the lady who ran your pals off?"

"That bitch." He spat into the dirt. "She's always tryin' to screw us up."

"She'd be Anita Torquay?"

"Yep."

"And in competition with Steve Janson."

"She's a rustler, sure enough."

"How you figure she got wind of what you boys were planning?"

"She's got ways of findin' out stuff. But I ain't sure how."

"Why'd she do it at all?"

"What do you mean?"

"Why keep you boys from doin' us in?"

The young outlaw shook his head. "Hell, I got no idea."

"Stay here until we're ready to pull out," said Spear. "I'll truss you up, so you won't get any ideas about borrowing some guns."

"Aw, I won't do nothin' like that."

"Not the way I'm going to tie you, no," agreed Spear.

The lobby of the Tascosa Manor Hotel was neat and clean and about the size of a parlor. It was crowded with sofas, armchairs, potted plants, claw-foot tables, knickknacks and assorted bric-a-brac.

Spear and Molly were sitting on a candy-stripe love seat, facing the dusty late afternoon street of Tascosa which lay out beyond the small, polished front window.

The red-haired woman said, "We could talk much better up in my room."

"I don't have time for a social visit. I've got to visit the town marshal."

"I wasn't exactly inviting you to go to bed," she countered. "Just because, once, out in the wilderness, I—"

"You'll be fairly safe here. I'll look in on you whenever I can."

"I see why you're behaving this way. You think I

had something to do with the attack on our party, don't you?"

"Nope."

"What exactly did that lout you turned loose tell you about my husband?"

"Said he was calling himself Doc now and not Sam Cartland," he answered.

Molly looked out the window as she weighed this information. A buckboard loaded with a ranch family coming into town went rolling by, trailed by a curious yellow dog.

"But why was he with that gang at all?" she asked with anxiety in her voice.

"Young fellow didn't know."

"I just simply don't understand what's going on," she murmured. "We had such fine plans, Sam and I, and now . . ."

"You know the location of your land, don't you?"

"Yes, I do."

"Might be a good idea to head out there and look around."

She put her hand on his. "I'm a damn independent woman. Still, I'd feel much better if you came along, Brad."

"Can't do that."

"I mean, I'm willing to hire you."

He shook his head. "Right now Peter Ramsey's my client."

"Peter wouldn't mind, I'm sure, if you took a day or two off."

"I don't do business that way." Spear got up, picked his Stetson off a small marble-top table.

Molly stood. "Aren't you concerned about me at all? After what's happened between us?"

"You mean what went off out in the wilderness?" he asked, grinning.

She made an angry face at him. "Oh, you really are a nasty bastard," she said, turning away.

"For all practical purposes I reckon I am." He walked on out into the street.

Chapter 9

Lightning crackled.

Seeing lightning on a clear afternoon was an unusual thing, especially since this bolt came sizzling horizontally down the center of Tascosa's principal street about five feet above the ground.

The flash had originated out of a strange and glittering contraption. It looked like a rifle that had gotten tangled up with a lot of glassware and wire. The barrel was silvery, stuffed with bolts and nuts. The device was being held by a small, wiry man of fifty some years. He was hatless and his sand-colored hair stood straight up to a height of six inches. He wore a rumpled and dusty white linen suit, which he'd probably inherited from someone a few sizes larger than himself.

". . . awesome power of electricity, my friends!" he was booming to the dozen or so townspeople gathered around the low platform he'd set up in the street. "For untold generations, if not longer, man has dreamed of harnessing this fearful source of power!"

Spear paused on the board sidewalk to take in

some of the little man's spiel. There was something vaguely familiar about him.

"I am proud to announce that I, Professor William Emerson Pepper, have succeeded in conquering lightning! Do you fully realize what that means, my friends? It means that I, by aiming the Searing Flash Bioptiscope at the heavens, can for a modest—considering the results—fee, produce rain. Aye, rain! Rain, which falls like a gentle gift from above, bringing blessed wetness to this parched land! Rain to fill the water holes, rain to feed the mighty rivers. Water for your cattle, water to bathe your cherubic tots in, water . . ."

Spear narrowed his left eye. Sure, he'd seen this bouncy little gent before. Out in San Francisco, which was the town the Pinkerton usually operated out of. The fellow was calling himself . . . what was it? Dr. Josiah Stevenson, he'd called himself then, and he was peddling Mystic Mahatma Magnetic Water. Two dollars a pint.

"For those of you not interested especially in rain, my friends," continued Professor Pepper, "I have, at great risk to my person, succeeded in bottling up the awesome power of electricity. Yes, and here it is! Dear people of Tascosa, I can offer you the miraculous Pepper's Lightning Water for the astonishing low price of just two dollars a pint!"

Grinning, Spear continued on his way.

The town marshal picked up a bowie knife. He used it as a bookmark and put the paper-covered novel he'd been reading down on top of his desk. "There's a feller can write," he told Spear.

"So I've heard." The detective was sitting in a straight-backed chair next to the marshal's desk.

"You take this one here," said the plump Marshal Beaven. "It's called *Six-gun Seymour, the Masked Fur Trapper; or, Lost in the Woods*. The darn thing's a crackerjack piece of reading." He picked up the book once again, opened it to the title page. "And I'm right proud of the inscription Mr. Stormfield wrote in it. 'To a stalwart minion of the law and a man of keen literary taste. Your humble servant, Thomas Alexander Stormfield.'"

Spear noticed the date scrawled under the inscription. "Stormfield signed that just three days ago?"

"Yep, sitting in that very chair you're now occupying. That was pretty exciting." Beaven chuckled at the memory of the occasion.

"Why's he in town?"

"He isn't exactly in town. He's about fifty miles out of town, staying as a guest of Wilbur Rudd at the Tumbling W," explained the lawman. "When he arrived in Tascosa, he dropped in for a visit, much the way you're doing."

"Did he tell you why he was in Texas?"

"Oh, sure. He's gathering material for a new batch of books. You an admirer of his work?"

"Who isn't?" Apparently Stormfield hadn't confided in the marshal, thought Spear, and also hadn't told him he was an undercover Secret Service agent. "Fact is, I've run into him before on my travels." Every time he'd bumped into the writer, Stormfield had turned out to be working on the same case he was. "I'll have to ride over and pay him a visit one of these days."

"Tumbling W is fifty miles due south," said Marshal Beaven, dropping the book on top of his desk. "Well sir, what can I do for you, Mr. Spear?"

Producing his identification papers, Spear said, "I'm an agent with the Pinkerton National Detective

Agency. Arrived in town this morning with an English gent by the name of Peter Ramsey and—"

"Two wagonloads of guns," the marshal finished. "Yep, I was planning to drop over to Mel Yauk's livery stable and inquire about that."

"Ramsey represents the Horesham cattle interests, investing group over in England," Spear continued. "They've gotten sort of anxious over all the rustling at Big Jim Phillips' spread, which they've invested pretty heavy in."

"You and Ramsey fixing to haul all them guns out to Big Jim's?"

"Ramsey has the notion he may be doing some rustler hunting. Intends to use the ranch as his base."

Beaven ran his tongue over his upper front teeth. "Don't know if that there is the greatest idea I ever heard."

"Why? Big Jim's supposed to be on the up and up."

After a few seconds the marshal replied, "Reckon he is, more or less. Thing is, we've been having trouble in these parts with shipments of arms being highjacked. And since Big Jim's been having lots of trouble with rustlers, his spread maybe ain't the safest spot in the world to cache weapons. 'Cause they might just get stolen, too."

"Big Jim's been hit hard?"

"Most of the big cattlemen have."

The kid he'd turned loose had told him that the Steve Janson gang hadn't touched the Phillips ranch in nearly six months, for as long as the kid had been with him, anyway. "Any idea who's behind the rustling?"

"Sure," answered the marshal. "Steve Janson's the biggest and most successful one. There's lots of others, including a couple gangs that come up out of Mexico every now and then." He spread his hands wide. " 'Course, as you've probably learned, knowing who a crook is and catching him are two different things."

Spear nodded. "What about this Anita Torquay lady?"

"That's a good question."

"Got an answer?"

"I don't imagine you know much about the girl."

"Not as much as I'd like to."

"Well sir, Anita grew up hereabouts," Marshal Beaven began. "Lived with her grandfather on a small spread southwest of here." He rocked slightly in his chair. "Two years ago a gang of about six men rode down on the place late one night. The old man got killed and Anita—she was nineteen then—she was . . . well, they raped her. Least five out of six of 'em did. Right after that, she left Texas. Supposed to've gone to stay with kinfolks up in Maine or some place like that."

"But she came back."

"Not officially. 'Cept about a year ago I started hearing about her. She's living in some little canyon out in no place, got herself a band of men and she's been raiding ranches."

"Stealing cattle?"

The marshal nodded. "Seems like that's one of her activities. Couple of times we've found dead steer out on the plains with their brands switched. The new one was the Circle AT. That was the brand she and her grandfather used to use."

Spear studied the older man's face. "You don't sound quite convinced."

"Guess I ain't," he admitted. "To be honest with you, Spear, I never been exactly sure what that girl is up to."

"What about her ranch, what happened to it?"

"Her granddaddy's place has water, which some spreads around here don't have. Quite a few of the neighboring ranchers had their eyes on the Torquay place. But he was stubborn, didn't care to sell."

"So somebody killed him."

"That's how I've always figured it, yep."

"Who owns the ranch now?"

The old man had a lawyer, fellow named Evan Marquand, handling his affairs for him. When Anita took off sudden for the East, Marquand up and sold the place on his own. Claims it was done all legal and upright, that the girl got her fair share of the proceeds." He shrugged. "I haven't talked to her since she come back, so I got no way of knowing if that's true or not."

"Who bought the property?" Spear asked.

"Big Jim Phillips."

"But you couldn't tie him in with those raiders?"

Marshal Beaven shook his head. "Nope. See, Anita was pretty much hysterical after . . . Well, I couldn't get no kind of sensible story out of her. Soon as she took to feeling better, she up and left."

"Now she's come back to get revenge on her own," Spear said.

"Yep, that's what I think. Anita is interested in a lot more than just stealing cattle."

"We were attacked yesterday morning by the Steve Janson gang," Spear revealed.

The marshal straightened up in his chair. "You sure it was Janson?"

"I'm sure. Also sure that Anita Torquay's bunch scared most of 'em off."

"Most of 'em?"

"All that were still capable of moving."

"Like I was saying, you can't always figure what the girl's up to." Beaven smiled grimly. "Might well be she's a bit crazy in the head."

"In order for Janson to attack our wagons, he had to know we were coming," Spear noted. "Was that information floating around town?"

"I sure as hell didn't hear it before you all pulled in," Marshal Beaven insisted. "And I make it my business to hear *all* the news." He sucked in his cheek. "This Ramsey fellow must have told somebody he was coming."

"Sure, he notified Big Jim weeks ago."

"Interesting."

"Also interesting how Anita found out what Janson was planning to do and got there to stop it."

"Sometimes she's almost like . . . one of them masked avengers Mr. Stormfield writes about. Comes and goes real mysterious."

"It's only mysterious till we find out how she does it." Spear stood up. "We'll be moving out for Big Jim's tomorrow morning early, Marshal."

"Need any help looking after them guns and all?"

"Nope, but thanks for the offer." He shook hands with the lawman.

"Appreciate it if you was to keep me informed," Beaven said.

"I'll do that," promised Spear.

Seamus Tuck was squeezing a tune out of his concertina. "Oh, come along, boys, an' drink your fill," he sang in his grating voice, "whiles I tells you 'bout me an' ol' Buffalo Bill. Come along . . . Howdy, brother Spear."

Spear crossed the stable yard to where the driver

was perched on a stump beside his wagon. "Everything going well?"

"Seen nary an outlaw since we unhitched the horses."

"Where's your pardner?"

"Wally? He's out huntin' up a sawbones."

"We checked him over, he wasn't really shot."

"Well sir, Wally claims he was and that there's a bullet rattlin' round inside him somewheres," explained Tuck while he lowered his wheezing squeeze-box to the dirt. "He ain't gonna rest till he finds it."

Spear grinned. "Ramsey been around?"

"Been here and gone. Mentioned as how he was fixin' to have himself a bite of dinner soon."

"Where?"

"Place named Rowdy Kate's."

"Sounds cozy."

"Food's supposed to be dang good," Tuck disclosed, spitting. "You aimin' to nursemaid the wagons tonight?"

"Yep."

"Me, too. Let's be careful we don't get skinned. Oh, by the way, I got to jawin' with Yauk. Found out an interestin' thing or two."

Spear leaned against a wagon wheel. "Such as?"

"Seems like this here Big Jim lives himself quite a high life out on his ranch. Yes sir, he's a great one for the ladies. And, so they say, he's got his own stable of whores."

"Don't tell me he's supposed to be running a bordello on the side?"

"Nope, these here ladies is all for his own personal use, you see," amplified the driver. "He's got three or maybe four of 'em livin' there in a special house of their own. They's exclusive for the use of Big Jim, and certain of his special buddies. Sounds like one of them harems they got over in China or wherever."

"The more I hear about Big Jim, the more anxious I am to meet the gent."

Tuck gave a cackling laugh. "I'd rather meet up with his collection of whores!"

"I'll be back here a little after sundown," Spear said. "Right now I'll look up Ramsey at Rowdy Kate's."

"They say everything's good 'cept the stew," warned Tuck as Spear went striding off.

Chapter 10

Spear made a short side trip to the Golden Door Saloon. Inside, it was long and narrow, and it smelled more like an outhouse than a place to drink. A wooden bar ran along one wall, with a large, milky mirror behind it. There was a poker game going on at one of the bigger round tables. A few other customers were scattered around the dimly lit, smoky room.

The bald bartender was on duty. He seemed out of place in these drab, run-down surroundings. His face was a healthy pink color, his candy-stripe shirt was fresh and bright, his mustache was smartly waxed. He was polishing a glass industriously and humming to himself.

At the far end of the bar an old muleskinner was slumped beside an empty glass, sobbing quietly into his elbow.

"Ah, top of the evenin' to you, sir," greeted the bartender.

This gent looked too jovial and carefree to be linked up with the Steve Janson gang. Yet the pug-nosed young outlaw had said the bartender at this place was a contact man for the rustlers. Spear wanted, without tipping his hand as yet, to get a look at him.

"Whiskey." Spear rested one booted foot on the bar rail.

"Would you by any chance be an Irishman?"

"Not quite."

"Pity, for you have the look of a black Irishman about you." He gave the glass a final swipe and returned it to its shelf. "And whenever I meet up with a true son of the Emerald Isle, why 'tis glad my heart is."

"You're Irish yourself, huh?"

"Through and through. My name is Patrick Terrence O'Malley." He produced a bottle of whiskey.

"I heard the bartender here was named Curly."

O'Malley rubbed at his hairless head. "Aye, there are those spalpeens as do call me that," he admitted ruefully. "But 'tis not a name I'm overly proud of." Filling a glass near to its brim, he passed it over to Spear.

"Join me?" the detective invited.

"Thanks, sir, but I never touch the stuff."

"And you an Irishman."

" 'Tis a shame, I agree." He shook his bald head. "Any sort of spirits play hob with my poor stomach."

Spear tasted his drink, winced, blinked and sat the glass down. "I can see why."

"Even good liquor makes me ill," O'Malley told him. "Passing through town, are you?"

"Yep."

"Would you be lookin' for work?"

"Might be."

The bartender nodded. "Worked with cattle before?"

"Out in Wyoming," Spear lied.

"Well, if you . . ." Some of the jolliness dropped from his face as he frowned over Spear's shoulder.

In the milky mirror Spear saw the reflection of the slim young man who was approaching. He was no more than five feet six, boyish in build though he was in his middle twenties. He had a delicate face, a handsome one, and he wore his shoulder-length black hair pulled back and tied with a twist of rawhide. His low-slung gunbelt sported twin .44s.

"You should have told him, Curly," the young man said in a pale voice.

The bartender swallowed. "Told him what, Angel?"

The handsome gunman smiled. "He's standing where I like to stand."

"Now, Angel, don't you go and start makin' trouble."

"Never mind. I'll tell him." Angel stopped at a spot a few feet from the bar and to the right of Spear. "You better move, mister."

Spear turned from the reflection and looked right at the black-clad youth. "I didn't catch what you said, son."

Angel kept smiling. "I'm willing to let it slide this time, you being new in Tascosa," he said in his murmuring voice. "See, you picked the spot at the bar where I like to park."

Chairs scraped on the raw plank floor. The poker game had ended abruptly.

"Angel," began the bartender, "this gent didn't mean—"

"I'll explain things, Curly," the long-haired young man said, a pitying look in his bright brown eyes. "Mister, it annoys me when some dude comes in here and tries to take my special spot at the bar. I mean, it makes me madder than hell. I start to see red. I get real damn angry at the no-good son of a bitch who's giving mc trouble."

"Maybe," suggested Spear amiably, "you ought to go out and soak your head in a water trough."

The rest of the Golden Door's customers, except for the sobbing muleskinner, left.

Angel chuckled. "You're trying to make jokes at my expense, I reckon," he said. "I allow that. Once."

Spear narrowed his left eye. "Son, I came in here for a quiet drink. After I finish, you can have the whole damn place to yourself."

"Afraid that won't do, mister. Because you're standing at my place *now*."

"Have a drink on the house, Angel," offered the anxious O'Malley. "Enjoy it over at one of the vacant tables."

The long-haired gunman was concentrating on Spear. "You going to move, you goddamn son of a bitch?"

Spear took a deliberate sip of the terrible whiskey. "Nope."

"I take that as a personal insult."

"Imagine you take most everything that way."

Angel took two wide-legged steps backward. "And I'm telling you, mister, that you're a no-good bastard." His fingertips were rubbing at the palms of his hands.

Spear said nothing.

"You're the kind of slime that gathers when the outhouse ain't been cleaned."

Spear grinned. "That's only one man's opinion," he said, finishing the drink. He placed the glass on the bar. "Good evening, O'Malley."

"Oh. Yes. Same to you, sir."

Turning his back on the angry young gunman, Spear walked toward the gold-painted swing doors.

"I knew you were a chickenshit bastard!" called Angel. "I had you pegged!"

Spear turned slowly with both hands in view. "Son, I want you to remember something," he said. "Tonight you got to play some of your games and you're still alive. But next time . . ."

He walked on out of the place.

"Jove, that's rum news," observed Ramsey, dropping his fork to the checkered tablecloth. "Bloke had in mind to goad you into a blooming duel, what?"

Spear was sitting across from his client in the large eating establishment run by Rowdy Kate. "Yep," he replied.

"I expect one must be constantly on the lookout for such things in the Wild West, you know. Short tempers, crazed blighters with blood lust coursing through their veins."

"This kid's a hired gun," Spear told him. "He never gets mad, no more than the gents who work in the slaughterhouses back East got it in for the cows they butcher. Just a job."

Ramsey blinked. "This young chap was hired to kill you?"

"Seems likely."

"Well then, oughtn't you to have shot it out with him? Kill or be killed, and all that?"

Spear grinned. "I want to find out who's picking up his tab."

"Ah, yes, I see. To be sure. That way we'll learn the identity of the mastermind behind all this." Ramsey nodded his blond head thoughtfully. "How exactly will you go about doing that, old man?"

"Later on this evening, I'll make a few inquiries." Spear leaned both elbows on the table. "That's why I'd like you to keep an eye on the wagons till I get back to 'em."

"Really, now? Do you think that's absolutely called for? I mean to say, we've got Tuck and Wally over there watching—"

"Wally thinks he's dying and Seamus could sleep through three earthquakes and the Battle of Gettysburg," said Spear. "If you want your little rolling arsenal to get safely to Big Jim's, you better sit up with it tonight."

"Very well." Ramsey looked downcast. "Thing is, old chap, I was intending to pay a call on Molly Cartland. The poor lass is quite beside herself."

"She'll do okay."

Ramsey frowned. "You two never hit it off, did you?" he remarked. "A shame, really, since she's a likable woman."

"You better get over to Yauk's stables in a half-hour—"

"You call that a tip, you walleyed clodhopper?" roared a brassy feminine voice across the room.

Both Spear and Ramsey looked up to see who was making all the noise.

"Listen here, Kate, I—"

"Who in blue bloody hell told you you could call me Kate? My name is Mrs. Pitt, you lop-eared runt!"

"Well, Mrs. Pitt, I ain't goin' to pay you no dang ransom ever' time I dine in this greasy spoon!"

"I won't take no sass and disrespect, Fuzzy!"

Rowdy Kate Pitt was a huge orange-haired woman of forty-odd years, tall and wide, with breasts like twin cannonballs. She wore a tight buckskin skirt, a checkered shirt and a dainty green bow in her wild orange hair. She was clutching at the shirt collar of a gaunt cowpoke and had him half up out of his chair.

"Damn it, Kate . . . Mrs. Pitt! It's gettin' so's a man can't even—"

"Cough up, you lump-jawed baboon!"

Fuzzy dug a two bit piece out of the change pocket of his denims and threw it next to the single one already on the table. "There. And that's absolutely all. I got a sick ma back in Newark, New Jersey, and I ought to be sendin' her more than what I paid for this here meal."

"Got no time for chitchat, Fuzzy. If you're finished with your chow, get on out. There's lots of others waiting for tables."

He jerked free of her grip, stumbled to his feet and glanced around. "This dump's half empty," he informed her as he edged toward the door. "Way you treat folks, it's a wonder you get even . . ." He dove out into the twilight, narrowly avoiding the saltcellar she'd sent toward his head.

Smacking her big hands together a few times, the proprietor came clumping over to Spear's table. "Got any complaints, bright eyes?"

"If I did, ma'am, I'd keep 'em to myself," Spear told her.

"You sure didn't eat much of your pot roast."

"Guess I got distracted by the floor show."

Rowdy Kate studied the Pinkerton agent for a few seconds. Then she laughed and slapped him on the back. "You're a wise guy, for sure. I like that." Uninvited, she plopped her bulk down at their table's empty chair. "Now take your friend the reverend here. He's all serious and sober."

"Madam," protested Ramsey, "I am not, let me hasten to assure you, a man of the cloth."

"Maybe not on the outside." She ignored him after that, keeping her attention fixed on Spear. "You're a handsome galoot."

"True," he agreed.

She let out another whooping laugh, smacking him across the shoulder blades once again. "Not modest either," she boomed. "Ever fool around with a red-haired woman?"

"Now and then."

"Could you go for one built along my lines?"

"Nope."

"Didn't think so." Rowdy Kate shook her head. "You should've seen me in my youth. My breasts were as big as they are now, but I had a waist you could just about circle with one hand. Pretty I was, and a natural redhead."

Spear eyed her improbable hair, saying nothing.

Rowdy Kate guffawed. "It used to be real authentic red. Now I got to help nature along," she explained. "Getting old is a pain, ain't it? I was thinking the other day . . ."

A clattering crash came from the kitchen. "Excuse me a moment, gents." The big woman grunted up out of her chair. Leaning over Spear, she whispered, "Don't skip out, honey. I got something important to talk over with you." Then she went steaming across the room and into the kitchen.

"Colorful," said Ramsey. "Typical of the Western spirit."

"Don't you have fat ladies in England?"

"Not with Rowdy's Kate's style and brio, no. The old girl seems to have taken quite a fancy to you, Spear."

Kate yelled out behind the white kitchen door, "Ain't you ever going to learn delicacy, you dimwitted coyote? That's the second stack of dinner plates you went and broke this month, you rum-soaked gink! I ought to stuff all them poor fragments of crockery up your droopy—"

"Colorful," repeated the Englishman.

Rowdy Kate had a small office at the rear of the restaurant. It was there that she and Spear had a private conversation. "Never marry a man smaller than you," she said, taking a cigar from the humidor on her roll-top desk. " 'Course, Rowdy Dan had a reputation for chewing nails when I first met up with him."

"Your husband's name is Rowdy Dan?" The rocker Spear was settled in creaked every time he moved.

"Rowdy Dan, Rowdy Kate. We're a team. Been married near twenty years." She bit off the tip of the cigar and spat it into a brass cuspidor. "Lately he's been getting damn clumsy. Dropping plates right and left."

"So that was Rowdy Dan you were chastising out in the kitchen a while ago."

"That lop-eared runt," she grumbled. "I wish sometimes I didn't love the cuss so much."

"You wanted to talk about something," Spear reminded her.

Rowdy Kate scratched at her huge left breast. "You're a Pinkerton, ain't you?"

"Right."

"I've heard of you. You was in Deadwood a few months back."

"That was me," he admitted.

"Some Pinks are yellow-bellied rats," the big woman claimed. "They work on the side of the folks who like to grind honest people into the dirt."

He didn't disagree.

"But they say you ain't that way," she went on. "You're pretty near to being honest."

"If there's something you want to confide in me, I won't pass it on," he told her. "If that's what you're getting at."

"It ain't my hide I'm concerned over," Rowdy Kate answered, lighting her cigar. "I may look like a cathouse madam, but I'm about as honest as anybody in these parts. I'm the sort who takes in stray dogs and feeds starving orphans."

"I noticed you being kindly to Fuzzy tonight."

"Aw, we was just kidding around. We're pals. Inside, I've got a heart of gold."

"Right now you're interested in helping somebody out?"

She nodded, her frizzy orange hair flickering. "There's someone who'd like to talk to you. I was on the lookout for you. If you hadn't come in here tonight, I was going to drop over to Yauk's Stables, soon as I got Rowdy Dan tucked in for the night."

"Okay, who wants to talk to me?"

"Suppose," she said, lowering her voice, one hand resting on an immense thigh, "suppose this someone was maybe someone some folks had pegged as an outlaw. Would you feel obliged to turn the person in?"

"Nope." He shook his head. "But Kate, I don't want to have any conversations with killers or—"

"She isn't a killer, no matter what anybody claims."

His rocker creaked. "You mean Anita Torquay?"

"The poor kid. You heard about what they did to her?"

"Yep, I heard."

"Drove her near crazy. Took turns with her, they

did. Two of 'em held her down while the other had his fun. They all watched, laughing. Except for one feller. He didn't have no stomach for it. Didn't touch her, but didn't have the guts to stop 'em. Nita was just nineteen, churchgoing, a virgin. She came to me next day, still wearing the bloody clothes she'd had on. Her old grandpap and me was friends, although I thought he was a narrow-minded Bible-thumping jackass most of the time. Nita I really liked. I felt sorry for her, having to grow up the way she did."

"Why'd she come back to Texas?"

"Hell, she never left," replied Rowdy Kate. "Story that got around, thanks to me, was that she'd gone up to Maine to live with relatives. That was all hogwash. I sent her to kin of mine in San Antonio. We do real well on this restaurant, plus what we take in off some land holdings. My idea was, Nita'd live quiet in San Antonio for a spell. Once she got over what those sons of bitches had done, well, she might go off to college somewheres and get herself a good education." The big woman sighed. "She wouldn't have none of that. Once she took to feeling well again, she went out riding every day and practicing with a six-gun and a rifle. I got me a pretty good idea, when my kinfolks wrote me about her, what the girl was fixing to do."

"Come back here for revenge."

"That's it exactly, Spear." Rowdy Kate nodded vigorously.

"Who raped her?" he asked.

Rowdy Kate spat away a fleck of tobacco from her lip. "She wouldn't never tell me. Claimed she didn't recognize any of 'em."

"But who do you think did it to her? Some of Steve Janson's gang?"

"Now I can't prove a damn thing, but I don't

think it was any of *them*. Not that they ain't done worse." She paused, gazing down at the glowing tip of her cigar. "I got me the notion the gang was working for Big Jim Phillips."

"Honest and upright Big Jim?"

Rowdy Kate snorted. She raised her head and looked Spear straight in the eye. "He's about as honest as a cross-eyed snake. If you're going to be visiting Big Jim, keep both eyes open and be damn careful who you turn your back on."

Running a thumb knuckle across his bearded chin, Spear asked, "Can you get up a meeting between me and Anita?"

"That's just exactly what I'm trying to do. But I got to have your word you won't do nothing to hurt the girl."

"You have it."

"Come back into Tascosa in a couple days," she instructed. "Drop in here for a meal and I'll tell you what you have to do. And remember, Spear, if you make any trouble for the girl, I'll skin you alive."

Chapter 11

Thomas Alexander Stormfield smiled and murmured, "Excellent, dear lady. Quite marvelous." After he turned his back on the piano, the smile dropped from his face.

Maude Rudd brought the Chopin piece to a galloping close, then said, "It isn't fair that I monopolize the entertainment, Mr. Stormfield." She was a plump, pink woman of thirty-nine, with a mound of curly blonde hair piled atop her head. She wore a lace-trimmed satin gown.

"Ah, but I have, I fear, never courted the muse of music," he told her as he paced the ranch house parlor. Outside, the dusk was darkening into night.

"You might, however," suggested Maude, "recite."

"From the works of the immortal Bard, or perhaps from the lays of Sir Walter Scott?"

"I meant from your own works, Mr. Stormfield."

He cocked his head to the left. "Eh? A little reading from the work in progress perhaps?" he inquired, pivoting slowly to face the portly pianist. "Ah, but I fear my humble efforts at prose would bore you."

"Oh, heavens, no," she assured him with a smile. "It would be quite a treat, most exciting. You see, I've never met an author before. Unless you count . . ." She let the words trail off.

Stormfield had crossed to the small desk he'd been working at that afternoon. "Unless you count whom, dear lady?"

"Well, he never actually told me he was an author," Maude replied, toying with one of her many blonde curls. "Yet I had reason to suspect he might well be."

"Who?" he inquired, fingers drumming on the most recent pages of his manuscript.

"Why, poor vanished Mr. Klein."

The writer straightened. "What gave you the notion Elisha Klein was an author?"

"Well, because I saw him at work. That is, I assume it was a manuscript of some sort he was writing in that large leather-bound notebook."

"Large leather-bound notebook," echoed Stormfield, taking several steps in her direction. "You saw Klein making notes in one, did you?"

She lowered her head, running a plump pink finger along the edge of the piano bench. "I don't believe he knew I was watching him. Not that I was eavesdropping, you understand."

"This incident, innocent as the driven snow I have not the slightest doubt, transpired here?"

"Goodness, no. It was up at the abandoned mine shack," answered Rudd's very widowed daughter. "I imagine Mr. Klein, poor soul, must have used the place to . . . how did you phrase it at supper this evening? Yes, to woo his muse."

Stormfield was standing over her now. "You say you saw the young fellow at work in this notebook up in this shack?"

"I don't believe he knew I was watching."

"How'd you get close enough to see what he was doing without his being aware of it?"

Maude coughed demurely. "Well, I used binoculars."

"Binoculars?"

"Mr. Klein was a very personable young man and when I chanced to learn he was in the habit of dropping by that deserted shack at the north end of Father's property, why, I decided to . . . watch him. I did that from a stand of alder trees about a quarter mile uphill. The binoculars are very powerful and I could see right into the shack, wherein he sat at an old wooden table and wrote. A shame he disappeared before finishing the book."

Stormfield lowered himself next to her on the piano bench. "He made entries in that book more than once?"

"I watched him write in it . . . oh, several times."

"The notebook. Do you have any idea where it is now?"

She shook her head. "Why, no. I imagine Mr. Klein took it with him when he vanished."

"Yet it might still be in that old shack."

"It might, yes," she answered, not sure. "You seem very eager to see his work."

"Let me confess something to you," he began. "Elisha Klein was indeed an author. In fact, I have been asked, by certain figures in the New England literary establishment who learned I was journeying westward, to look the young fellow up. Yes, a noted publisher residing in Boston is most anxious and eager to negotiate with Mr. Klein for the publication of his book. The very book, I suspect, you so often witnessed him composing." He stood up. "I'll visit the shack in the morning."

"But if Mr. Klein has disappeared without a trace, won't it be difficult to come to any sort of agreement?"

"We'll let the publisher worry about the technical matters, dear lady. All you need concern your lovely head about is telling me how to reach this deserted mine shack."

"I'll do better than that." Maude gave him a broad smile. "I'll take you there myself, first thing in the morning."

After a few seconds Stormfield said sourly, "That will be delightful."

Chapter 12

Angel concentrated on rolling a cigarette. The oil lamp hanging over his head caused his low-crowned black sombrero to throw a band of deep shadow across the upper half of his handsome face. "You got to learn to relax, Curly," he advised.

"That was a damn fool thing to try," the bald bartender fumed.

The two of them were in the small storeroom at the rear of the now shut Golden Door Saloon. It was a few minutes this side of two a.m.

"Why?"

"Shooting that Pinkerton out in the open would've been a mistake." O'Malley's smiling manner had deserted him. "It'd link you with him."

"Horsefeathers." Angel licked the cigarette paper. "It's my job to kill Spear. When he come strolling into the place tonight, I seen my chance."

"Maybe he had a reason for coming in. Maybe he suspects something."

"Aw, the hell he does. He ain't got no more brains than a meatball."

"You're supposed to kill him quietlike," reminded the bartender, rubbing his palm over his scalp. "So as not a soul knows who done it."

"Listen, Curly, if I'd killed him tonight, you'dve just swore it was a fair fight." Striking a match on the side of a case of whiskey, he lit his cigarette. "Trouble was, he wouldn't try. I wasn't figuring he'd turn out to be so yellow."

"Spear's no coward. He's just not a hothead. And not dumb enough to let you nudge him into a fight."

"Next thing you'll be saying, old buddy, is that he could have outdrawed me."

O'Malley shrugged one shoulder. "Maybe he could have, maybe he couldn't have."

"He ain't going to get no more chances," promised the handsome gunman. "Because I'm aiming to take care of him tonight, while he's sleeping with his wagonload of guns."

"You botched that once before, back in Dodge."

Angel blew out a thin stream of smoke. "I'm getting sort of tired of you putting me down all the time, Curly."

"I don't mean nothing," the bartender assured him quickly. "I'm just after making sure you don't go off halfcocked. This Spear is a lot smarter and a lot tougher than you're giving him credit for."

"Aw, he's a— Hold on!" Angel spun, long hair whipping, and ran to the room's single small window.

"What in the hell is it?"

"Keep your mouth shut for a minute!" The young man put his fingertips to the dark pane, listening.

"Hear something?"

"Not with you shooting off your bazoo." He inched toward the rear door, sliding out one of his ivory-handled .44s. With a darting dive, Angel threw the door open and lunged out into the darkness.

A half block away a dog gave a few grumbling barks.

"What is it?" asked O'Malley, watching the black rectangle the gunman had stepped through.

Angel returned, shut the door, holstered his gun. "Thought I heard something."

"You're jumpy."

"Maybe." He glanced at the window. "Nobody out there now anyways."

"Might be a good idea to hold off on Spear until he's out of town."

"Hell, no." Angel took a deep drag on his cigarette. "I mean to get the bastard tonight."

Things didn't go exactly as Spear had planned.

When he'd worked things out in his head, after overhearing Angel and Curly, everything had sounded just fine to him. He'd roused Seamus Tuck and explained the idea, so they wouldn't go bumping into each other in the dark this time. Wally Anderson wasn't around, having gone to spend the night in a boarding house which was right next to the offices of one of the town's two doctors.

Spear, holding a Winchester rifle taken from their stockpile, was spread out on the roof of a shed that overlooked the corral.

He'd strung wires across the front and back of each wagon. If anybody tried to slip inside either one of the wagons, the wires would yank down enough pots and pans to make one hell of a noise. There was also a trip wire strung across the doorway leading from the stable into the yard and one rigged up to the gate of the corral.

As soon as Angel showed up in the pitch dark below, Spear would know it. So would Tuck, who would then light up a couple of oil lanterns and duck out of the way. Spear would then tackle the handsome young gunman, taking him alive and kicking, so they could discuss exactly who was behind this ongoing effort to do Spear in. Listening outside the storeroom window hadn't given him even a hint as to who was paying the kid.

Inside the dark stable, old Tuck was performing an excellent imitation of a sleeping man. His growling snore was so good that Spear wondered if he really was dead to the world.

The night had grown colder, and the darkness pressed down on Spear. Must be getting close on to three, he thought.

Eyes narrowed, Spear searched the night below, trying to make out any sign of movement. Nothing stirred.

Several blocks away, two drunken cowhands began hollering at each other.

"You're the stubbornest son of a bitch I ever met!"

"Aw, shut up, ya bowlegged bastard!"

Then silence again, except for the wagon driver's realistic snores.

Spear didn't much like this whole job. The way he saw it, Peter Ramsey wasn't more than two or three steps away from being a damn fool, what with his hauling all this artillery around and parading it all right through some of the toughest towns in the country like a circus on the move. Spear didn't mind risking his neck—that was one of the things the Pinkerton Agency paid him for—but being just plain foolhardy was something else again.

"You're getting old," he told himself. "Old and crotchety. Hell, pretty soon you'll—"

Pots and pans rattled in the neighborhood of the stable. Someone gasped, fell out onto the corral ground with a loud thump.

Spear dropped from the roof of the low shed, landing wide-legged, rifle ready.

"We got you this time, you consarned varmint!" shouted Tuck.

A lantern blossomed in the darkness, then it floated down to the ground and a second one came to life.

Sprawled there on the dirt was Molly Cartland, tangled in her dark velvet cloak.

Spear made no move to help her up. He eased over until his back was against the side of one of the covered wagons. "What brings you here, ma'am?"

Brushing back a stray lock of her auburn hair, she glared up at him. "Exactly what the devil is this all about?"

Tuck took a few tentative steps toward the sprawled young woman. "She don't seem to have no weapons, Spear."

"Why would I have a weapon?" Molly pushed at the ground with both hands, got to her feet. She began brushing straw and smears of dirt off her cloak. "Why are you pointing that rifle at me, Brad?"

He lowered the barrel. "We were expecting . . . someone else."

"Hell." Tuck spat on the ground. "We sprung our goldang trap and didn't catch us no fox."

Molly crossed to where Spear was standing. "I don't understand what I walked into."

"Don't you?"

She sighed, dropped both hands to her sides. "You don't honestly think I'm part of some plot to kill you and steal all of Peter's guns?"

"Why are you here, ma'am?" he asked.

"So it's ma'am again instead of Molly." She shook her head. "Really, Brad, being involved with you is most exasperating."

"Why are you here, Molly?"

"I couldn't sleep."

"So you figured a walk around a dark livery stable would make you drowsy."

"No, damn it. I thought making love with you would be a nicer way to spend the sleepless hours than counting the cracks in the plaster."

Tuck snickered, then asked, "We going to reset our snares, Spear?"

"Nope."

"Then I'll mosey back to bed."

"Do that, but keep an eye open."

Molly said, "I seem to have spoiled something."

"Probably," Spear answered.

She touched his chest. "I'm sorry. I'll make it up to you."

"Not now, not tonight." He pushed her, gently, back from him. "I'll be sitting up the rest of the night. Just in case."

"Can't I at least sit up with you?"

"Nope."

"But—"

"I don't want any distractions."

"You're mad because I accidentally—"

"You hustle on back to your hotel. Now."

"You're leaving tomorrow. I may not see you for weeks."

"Even so."

Molly gave an angry shake of her head. "One day soon, Brad Spear, I'm going to cross you off my list entirely!" Angrily, she strutted away from him.

There were no further visitors that night.

Chapter 13

Big Jim Phillips was big—six and a half feet high, broad-shouldered and thick-necked. He was fifty-two years old and his dark, shaggy hair was speckled with grey. At the moment, two hours before dawn, he was wearing a grey flannel nightshirt. He was stretched out beside a young and relatively pretty blonde named Inga.

Inga was plump and her breasts were large. One of them was peeking out over the top of the quilt, jiggling provocatively as she snored.

Big Jim fought off an urge, centered in his crotch, to grab that breast and give it a hearty squeeze. Shaking his head, he eased out of the four-poster.

Inga murmured, "Big Yim . . . vhere you go?"

The rancher said nothing.

He took his crimson silk robe off the back of the sleeping blonde's vanity table chair and slipped it on.

"Look like a madam in this thing," he muttered to himself. "Still, it's got style and class."

He let himself out of Inga's room and moved quietly down the hall. The hardwood floor was chilly underfoot until he reached the Oriental carpeting. Two oil lamps, gilded and with stained-glass shades, dimly lit the second floor corridor.

It was all very stylish and high-class. Indeed there was not another house like this in all the Texas panhandle. What it was based on was a bordello Big Jim had visited in St. Louis some years ago, back when he was still scuffling for a living. A night in that ornate brothel had set him back a month's pay. Right then and there he'd decided he'd like a place like that of his own someday, well-stocked with fine food, liquor and women.

He had been able to build such a house on his spread two years before, not to live in but to keep his ladies in. There were five in residence just now; a sixth had run clean off recently, an absolutely lovely Chinese girl who would always keep him awake until dawn.

No use crying over spilled milk, he thought to himself. Big Jim, without knocking, let himself into another bedroom.

"I'm not feeling at all well," announced the slim, dark-haired girl who sat up in bed the moment his first heavy footstep had touched on her side of the threshold. "Maybe later in the week, when my headache's better, we can—"

"I'm not here for fooling around, Yvonne," he told her. "So save your excuses, hon."

"I really am under the weather, Big Jim, and wouldn't for a minute think of making up a lie."

"Yes, I know, darlin'." He sat on the edge of her bed. He could just make out her pretty face in the near darkness. "I'm hoping, though, you'll be feeling better by tonight."

"When I come down with one of my spells I sometimes—"

"It isn't me I have in mind for you, Yvonne."

"Oh?" She hugged herself, arms forcing her small pert breasts closer together beneath her frilly nightdress. "You have in mind my entertaining some old goat who's going to be visiting the Circle BJ?"

The cattleman gave a rumbling chuckle. "This gent's young and not bad-looking, so I hear."

After a few silent seconds she asked, "So what's wrong with him? You almost never give me the young, halfway passable ones to work on. I always get stuck with the humpback, bandy-legged, squinty-eyed—"

"I'm expecting a visit from the British folks who dumped a considerable piece of money into the ranch."

"Englishmen are lousy lovers."

"I want you to go after the Pinkerton agent who's traveling with the limey," Big Jim explained.

"A dick? Really, Big Jim, I ought to draw the line somewhere."

"His name is Brad Spear."

"You're kidding? Nobody has a name like that."

"He is rumored to be quite a devil with the ladies."

"I'll just bet."

"Be that as it may, darlin'," Big Jim continued, "you are to worm your way into his affections. Of my five ladies, you are the best suited for this type of hombre."

"You want me to find out what he knows?"

"Most assuredly," the rancher responded. "And I want Spear completely occupied from bedtime to dawn tomorrow night. Do anything you have to to keep him out of the way."

She smiled. "What'll you be up to while I'm distracting Mr. Spear?"

"Business," he answered. "No need for any of my girls to worry about business."

"Suppose he's not interested in my brand of romance."

"He'll be interested in you. I hear he's very chivalrous."

"Like a knight in armor, you mean? Sounds dull as ditch water."

"He's been known to get involved with ladies who're in trouble, ladies who've been mistreated," explained the big rancher. "He sort of takes them under his wing."

"How am I going to convince him that I've been mistreated?"

"You're going to ask him to help you, simply tell him I treat you real bad." Big Jim stood up. "You'll make his hair stand on end by telling him how often I beat you for the fun of it."

"I may not be able to make him believe that."

"Sure you will." He swung out suddenly, slapped her hard across the cheek. "I'll see to that."

Sam Cartland was shivering. Shivering bad, his arms jerking and his teeth chattering. He turned up the collar of his pea jacket, tugged down the brim of his grey Stetson and then blew on his hands.

It wasn't that cold. In fact, there was a touch of warmth in the night air. Didn't matter, he always got to shaking like this before they went on a cattle-stealing raid. Standing there in the dark of the narrow little canyon, holding on to the reins of his saddled bay mare, Cartland said to himself, "I'm not meant for this kind of life." It scared him, scared the hell out of him.

Funny, because back in the war he'd never been afraid of anything.

That was a long time ago, he reminded himself.

He was getting old now, was losing his nerve.

Someone came walking across the hard earth toward him. It was Steve Janson, small and stocky, his flat face blurred with pockmarks and his left eye locked in a perpetual wink.

"Let's get going, Doc," said Janson, his breath well-laced with the smell of whiskey.

"Sure, Steve, okay." Cartland put his foot in the stirrup.

"Anything wrong with you?"

"No. Hell, no. I'm fine." He swung up into the saddle.

"You sound funny, that's all." The outlaw was looking up at him. "I don't want any screwing up tonight."

"Don't worry."

"And remember what I told you boys," Janson said to the group. "No killing, no shouting. If you see any of Big Jim's crew, leave the buggers alone."

"But suppose they start shootin' at us?" Cartland asked.

"They won't." Janson walked away and mounted the ornery black stallion he always rode.

Five other members of the gang were in the saddle. At a signal from Janson, they urged their horses into action.

Cartland brought up the rear. The shivering wasn't quite so bad now. It usually did get better once he was moving, doing something.

I'm a damn fool, he thought. I ought to be with Molly right now. Living in my own place, living well on our own ranch. Cartland knew cattle and he'd raised shorthorns up in Kansas a few years back, before he got married. He was damn near sure he could do well with Texas longhorns.

Trouble was, he didn't have the ranch anymore. He lost it just like that, just like snapping your fingers or blinking your eye. Lost the whole damn ranch in a poker game. The game hadn't lasted more than an hour. And he'd come out of it flat broke and without the deed to their fifty thousand acres.

Cartland never could quite explain to Molly why he liked gambling so much. The way some men got a craving for liquor, that was how gambling worked on him. Even stronger than that, maybe. You couldn't help it. You just had to do it.

Even so, you couldn't have gone back to Molly, he thought. Earlier maybe, right when he'd lost everything, their ranch and all, in that damn poker game in Buffalo Springs. Sure, he could've rounded up enough cash somehow to get himself to Dodge or Abilene. Hop a train there and go back to his wife.

Except he just simply couldn't face her. Couldn't stand up to Molly and say right out what a damn fool thing he'd gone and done. Cartland couldn't even bring himself to put it in writing. So what he'd decided to do was make as much money as he could as fast as he could. He'd take that money and parlay it somehow into a small ranch for him and his wife. Not any fifty thousand acres, but something.

When the chance came along to tie up with Steve Janson, he'd taken it. Most of his life he'd been fairly straight. But he was getting old and he had a young wife and he wanted money fast.

Wonder if she's waiting for me, being faithful.

Well, hell. He knew the answer to that. Molly was a beautiful woman. Smart, too. And he was just a big ugly man with average brains and not much luck. Sure, he knew she'd slept with other men since they'd been married. He knew, but he worked hard at not letting on to Molly. She was the best thing ever to come along into his life and he didn't want to risk losing her.

She hadn't taken to a lot of other men. Just one every once in a while. The first time he realized what was going on, three or four months after they'd gotten married, it really tore at him. He felt like somebody he knew really well had suddenly died. He never, though, let on.

Cartland pulled up on his reins. The gang had reached its destination. He dropped from his saddle, tethered the bay on some scrub brush and moved across the predawn darkness.

He kept on thinking of Molly as he worked with the strong wire cutters he'd brought, snipping the barbed wire that fenced in this quarter of the Circle BJ rangeland. Absently he noticed that this was a new brand of wire. Scutt's Arrow Plate, they called it.

Imagine getting rich on something as simple as barbed wire. They said Joe Glidden was pretty near a millionaire already from more or less inventing the stuff. Maybe Scutt, whoever he was, was rich, too. Stick some metal thorns on a length of wire and you rake in a fortune. Didn't seem fair.

"Hurry it up," urged Janson in a harsh whisper.

In another few minutes enough fence was down. They remounted and went riding over onto Big Jim Phillips' land.

Cartland glanced to his left and automatically started to go for his gun.

"No shootin'," reminded the man riding on his left.

"But those hands are sure to—"

"Forget 'em!"

The two Circle BJ riders Cartland had spotted some five hundred yards to his left didn't do a damn thing. They kept on riding off in the direction they'd been heading.

"I don't understand this," said Cartland.

"You don't have to, pard."

Chapter 14

"You ride very well, Mr. Stormfield," Maude Rudd insisted.

"I fear you flatter me, dear lady," said the moderately bouncing author. "I am no centaur."

The two of them were riding through the hazy yellow morning, across flat prairie toward low foothills. The hefty woman shifted in her saddle, smiling across at Stormfield. "It is truly a pleasure to be able to converse with a well-read man such as yourself," she told him. "My second husband, the poor late Mr. Estling, was also a cultured man. I sometimes think I miss him most of all of them."

He coughed, then asked, "How many have there been?"

"How many?" She bit at her tongue while she thought. "Heavens, the total so far must be six at the very least. Let's see. . . . There was poor Mr. Kolb, he was first. Then after Mr. Estling came Mr. Clark. . . . No, I take that back. Poor Mr. Lumbard was second, he only lasted three months. Clark was fourth. . . . Who was number five? Oh, what *was* his name? Yes, I have it. . . . Mr. Sederholm. A very handsome man, poor fellow, until the horse kicked him in the head. Next came Mr. Thompson, poor dear, and the last was the late Mr. Baumhofer. He's the one, as you may have heard, who had such an unfortunate encounter with those awful buffalo."

" 'Tis a sad life you've lived," said Stormfield. "They all died in accidents?"

"Yes, yes," sighed Maude. "I can't sometimes help but think that I'm a jinx, a Jonah, a—"

"There, there, dear lady. Don't blame yourself for the unfortunate spins of the wheel of fortune."

"I wish poor Mr. Baumhofer, my most recent, had shared your views. When he was in his cups, which was often, he was fond of calling me a hoodoo."

"Tippled a bit, did he?"

"Why else would he have taken a nap in the path of a buffalo stampede?"

"One wonders."

They rode on in silence for a few minutes, Maude on her grey mare, Stormfield on the docile, though still bumpy, roan gelding.

"There's the shack," said Maude finally, pointing.

It was near a stand of alder trees. The shack was made of sod blocks and had a slanting plank and tarpaper roof. There was a low, narrow doorway and one large rectangle of a window. The plank door stood slightly ajar, and before they reached the place, something small and grey came darting out of the doorway to vanish in the scrub and bluestem grass nearby.

"Far from palatial," Stormfield observed, reining up.

"Poor Mr. Klein seemed to enjoy it. He came here often to contemplate and compose." She dismounted and tethered her mare. "I haven't been by here in quite some time." From the saddle boot she slid out her Springfield rifle.

"What are you anticipating inside, dear lady?" he inquired as he dropped to the ground amidst clumps of grass.

"I have a hunch coyotes and such have been breaking in." Maude strode up to the sod shack and booted the door all the way open.

Several small scurrying sounds spilled out into the morning, followed by silence.

Stormfield ventured to the threshold to peer inside. "Fragrant," he decided.

The single room smelled strongly of animal droppings and soot. It contained a roughhewn table, two chairs and an oil lantern. There was a small sod-brick fireplace and three wooden crates against one wall.

"We may as well go on in," suggested Maude, edging by him with her rifle pointing into the shack.

He followed her inside.

"Heavens, this is going to need a good airing and a real cleaning up before we can look for—"

"Touch nothing, dear lady."

"But why?"

"Indulge my whim, please." He took her arm, led her back to the doorway and stood her there. "I want to poke about a bit, see the place just as it is."

"For some artistic reason, you mean?" She lowered her rifle, puzzled.

Stormfield was crouching, scowling at the stains he'd already noticed on the plank floor at the center of the room. There were also faint traces of bootprints in the dust, scribbled across with the tracks of small animals. Even so, he could make out the signs of two—possibly three—men struggling. And the dark splotches were unmistakably blood.

"I just realized," Maude gasped. "That's blood, isn't it? Do you think poor Mr. Klein met with foul play?"

"It may just be animal blood," he lied blandly, rising and rubbing his plump hands together. "He worked at yon table?"

She nodded. "You're certain it wasn't Mr. Klein who bled all over the floor?"

"Don't worry your dear head," he advised as he crossed to the table.

There was the stub of a pencil next to the lantern. Nothing else was on the slightly warped top.

The author glanced around, then made his way to the fireplace. "Ah, too late, I fear." He knelt, fished a chunk of blackened leather out of the ashes. "The cover of his notebook, mayhap?"

Maude took a few steps forward. "Looks as though it might be," she decided, squinting. "But why ever would poor Mr. Klein destroy his manuscript?"

" 'Twasn't Klein did this." He poked his fingers in the soot, locating another fragment of the burned cover. "Ah, eureka!"

Clinging to the charred piece of notebook cover was a fragment of white paper, nearly three inches square and unburned. There was writing, neat script done in pencil, on both sides. One side read, ". . . not only guns but cattle, running both South to . . ." On the other side of the scrap of paper was, ". . . tender at the Golden Door is tied in. Am almost certain whom he and Angel are working for and . . ."

Nodding, Stormfield preserved the fragment carefully in his flat wallet. He went back to probing the ashes until both his hands were black to the wrists. He found no more of Klein's notebook.

From the doorway Maude asked, "Was he working on a novel?"

Drawing out his crisp breast-pocket handkerchief, Stormfield stood and began wiping his fingers. "His work was more in the line of reportage, dear lady."

"Now it's lost forever."

"Perhaps not." He gave her a thin smile. "It's always possible to go out and collect the same facts over again."

Chapter 15

"Now you take that business with the Molly Maguires," said Big Jim Phillips, snapping his fingers at the grey-haired Mexican servant standing near the large oak dining table. "Seems to me, meaning no offense, that the Pinkertons acted like Judas goats in that little affair. They certainly weren't on the side of the common man."

Spear grinned across the dinner table. "Common men such as yourself, you mean?"

"I grew up dirt-poor," the big rancher responded. "*Más vino,* Ramon. What I have now, I worked hard to get. You Pinkertons always seem to be on the side of the snooty bastards who grind our faces back in the dirt."

"I say, Phillips, Spear isn't involved in grinding any poor blokes into anything," put in Ramsey.

He and Spear, along with Seamus Tuck, Wally Anderson and the two wagonloads of guns and ammunition, had arrived at the vast Circle BJ Ranch at sundown. Now the two of them were finishing up a lavish dinner with Phillips in the big, beam-ceilinged dining room of the main ranch house.

"I'm not trying to ride anybody," protested the rancher. He paused while the old Mexican placed a fresh carafe of red wine on the white tablecloth before him. "Simply speaking my mind. You understand that, don't you, Spear?"

"Sure, and I appreciate your forthrightness, Phillips. Now that we've gotten your feelings and opinions about the detective agency I work for out of the way, we can have ourselves some forthright palaver about what's wrong here at the Circle BJ."

Big Jim laughed, nearly spilling the wine he was pouring. "That is getting right to the point. Well sir, what's wrong is these goddamn rustlers. In the past six months they've made off with near to three thousand head of cattle. Matter of fact, the sons of bitches hit me last night for another two hundred head."

Ramsey half stood. "Last night? You mean the blighters were taking cattle just last night? You should have mentioned it!"

"I'm mentioning it now." Big Jim poked the stopper back into the carafe. "You see, Ramsey, a raid isn't all that much in the way of news anymore."

"How many times've you been hit in the last few months?" Spear asked him.

"Seven, maybe eight," the rancher fretted. "Jake Berril, my foreman, can give you all the details."

"Who's responsible?"

"Our biggest troubles come from Steve Janson. But there is also a wild woman named Anita Torquay, and she accounts for quite a few of my cattle, as well as those of my neighbors."

"You can't stop them?" asked Ramsey.

Big Jim drank down half his glass of wine. "This

isn't exactly merry old England, Ramsey. We can't catch rustlers with spring gun traps and gamekeepers. I got near to two hundred thousand acres, and policing all that is one hell of a job. Janson, the Torquay girl and some of the others, you know, who come up over the border or from New Mexico . . . well, they're smart and mean. They come down like the proverbial wolf in the fold. They hit, take themselves several hundred of my longhorns and vanish. Brands get switched, cattle end up in some other state or down in Mexico."

"Certainly, old man, you've taken steps to prevent or at least discourage these raids."

"Hell, I've hired a dozen new hands this year, merely to patrol the fences day and night," Big Jim informed them. "All the cattlemen have done the same." He rested a rough fist on the table. "You've heard about the cattle raisers' association we formed. And about things like McNelly's Rangers."

"Haven't they helped?" Spear questioned.

"A little. The association set up patrols, hired a few range detectives. But the rustling goes on. This hotshot Captain McNelly has been pretty active, but he sure never has brought one of my cows back to me."

"What I mean to do, you know, is actively pursue these rustlers," said the Englishman. "I want to hire men, unless you can provide me with some of your own staff, and go after the blighters."

"That why you dragged all that fancy artillery here?"

"Indeed it is." A grim look of determination touched Ramsey's young face. "I've had a bit of experience, you know, and I'm confident we can run these fellows to ground."

• "Well sir, you are sure welcome to try. God knows, we got to do something."

"This latest raid," Spear mentioned. "I'd like to see where it took place."

"Nothing to see," the rancher replied. "They cut my fences, herded off my cattle. The barbed wire's been restrung, cows are long gone and you won't see a single damn thing."

"Also like to talk to the hands who were watching that part of your range."

"They didn't see or hear a damn thing. I already grilled 'em both good," said Big Jim, pouring himself more wine. "They're both boys I trust."

Ramsey was frowning. "It strikes me, you know, that you are taking all this very well, old chap. You're losing cattle in droves, Horesham is losing money. It's a state of affairs that one usually finds a bit alarming."

"Listen, Ramsey, when I catch any of the guys who've been making off with my beef, I'll personally string 'em up," Big Jim assured him. "That goes for the Torquay woman as well. While you're here nosing around, you can go over my ledgers, talk to my book-keeper and read every damn memo in my files. There hasn't been a drop of profit since your outfit bought in, Ramsey, and the main reason is rustlers. Nobody's ever accused me of being dishonest or incompetent, and I don't aim to let anyone start accusing me now!"

"Here now, old man," he said, raising a calming hand. "I am not accusing you of a blooming thing. I want those rustlers stopped and I'm counting on you, don't you know, to give me your full cooperation."

"You've got that." Big Jim pushed back from the table. "If we're able to leave off discussing business for a spell, I'd like you to visit a special part of my ranch.

I'd like to adjourn over there for a little entertainment." He got up.

"What kind of entertainment?" asked Spear.

"Female entertainment."

Ramsey gazed around the gaudy parlor, at the crystal wall lamps, the marble tabletops, the small, pink-tinted Venus posed demurely beside the white upright piano. Rubbing the sole of his boot over the bright Oriental carpet, the Englishman said, "I say, this must've cost a pretty penny."

"Bought and built," Big Jim was quick to explain, "before we began having all our financial woes here at the ranch."

"What about the ladies' salaries?" asked Spear.

Big Jim cleared his throat. "Very nominal."

Spear sat on the edge of the white-and-gilt piano bench. "Why don't you give Ramsey the tour of your private bordello," he suggested. "Think I'll just turn in for the evening."

The rancher pointed a big, blunt thumb at the ceiling. "Surely, just go on up and settle into one of the empty bedchambers. I'll send one of my best girls in to see what's your pleasure."

"You're missing my drift," said Spear. "I aim to turn in solo, over in the main house."

"You aren't interested in meeting my girls?" Big Jim gestured toward the door. "Why, they're prettying themselves up right now, anxious to come on in when I call 'em and meet you two."

"Nevertheless—" Spear got up.

"I hear you're supposed to be something of a lady's man," persisted the big rancher, giving Spear a wink. "Now, here in Texas, when a host offers you hospitality—"

"Maybe later in my stay." Spear yawned, headed for the parlor doorway. "See you gents in the morning."

Ramsey absently patted the pink Venus on the top of her head. "If you don't mind, Spear old boy, I'll linger here and . . . um . . . enjoy the hospitality, as it were. I'm, don't you know, curious as to how this sort of thing is managed in this part of your country."

"Sure, you might as well take advantage of all the tourist attractions." He went striding out.

When the front door of Big Jim's private bordello closed, the rancher shook his head. "Can't quite figure out that hombre."

"He's simply tired out," said the Englishman, moving to the piano bench and sitting down facing the keys. "We've had rather an eventful journey."

"From what I've heard of Brad Spear, he hardly ever misses a chance to have his way with women." Frowning, Big Jim went over to the doorway. "Excuse me for a moment, Ramsey. I'll see what's holding up the ladies."

"By all means." He began playing an English drinking song, but very quietly.

"Vhich vun was you?"

Ramsey jumped.

A plump young blonde woman had silently entered the room. She was wearing a silken kimono and little else, and her impressive left breast was very close to popping free into full view.

"Beg pardon, miss?" He got to his feet and bowed.

"Vas you the Pinkerton or the limey?"

Ramsey smoothed his tweedy Norfolk jacket. "I am the limey," he replied politely. "You, I take it, are one of the . . . um . . . residents."

"Yah, I'm vun of the floozies," she replied, coming

closer to him. "My name vas Inga Reisberson. I come over from Hammerfest, Norway, five years ago."

"Ah, yes. I can see your Nordic heritage."

She pulled her kimono tighter. "Yah, dey is alvays flopping out."

Ramsey chuckled politely. "Well. And how, Miss Reisberson, do you like . . . um . . . that is, do you enjoy Texas?"

"Sure, is great place." She came several steps closer, her blonde head tilted slightly to one side. "I'm vunderin' vould you like better Irene or Sophie."

Blinking, the blond Englishman muttered, "As a . . . um . . . partner, do you mean?"

"Yah." Inga nodded and her left breast escaped completely. "Irene vas skinny, but she come from Glasgow. That's England, isn't it?"

"Well, quite near actually, yes," he answered. "When you say skinny, what exactly do you imply?"

"Small breasts."

"Ah, yes, I see. And Sophie, I presume, is better . . . um . . . endowed?"

"Big breasts."

Ramsey pondered this, dropping back to the piano bench.

"Sophie, however, ain't got much brains," Inga imparted.

"Whereas Irene is smart?"

"Smarter than Sophie."

Brightening, Ramsey said, "I say, suppose I try them both?"

Spear circled the wagon, puffing on his cigar. Both the covered wagons, still loaded with weapons and ammunition, had been parked in a large barn to the rear of the main house.

"Dagnab," Seamus Tuck exclaimed, spitting on the wooden floor. "I had me in mind to sleep in a feather bed tonight."

"After two a.m. you can sleep anyplace you please."

"It was my notion we was safe, now that we've arrived at this enormous large ranch."

"Might be we are," Spear speculated. "Come tomorrow we'll get all of Ramsey's war toys unpacked and locked up. Until then I want to keep an eye on all of them."

"Go right ahead," invited the grizzled driver. "Start now and I can maybe sneak up there—"

"Despite the Pinkertons' motto about never sleeping," cut in the detective, "I find I need a nap every few days. I'll take over from you in about four hours from now."

"Well," replied Tuck, spitting again, "I s'pose I can help out to that extent. Who you expectin' to show up? Not somebody with a buffalo knife?"

"Not sure." Spear took another puff on his thin cigar. "How's Wally faring?"

"Sound asleep in a feather bed."

"Still think he's wounded?"

"Nope, it is now his half-wit notion that he passed the bullet shortly after supper. I didn't bother to trot on over to the outhouse to confirm that."

Spear grinned. "See you in a few hours."

Tuck caught at his arm. "Have you seen 'em?"

"Which?"

"Big Jim's ladies. Word is he got a half dozen or more and every one a ravin' beauty."

"I didn't get around to looking over his collection," said Spear, "but Big Jim claims his ladies are indeed lookers one and all. There are only five of 'em, by the way."

"Right now," Tuck chuckled, "I'd settle for just one."

Chapter 16

Spear, minus boots and Stetson, was dozing in an armchair in his room in the main house. He was dreaming that he was back home in the Oregon timber country. His father was alive and they were walking together in the pine woods. Spear's dad had something damn important to tell him. Something about self-preservation. . . .

There was a tapping on his door.

Spear got up, wide awake, and tugged out his pocket watch. Three minutes beyond midnight.

The tapping was repeated and a voice whispered, "Spear?"

Staying clear of the doorway, he reached over and turned the knob. The door opened a few inches, swinging inward with a faint creak.

"Spear? I have to talk to you."

The moonlight from the narrow hallway windows revealed a slender young woman, dark-haired and pretty. She had high cheekbones, large dark eyes and an ugly bruise across one cheek. She wore a short-skirted frock trimmed in black lace and a dark cloak over her slim shoulders. She was carrying no visible weapon.

Spear's hand moved away from the vicinity of his holster and pulled the door open wider. "Something I can do for you, miss?"

The girl shivered, looked back over her shoulder furtively. "Be a lot better if I come in," she whispered. "I'm risking my tail out here. If he sees me . . ."

"C'mon in then," he invited, stepping back. "*He* would be Big Jim?"

The dark-haired girl closed the door, leaned back against it and sighed out a breath. "They're still carrying on over at the other house, him and your British friend." When she brushed back her hair, he noticed a large purplish welt on her forearm.

"You're one of the girls?"

She nodded. "My name's Yvonne."

"That's all of it?"

"Yvonne, yes. That's all the name I've had for a while."

Spear moved to the kerosene lamp on his bureau. "What exactly did you—"

"No lights, please," Yvonne insisted.

Spear shrugged, turned to face her. "Okay, let's talk."

She walked, tentatively, over to his bed and sat on its edge. "I'd been hoping I'd get to see you earlier, over there."

"My visit was sort of brief."

"You're a Pinkerton."

"Yep." He leaned against the wall, folded his arms and studied her face as she sat there in the pale moonlight.

Yvonne kept her dark cloak tight around her shoulders. "And you get hired to help people."

"That about sums up my job."

"Could you help me?"

"Depends," he answered. "What sort of trouble you in?"

"I'm just about a prisoner in that house," she murmured.

"Didn't you volunteer?"

The young woman lowered her head. "That was five long months ago. And then the deal here sounded better than what I had going in Abilene."

"But now?"

"Big Jim . . . well . . . he's really been treating me badly." Yvonne touched the bruise on her face. "I guess, being one of his private ladies, I don't have too many rights, but . . . but he hits me all the time now and . . . makes me do awful things."

"Why can't you leave?" Spear asked.

"You only leave when Big Jim's tired of you. He's not tired of me yet."

"What do you have in mind? You want my help in getting clear of him?"

She nodded. "You can do that, can't you? Alone, I don't stand a chance."

"Where'll you go?"

"Home, probably," she replied. "I still have relatives in Pennsylvania. And I've saved a little money. Enough for my train fare and to pay you a little something for your trouble."

"Nope, if I help you, there won't be any charge."

She rose up, the cloak falling away, and ran over to him. "Then you will help me." Both arms went around him and she stretched up to kiss him on the cheek. "He won't be able to stop you, I know it."

"He isn't going to get the chance," said Spear, "because he won't know a damn thing about it until you're long gone."

"How soon can we start planning?"

"I've got to handle things here first," Spear responded. He was becoming increasingly aware of her body rubbing against his. "You'll have to hold on for a few days."

"I can do that, now that I know you'll be on my side." Yvonne kissed him again, on the mouth this time, pressing her slim body hard against him.

Spear put one hand on the small of her back, feeling the warmth of her smooth flesh through the thin cloth. His other hand was easing into her low-cut bodice, finding her small sharp breasts and caressing them in turn. Her dark nipples swiftly grew erect.

"For you," she whispered warmly, "I'll do anything you want."

"Nothing fancy," he said. "I'm a man of simple tastes." He helped her out of her black silk dress and then out of the chemise she wore beneath it.

Yvonne held tight, naked against him.

He pushed her, gently, back from him and admired her.

"I look like a scarecrow," she sighed.

"Any self-respecting crow'd be pleased to perch on you." Grinning, he guided her over to his bed and arranged her atop it with her long legs spread wide.

She watched him undress, rubbing her own palms over her breasts and her stomach and finally her thighs as she waited. "You can be kind of rough, if you like."

Shedding his long johns, Spear replied, "Not my style, but I appreciate the offer." He straddled her and stayed kneeling over her body, his erection pointing to the wall behind his bed where there was a sentimental print of a lone cowboy dying beside his dead horse.

Yvonne closed one hand around his staff and began to slowly stroke it. With her other hand she fingered the tip, rubbing it softly so that it swelled even larger.

Sitting up, she licked it from the base to the top and then ran her tongue all around it. She repeated this, over and over, slowly and lingeringly, working on his staff until it glistened and was throbbing.

She then took it into her mouth.

Spear put a hand on each of her bare shoulders and began thrusting up gently. She sucked at him, stroking with both hands at the same time, running her hands up and down the length of his smooth, wet shaft. The rhythm of her sucking and stroking grew more and more intense and frenzied.

Spear kicked up the pace, too, easing up into her soft, willing mouth, humming with sounds of ecstasy. Then he was going off, shooting fluid into her.

She murmured with pleasure, swallowing, sucking, licking at him. Her lips were wet with his release.

She slowed, let go of his staff at last and wiped at her lips with the back of her hand. Settling back on the bed, she urged him down beside her. "That was only the start," she promised.

At exactly 1:15 a.m. Spear rolled out of bed.

The dark-haired girl opened her eyes. "What is it, Brad?"

"Got to visit the outhouse," he explained, getting into his underwear.

"You can use the chamber pot, it won't bother me."

"Nope, that goes against my upbringing." He was already into his trousers. He tugged on his socks and boots, then strapped on his six-gun.

"How come you need a gun to go to the outhouse?"

"Habit."

"If they haven't missed me by now, they aren't likely to for the rest of the night," she told him, rising up on one elbow. "I can stay with you all night. We can make love as many times as you'd like—or can."

"Soon as I come back, Miss Yvonne, I'll take you up on that," he smiled. He buttoned the last button on his shirt, put on his Stetson and crossed to the door.

"You'll be right back?"

"Give you my word." He eased out into the corridor. Shutting the door, he set off for the barn where the ammunition was stored.

Chapter 17

The night was cloudy, the moonlight dim.

Spear stood near the rear of the main house, looking toward the barn where the wagons were. He saw five horses standing silently near the big barn, about a hundred yards from him. Four were riderless. In the saddle of the fifth sat a husky man in a dark duster and a low-crowned sombrero. He was puffing on a cigarette, and in the red flashes his bearded face showed. It wasn't much of a face, flat and scarred. The lookout had his collar turned up and was hunched in the saddle watching the barn. He wasn't aware of Spear yet.

Nodding, Spear moved quietly across the chill ground until he was at the rear of the barn, where the bearded man couldn't see him. He edged up to the narrow rear door, stopped and listened.

Men were talking inside.

". . . least cut off an ear," one was pleading. From the inflections, Spear guessed he was an Indian.

"We got no time for games, Pinto." This one was Mexican.

"Aw, but Paloma, it's in my blood," persisted the

Indian. "I got to collect me souvenirs on a raid, you know. Ears, scalps——"

"This ain't no raid," Paloma told him. "It's a pure and simple business venture, amigo. Now get them damn horses hitched up to the wagons."

"You better do somethin' drastic to me, you goldang half-breed," said Seamus Tuck. " 'Cause if I ever get loose I'll skin you alive and use you for a rug."

"Another minute and you ain't gonna have no nose, old man."

"Pinto! Get to work!" ordered Paloma. "Help Sonny up front here."

"Hell, I do twice the work he does. And you still don't let me have no good times."

"C'mon, c'mon," urged a gruff-voiced older man.

That would be Sonny, thought Spear. Meaning there were at least three of them inside. The fourth man was with the horses and the fifth—since there were five mounts, there ought to be five riders—might be in the barn, too. Or he might be a lookout somewhere else. Out near the bunkhouse, most likely. And how come all of Big Jim's boys are such damned sound sleepers? he wondered.

Judging by the voices inside the barn, the Indian was nearest the rear. Paloma and Sonny sounded to be up near the front of the wagons.

Spear eased out his six-gun.

"Get a move on, Pinto. We ain't got all night."

"I got to tie up this old man good, don't I?"

Spear turned the handle of the door. They hadn't yet had time to rig up locks, and the door opened a few inches.

The highjackers were working by the light of a single oil lantern, and that was up toward the front. Back here it was all deep shadows.

Spear eased into the barn, ducking behind a bale of straw. Thirty feet away, with his back to him, was a lean Indian in buckskins and a dirty white Stetson. He was bending over the sprawled figure of Seamus Tuck.

"You're tyin' them dang ropes too tight, you goldang redskin!"

"Keep talkin' back and I'll slice your tongue out for you, old man."

The two wagons full of guns and ammunition hid Paloma and Sonny from Spear. And, equally important, hid him from them. Spear, crouched low, went stalking toward the preoccupied Pinto.

The Indian sensed him finally, but not quite soon enough. He was turning, knife coming out of its sheath when the butt of Spear's gun cracked across his temple. Pinto made a small, angry sound and dropped to the floor.

Spear knelt and used the unconscious man's knife to cut Tuck free. In a few seconds Tuck was on his feet. "Truss him up quick," Spear ordered in a whisper. "Then start yelling that he's cutting off your ears."

The grizzled driver winked, rubbing at his legs. Squatting in the straw, he nudged Pinto over onto his face and swiftly hog-tied him.

Spear, meantime, swung up over the tailboard of the wagon nearest Tuck and the bound Indian.

"Help!" hollered the old man. "Help! This bloodthirsty Injun is loppin' off my dang ear! Ow! Ow!"

"You stupid bastard!" Sonny came running back to the rear of the wagon. He was a fat man, pale and blond. It took him about ten seconds to realize he'd been suckered. And in that same ten seconds Spear had stretched out and conked him a good one over the skull.

Tuck, chuckling softly, caught the falling gunman.

He stretched him out next to Pinto and used the left-over rope on him.

"Stay here," instructed Spear.

He moved cautiously through the artillery wagon.

When he was five feet from the front end a slug came chuffing through the canvas. It missed him by about four feet. Spear ducked low.

"Don't know who you are, amigo!" called Paloma. "But you better come out of there pronto!"

Spear spotted the oil lantern sitting on a nail keg. He fired at it. Glass exploded and then darkness flooded the barn. He moved swiftly to the far side of the wagon, undid the canvas and dropped out into the blackness.

"Adios!" shouted Paloma. "We take this up again later!"

Boots thudded on the ground, the front door creaked and then the raider was out in the night.

Spear ran, his eyes getting used to the dark. He booted the barn door open wide and dove out, throwing himself flat on the ground.

Three horsemen went galloping away, followed by two riderless nags.

Shaking his head, Spear got to his feet. He'd scraped a little skin off his left hand.

"Stop right where you are, you son of a bitch! Or I'll drop you in your tracks."

"Better not, Big Jim," advised Spear to the big dark shape that was lumbering toward him. "Or you'll have one hell of a lot of Pinkertons right sore at you."

"Spear?" The rancher lowered the shotgun he was hefting. "What the devil's going on? I heard shooting and come out as quick as I could."

"Glad somebody heard something. Your hands slept through the whole mess."

"What's going on?" He was wearing a candy-stripe nightshirt with a hurriedly pulled on vest over it. "I hopped right out of bed."

"Ever hear of a gent by the name of Paloma?"

The rancher scowled. "That son of a bitch. Sure, I know about him. He's based down in Mexico, comes up into the Panhandle to steal my cattle every so often."

"He was after guns tonight."

"You mean he was trying for Ramsey's hardware?"

"Interesting, isn't it?" Spear grinned and dropped his six-gun into its holster. "How he got wind of the guns so soon and knew right where to find 'em?"

"Hell, by now half of Texas knows about these wagons, Spear." Big Jim nodded at the barn. "You ain't suggesting that I—"

"Nope, not suggesting anything, Big Jim," he replied. "Merely ruminating." He went walking toward the barn door. "Since we caught us a couple of 'em, I'll save all my inquiries for—"

"Dang it all to hell!" From inside Tuck could be heard groaning and muttering.

"What's wrong, Seamus?" Spear hustled inside.

"Well, I been bushwhacked." A lantern blossomed on the left and Spear saw the driver walking toward him. Tuck was unsteady on his feet and there was a bloody gash on his forehead.

"One of 'em got loose?"

"Hell no, Spear." The driver spat into the straw. "When I tie 'em, they stay tied. Nope, this was some other hombre, snuck up on me and thunked me a good one."

"Obviously one of them doubled back to rescue

his pardners," said Big Jim from the doorway. "Now we won't be able to find out anything."

Eyeing Big Jim, Spear said, "No more than we already know."

Spear sat on the edge of his bed to tug off a boot.

"That was one long visit out there," remarked the naked Yvonne from under the covers.

"Got distracted." He pulled the other boot free.

"I thought maybe I heard some shooting." She sat up, the sheet sliding away from her breasts.

Grinning, Spear answered, "You know, I've paid good money in New York and Frisco theaters to see ladies who can't act nowhere near as good as you."

"What the devil are you talking about?"

"Who suggested you call on me this evening?"

"Nobody," she insisted. "I heard you might be somebody I could trust."

"The idea was to keep me and Ramsey otherwise occupied," he said. "When I didn't settle down in Big Jim's private whorehouse yonder, he sent one of his crew over here to distract me."

"Oh, and I suppose I beat myself to make my act convincing."

"Nope, I reckon Big Jim really did smack you around." He shed his trousers.

Yvonne folded her hands atop the quilt. "If you suspected I was conning you, why'd you go ahead and make love to me?"

"Because I figured nothing was going to happen out at the barn until the middle of the night," he told her. "And you're an attractive lady."

"Thanks. Were they shooting at you out there?"

"A mite."

"You could've got killed."

"Yep, that is one of the frequent side effects of gunplay."

"Well, I'm sorry."

"If I'd been shot dead, I bet you'd have come and put fresh flowers on my grave every day."

"Listen, you conceited son of a . . . hell, never mind."

Spear got under the covers. "I'm going to sleep for a few hours," he told her. "You can stay here or trot on home to report to Big Jim." He stretched out on his side, his broad back to her.

"I thought we still might . . . I mean, aren't you interested in maybe . . ."

"There's something about getting shot at that cools my ardor."

She made an angry sound and hit him on the back with her fist. "You're so damn smug. It's easy for you to do the right thing all the time. You've had the breaks. Sure, being lucky makes all the difference."

"Nobody in this world is lucky or unlucky."

"Oh, sure. But you don't know what it's like, growing up in a coal mine town, having your damn father the town drunk. Or having your mom run off when you're seven or eight and your father trying to sell you to his friends for drink money."

"That's all over." He sat up, looked into her face. "What you do now only has to do with you."

She shivered, folding her arms under her breasts. "Well . . . well, Big Jim did send me over here. He told me first to find out what you were up to, what you suspected and all. Then I was to be damn sure you stayed in all night."

"Why?"

"I don't know. He's not the kind of man who gives you reasons," she replied. "You just do what he tells you." She held her breath briefly, then let it out slowly. "Could you really do what you said? Get me clean away from here?"

"Were you on the level about that?"

"Big Jim only ordered me to keep you here," Yvonne answered. "The bruises were to make you feel sorry for me. But the story I told you, about wanting to get free and clear of here . . . thing is, when I got to spinning that yarn for you, it got to sounding pretty damn good. I really do want to leave."

"Okay, my promise still goes. I'll help you out."

"I was conning you some earlier," Yvonne told him. "I'm not now."

"Doesn't seem like you are."

"When we were making love, that wasn't exactly pretending either. What I mean is . . . I really did enjoy it."

Spear stretched out on his back, locked his hands behind his head. "I appreciate your sincerity."

"Now you're making fun of me, but I do mean it."

"When you see Big Jim again," he said, "tell him I took a liking to you. Even though I managed to slip out and make trouble, you think you can get more out of me in time. That way he won't get too mad at you maybe."

She leaned down and kissed him lightly on the lips. "Thanks," she murmured. "If you'd like to begin all over. . . ."

Putting an arm around her smooth bare shoulders, he returned her kiss. "Think I better sleep for a few hours," he sighed. "But if you're still here at sunup, bring up the motion again."

"I'll be here," promised Yvonne, snuggling down close beside him.

Chapter 18

Spear left the warm, dry afternoon and went striding into the shadowy barn. It looked very much like an armory now, with the cargoes of both the wagons unpacked and stacked.

On a case of Winchester rifles sat Seamus Tuck, squeezing a tune out of his concertina. "Let's look lively," he urged Wally Anderson and the two Circle BJ hands who were unloading the final wagon.

"A recently shot man," complained Wally, "oughtn't to lift nothin' heavy." He was hefting a case of dynamite over to the corner of the big barn.

"Exercise is the best dang thing in the world, Wally. Why I knew an hombre once in Beaumont who got himself shot right smack in the brain. But by jumpin' around a whole lot he . . . oh, howdy, Spear. Just wind up your tomcattin'?"

"Been out exercising. Where's Ramsey?"

Tuck ceased playing so he could jerk a thumb at a stall across the way. "In there snoozin'," he explained. "He straw-bossed us for a spell before decidin' he needed a nap or two." The grizzled driver chuckled. "Them ladies of Big Jim's must be really somethin'."

"Want to chat with you later about getting this place locked up proper." Spear crossed over to the stall and looked in.

The young Englishman, blond hair tousled and mouth agape, was asleep on his back. An ancient army blanket was spread out beneath him.

Spear kicked at his nearest foot. "Hey, Ramsey."

". . . delightful country . . ." murmured Ramsey, eyelids fluttering.

"Ramsey!"

"What? Are they acting up again in . . . ah, I say, it's you, eh, Spear?" He yawned, rubbed at his eyes, sat up. "Thought for a moment, don't you know, that I was back in India and we had a blooming mutiny on our hands."

"Did Tuck tell you about last night?"

The blond Englishman blinked. "Yes, and I'm damned chagrined, old boy, that I wasn't on hand to help fight off the blighters." He got to his feet like a groggy prizefighter. "Jove, the whole bloody barn is spinning."

"Tonight I may not be around," Spear told him. "So you're going to have to watch."

"Of course, old man, of course." He leaned against a post. "I know my duty, after all. Fact of the blooming matter is, I'd have been here last evening to give those swarthy scoundrels a bit of what for had I not been distracted by the fleshy charms of two of the most intriguing young wenches I have ever had the pleasure of knowing."

"If this cache of weapons gets swiped, even if it's because you were busy with two women when you should have been watching, it's going to be trouble for both of us."

"See here, old man, there's no reason to chastise me as though I were a public school lad," moaned Ramsey, a deep frown wrinkling his forehead. "I mean to say, if it comes to that, where have you been all the bloody morning? I understand you formed a bit of a friendship with one of the birds named Yvonne."

"I rode out to the spot where the latest raid on the Circle BJ stock took place," Spear told him.

"Really, old boy? Did Big Jim accompany you?"

"Big Jim doesn't even know I went. I found out the location from one of the hands, gent named Tom Curry."

Ramsey ran his tongue over his lips. "Your Western liquor is . . . but let's get down to business," he decided. "Did you learn anything, old boy?"

"It was a very neat and efficient job. And I'm fairly certain that at least two of Big Jim's boys witnessed the rustling and didn't do a damn thing about it."

"How can you be at all sure of such a serious charge?"

"By reading the signs," said Spear.

"But then, I say, if that's true, we have to locate the two blokes and alert Big Jim to—"

"Listen." Spear took hold of his arm. "I don't want to tell anybody anything yet. Don't go babbling to Big Jim or any of his women."

"Come now, I am not in the habit of babbling to whores."

"And you're probably not in the habit of sleeping off a drunk in a barn, but that's where I found you," Spear countered.

"A most unusual situation, brought about by a

combination of excessive liquor and physical fatigue, both most disorienting."

"Yeah, okay. Whatever the reason, Ramsey, I'd like it not to happen anymore."

"Spear, you work for me. I don't see how you're in a position to tell me what to do."

"We both work for Horesham. I don't want to have to ship your carcass back to 'em in a pine box," he said evenly. "It wouldn't look good on my record."

"I say, you don't honestly think that I might be in mortal danger?"

"I think you'd better listen to what I'm saying and then keep it all to yourself."

Ramsey straightened up. "I shan't let you down," he promised. Lowering his voice, he asked, "Surely, Spear, you don't suspect Big Jim himself of any direct connection with all this? I mean to say, he's been most cordial and hospitable to the both of us."

Spear grinned. "I'm reserving judgment on him. But he wouldn't be the first whorehouse proprietor to deal on the shady side."

Molly Cartland touched her napkin to her lips. "This is what I call an amazing coincidence, Mr. Stormfield."

"Life abounds with them, dear lady," said the plump author, resting his elbows on the checkered tablecloth.

"Imagine running into someone here in Tascosa who's an old friend of Brad Spear's," the red-haired woman exclaimed.

The hotel restaurant was nearly empty, but the smell of beefsteak and onions was fragrant in the air.

"Yes, as a man who writes of fictional heroes, I make it my business to acquaint myself with some of the heroes of real life. Men like Buffalo Bill, Ulysses Grant, Bradley Spear——"

"You actually consider Brad heroic?" Her pretty nose wrinkled.

"In his way, most assuredly." Stormfield fluffed his side-whiskers. "Spear is not flamboyant, as is Bill Cody. Yet in his own calm, determined way. . . ."

"He's an interesting man," Molly admitted, toying with the handle of her coffee mug. "But . . . well, I can't help feeling he let me down. In fact, the reason I was forward enough to approach you, when I noticed you sitting out in our hotel lobby, is that I was feeling abandoned."

"A lamentable state for anyone to be in," he said. "I'm most pleased and gratified that my invitation to dinner was accepted and that I have perhaps brightened your lonely vigil, Mrs. Cartland."

"It isn't only that," she told him, her eyes gazing at his plump face. "You see, I sensed you were some-one I could count on."

Stormfield smiled. " 'Twould be an honor, dear lady, to act the champion. Do you find yourself in some dire predicament? I trust my long-time friend, Bradley Spear, is in no way responsible for your unfor-tunate situation."

"Well, not exactly, no," Molly answered. "He's doing a job and didn't have time for me."

"A job, eh?" said Stormfield casually. "Pinkerton work, do you mean?"

"Yes, he's here with a very thoughtful and helpful young Englishman named Peter Ramsey. Peter represents the Horesham Cattle Estates."

"Who've invested rather substantially hereabouts, have they not?"

"Yes, they have. Peter was sent over to find out why the ranch they invested in is losing money."

"Which ranch is this?"

"The Circle BJ, run by a man named—"

"Big Jim Phillips," Stormfield finished. "Yes, I've heard of the gentleman."

"Peter brought two wagonloads of arms down here from Dodge City," Molly told him. "He was kind enough to allow me to travel along with them."

"Guns and ammunition, eh?"

"Peter intends to run down the rustlers who've been stealing so many of the Circle BJ cattle." She paused, drew out her handkerchief and dabbed at her nose.

"Why does it cause you pain to discuss guns and bullets, dear lady?" He reached across the dinner table, put a plump hand over hers.

"It's not the guns and bullets," she answered, sniffing. "It's what he's going to do with them. When I imposed on Peter for a ride here, well, I didn't know that among the very gang of rustlers he'd be going after . . . well, that my husband might be involved."

"Surely, Mrs. Cartland, you don't suspect that your missing spouse is in cahoots with brigands?"

She wiped at her eyes. "I . . . I saw him with them."

"With a band of rustlers?"

"They weren't rustling at the time." Molly twisted the damp handkerchief between her fingers. "They were trying to kill us and steal the wagons."

"Encountering your beloved spouse under such circumstances must've been vexing." Stormfield clucked sympathetically. "What was . . . Sam, is it? What was Sam's reaction to this strange confrontation?"

"Oh, Sam never saw me. I was hunkered down in a wagon, shooting through a vent in the canvas." She used the handkerchief on her eyes again.

"This marauding band, do you have any notion who they might be?"

"Part of the Steve Janson gang," she replied. "I simply don't understand what Sam is doing with them. Because, as I told you earlier, we're supposed to own a beautiful piece of ranchland in this part of Texas."

"Yes, and I believe you mentioned that Bradley Spear had advised you to find out exactly where the acreage was and journey there in search of some clue as to your husband's whereabouts, and now, most assuredly, his behavior."

"There's ever so much red tape involved in doing that," Molly told him. "While I've been waiting for that to work out, I've found out a few things. I think the bartender at the Golden Door Saloon can get a message to the Janson gang."

"Do you now? Isn't that fascinating." Stormfield had come back to Tascosa for the purpose of getting a look at this very bartender, the one mentioned in the fragment of Elisha Klein's journal.

"The Golden Door is a wild place," she continued as she wound the handkerchief around her forefinger. "I've been trying all day to work up enough nerve to venture in there. I must get a message to Sam, let him know that I'm here in Tascosa and anxious to see him."

The author stroked his chin. "Dear lady, I should be most happy to escort you into that low den," he offered. "Even though I firmly believe it is not a desirable place for so fair a flower as you."

"I have to get in touch with Sam."

Stormfield bowed slightly. "I shall escort you,

dear lady, to the Golden Door. Or into the very jaws of Hades if you so command."

Stormfield and the red-haired young woman were several paces from the bar when Angel accosted them. He'd been sitting alone at a table with his booted feet up on it. His long hair wasn't tied and it hung down to his shoulders.

"I've seen you around town, Rusty," he said to Molly as he moved in their direction. "Been intending to invite you to have a snort or two."

"Ignore the lout," Stormfield advised in a whisper.

"What're you telling her, grandpa?" Angel's spurs clanged as he walked even closer.

The author guided Molly up to the bar, not cheered by the fearful look on the face of the bald bartender. "Speak your piece to this far from hirsute gentleman, my dear, as rapidly as you can."

"Hey, you old geezer, I asked you a question." Angel had halted about ten feet from them.

"Maybe you better do your drinking elsewhere, folks," suggested O'Malley as he wiped at his hairless head with a bar towel. "This isn't exactly a place for bringing ladies anyway."

"I had to come here," Molly began to explain, "because I—"

"C'mon, I'm waiting!" Angel shouted angrily.

One chair fell over as three of the patrons hurried for the saloon doors.

"Young man," Stormfield responded as he glanced disdainfully toward the gunman, "I suggest you run home to the bosom of your family, ere you find yourself in dire trouble."

"You got no right to talk to me like that," Angel

complained. "I see you got a gun strapped on under that frock coat of yours."

"I do indeed," acknowledged Stormfield.

"Then you better unbutton your damn coat and get ready to draw against me."

Two more customers went scooting outside into the night.

"Now, Angel, you got no call to threaten him like that," O'Malley cautioned.

"Shut up, Curly, or I'll put a slug in your fat belly for you," warned Angel, rubbing his fingertips on his palms. "You, grandpa, I told you to go for your gun."

"I have no intention, my boy, of entering into a gun duel with a callow whelp who's barely weaned." Stormfield urged Molly to move clear of him.

"I don't give a damn what your intentions are," Angel grumbled. "I'm going to count five and draw. You do whatever you want. One . . . two . . . three . . . four . . ."

Chapter 19

Big Jim Phillips let go of Inga's right breast and, after rubbing his fingertips along his nankeen trousers, he tugged his filigree gold watch from his vest pocket.

"You got something else on your mind, Yim?" inquired plump, blonde Inga while rearranging her substantial breast back inside her kimono.

"What?" He held the watch up close to his eyes, squinting.

"Yim, I hope you haven't tired of me." She slumped on the sofa she was sharing with the hefty rancher. "I hate to get booted out like some of dem udder girls you—"

"Now, Inga, you're still number one in my book. Don't go fretting none." Putting the watch away, he stood up.

"Number vun?"

"Why sure, hon." He bent, kissed her on one plump pink cheek. "Tell you what, sweetheart, you get yourself arranged in your bed yonder. I'll be back in a few shakes of a lamb's tail."

"You're not going to visit vun of dem udder floozies?"

"Nope, I am not," he assured her as he backed for the door. "And even if I did, darlin', you know I'm the kind of gent who saves the best for last. You're dessert to me."

"Yim, you're sveet." She smiled at him and spread her arms wide. "You sure you haven't time for yust a qvick one?"

"Soon, pet. Right now there's some business I have to take care of." He left her room, shut the door softly, glanced around and then went hurrying toward another door.

He hesitated at the door before tapping three times. Then he went in.

Sitting on the edge of the bed was a large, dark haired man. He was clean-shaven and had faintly Indian features. He wore his hair long. The makings of a cigarette, Bull Durham sack and paper, had been dropped on the bedspread. There was a Colt .45 in his left hand. "*Buenas noches*, Señor Phillips," he greeted with a smile.

"Put that damn shooting iron away, Paloma. Who the hell'd you think was going to come in here?"

Paloma shrugged. "One of your *putas* could be, or maybe that Pinkerton." He spun the gun once and thrust it back into the silver-trimmed holster.

"Don't go shooting any of my girls, thinking they're Pinks."

"You can always buy new whores, amigo. The supply never runs out." Paloma forked up the cigarette paper with two fingers and shook tobacco into it. "Did your Pinkerton indeed go?"

"Yep, left a couple hours ago for Tascosa." Big Jim sat down in an armchair. "I told you he was going, in that note I sent you. Telling you to slip in here for a meeting."

Nodding, the Mexican said, "I like to be sure."

"Afraid of him?"

Paloma rolled his cigarette and licked it. Then he laughed. "He's a little tougher than the last one," he replied, swinging his fancy boots up on the bed.

"Damn it, Paloma, don't go getting cow dung on the bed."

"I never step in it, Señor Jim," he assured Phillips. "Now let's talk of these guns which rest in your barn."

"You ought to've had them last night."

"Last night, amigo, I was not expecting the Pinkerton," reminded Paloma. "No, I had been informed that all your gringo guests would be here in your little bordello."

"One damn detective. Seems to me you and your men could've handled one damn detective."

"You know how old I am?"

Big Jim coughed. "What the devil does that have to do with anything?"

"Guess, señor."

"Thirty."

"Thirty-five," corrected Paloma, putting his freshly made cigarette between his teeth. "That is very old for anyone in my line of work." He lit the cigarette. "I got to be so very old, amigo, because I don't take chances. *Sabe*?"

"Well, Spear's in Tascosa by now," the rancher said. "The English dude's over in the barn with one old muleskinner."

"Can I kill them?"

"No," answered Big Jim, shaking his head. "I

don't want those damn English sending a whole army over here."

"It's going to be harder if I can't kill nobody." Paloma blew smoke toward the ceiling.

"Use a few more men."

"You know what I been thinking?" the Mexican asked.

"No. But my instincts tell me you're going to tell me."

"I been thinking you're going to get five hundred dollars less than I told you."

"Listen, Paloma!" Big Jim was on his feet, hands tightening into fists. "We got us a deal."

The dark man laughed softly. "You going to take me to court?" He shook his head. "No, amigo, you ain't going to do a damn thing. I pay you what I figure is fair and you keep your mouth shut. Just like on our other gun deals."

"But this time, Paloma, you don't have to worry about the army or the Secret Service," the rancher reminded him. "Hell, it's like shooting fish in a barrel. I don't see why you think you have to do this."

"Five hundred less because it's more trouble than I expected," Paloma said softly. "Otherwise I get mad. And then our friends down in Mexico, they get mad and that's *muy malo para usted.* You understand?"

"Okay, I'll settle for less." He sat down. "This time."

Lightning danced along the night street. Up on the lowered tailboard of his brightly painted wagon, Professor William Emerson Pepper, frazzled hair standing higher than ever, was addressing a small crowd of drifters and loafers. "My friends, noble denizens of Tascosa," he boomed, holding the Bioptiscope high, "tonight is the night of nights! Aye, for comes the rosy-fingered dawn and I depart your fair community for far horizons and greener pastures. You are witnessing, therefore, your last golden opportunity to purchase a bottle of Lightning Water for the fantastic low price of only *one dollar* per bottle!"

Grinning to himself, Spear walked on toward his meeting with Rowdy Kate.

His course took him by the Golden Door Saloon. As he passed, several customers burst forth into the street. They hurried away from the drinking establishment, casting anxious looks back.

Curious, Spear glanced in over the swinging doors.

He was just in time to hear Angel count ". . . three . . . four . . ."

"Before you go any further," Spear cut in, pushing through the swinging doors, his six-guns still holstered, "you better deal me in."

Angel's eyes flicked, taking in Spear. "The Pink, huh?" he sneered. "You two going to gang up on me?"

"Nope," Spear told the young gunman. "I'll just take over for Mr. Stormfield."

"I appreciate your kind offer, Bradley," the portly author put in, "but this youthful lout is challenging me and not you. Good to see you after lo these many months, I might add."

"Brad," said Molly, "he means to gun us down."

"Angel," said Spear, "I got me a hunch you and I met in Dodge a few weeks back."

"Yeah, and I should've spilled your goddamn guts then," replied the long-haired Angel. "You were lucky, damn lucky."

"Who put you up to that job?"

"None of your damn business."

Spear took a few steps across the planked floor. "Okay then, Angel, here's the deal. My friends are going to walk on out of this joint. Then I'm going to follow 'em. Should you make a move to stop any of that, things'll turn sort of unfortunate for you."

Angel's laugh sounded like a bleating animal. "Like hell!" he yelled.

Nodding in the direction of Stormfield and the red-headed young woman, Spear said, "Thomas, take her out of here."

"Yes, I've come to realize that's the wisest course to follow." He offered his arm to Molly. "Allow me, dear lady."

"Nobody's leaving!" warned Angel. His hands were floating at his sides, his fingers stroking his palms anxiously.

"Go on," Spear told the author.

"With alacrity, Bradley, my boy." Stormfield took hold of Molly's arm and pulled her back along the bar.

"Don't try to draw," Spear cautioned Angel.

The young gunman was running his tongue over his upper lip and grinding one boot sole on the saloon floor for better balance and leverage. "Can't nobody outdraw—"

That was the last thing he ever got to say in this world. Angel had gone for both guns at once. Before his fingers had even closed on the butts, Spear's six-gun was out and firing.

The first slug took Angel in the left arm, ripping away cloth and flesh.

The second one drove into his chest, raking across a rib and then tearing through a lung. Blood came spewing out of his chest and then bubbled out over his lips.

He was tottering backward, then dropped to one

knee. He was glaring up at Spear, trying to drag out his guns, struggling to at least curse him once more. But his hands didn't belong to him anymore and they only clawed air. And all that came from his throat was blood. He fell over on his side, his booted feet kicking and jerking until death stopped him.

Spear shook his head. "Damn fool kid." He glanced over at the bar, gun still in his hand.

Curly O'Malley was not in evidence. The bald bartender had gone scooting out of there while Spear's attention was elsewhere.

He heard Molly sobbing and looked over toward the doorway. She was standing there, her face very pale, with Stormfield's arm around her.

"Thomas, I've been intending to look you up out at the Rudd ranch," he said, walking over to them. "Figure we might have a few things to talk over."

"We do indeed," agreed the portly author. "First, however, I suggest I escort this lady to her suite at yon hostelry."

"I want Brad to see me home," Molly said in a weak voice.

Spear considered. "Thomas, I'll meet you at a café down the street called Rowdy Kate's," he told Stormfield. "In a half-hour or so."

"Do you recommend the viands? This little set-to has made me quite ravenous again."

"The food won't kill you," Spear replied.

"That's high praise," said Stormfield. "If one can say the same for the customers of Rowdy Kate, I'll see you in a half-hour . . . or so."

Chapter 20

"You threw me aside like an old shoe!" Molly accused Spear.

Spear grinned. "You've got me mixed up with your husband, ma'am."

She raised a hand, then let it drop back into her lap. "Oh, I'm too weary to come over there and slap your face." She was sitting in a threadbare armchair in her hotel room.

Spear was leaning against the wall near her iron-frame bed. "What were you doing at the Golden Door?"

"I'm still trying to find my husband," she explained. "I'd heard that the bartender there might be able to get a message to the Janson gang."

"Yep, Curly's a go-between for the Steve Janson bunch. But that saloon isn't exactly the sort of place for ladies like yourself."

"Your friend Mr. Stormfield was gentleman enough to offer to assist me," she said. "After you and Peter Ramsey abandoned me here, I was grateful for any help I could find."

"Nobody abandoned you. Ramsey agreed to give you a ride this far. That was all. As for me, I'm working for Ramsey's outfit."

"Yes, I know. And even though you took advantage of me out on the prairie, I can't expect you to help me now."

"Best help I could be is to see you get headed out of here."

Molly rose to her feet. "I won't leave until I find my husband."

"Trying to get in touch with Steve Janson is only going to get you in more trouble." He pushed up the brim of his Stetson with his thumb.

"I know what's the matter with you." She took a few steps toward him. "You're not used to dealing with a really independent woman. Someone who's unwilling to sit around doing embroidery all day while you're off chasing after God knows what—or whom."

"If you're so all-fired independent, Molly, then quit trying to get other folks to find your wayward husband for you."

"Oh, you arrogant—" She lunged, took a swing at his grinning face.

Spear caught her fist in his palm. "I've already done all the fighting I aim to do tonight." He slid his other arm around her shoulders, drew her to him and kissed her on the mouth.

She struggled, murmured and then gave in. She put her arms around him and returned his kiss, sending her tongue darting around his. "I wish," she said after a long moment, "I didn't want you so much. . . ."

Spear got rid of his hat and gunbelt while Molly shed her dress. Her lacy undergarments they both worked on.

When she stood naked against him, Spear unbuttoned his pants and his erect staff snapped out.

Molly rode it, running her scarlet triangle over it again and again, wetting it with her own love juices. Then she backed off and helped Spear out of the rest of his clothes.

They stood together, naked bellies touching, his erection between her thighs as they hungrily kissed each other. Spear reached down and drew up one of Molly's legs. His stout staff parted her soft wet lips as he rocked his hips against hers. Molly locked her arms around Spear's neck and bit into his shoulder. It was then that Spear, each hand cupping a full firm buttock, lifted her off the ground and onto him. Molly moaned with delight as Spear slid in smooth and deep.

'She pressed her lips against his, began probing her tongue into his mouth in time with the stroking of his staff deep into her.

"Now," she urged, "now!"

He went off, pumping a dozen rapid strokes, squeezing the flesh of her hips, feeling her breasts flatten against his chest as she clung to him. She stayed locked to him, kissing him, laughing at how good she felt.

With his strong rough hands still cupped to her bare buttocks and his staff still hard inside her, he carried the red-headed woman over to the bed.

"Don't leave me yet," she begged.

"Wasn't intending to," said Spear.

Stormfield pushed aside his coffee mug. "Ah, youth," he sighed as Spear sat down opposite him at the restaurant table. "Would I were as steadfast as . . . and so on."

"After I saw Molly Cartland home," said Spear, "I dropped in on Marshal Beaven."

"Yes, I thought it best to leave the explaining of that unfortunate young lout's sudden demise to you," the writer returned. "Since, so far as the town marshal knows, I am naught but a humble scribe."

"He doesn't know that you're also a Secret Service agent?"

"I didn't deem it necessary to inform him just yet. Ofttimes I can learn more when my governmental function is unknown."

There were few other diners in the place and Rowdy Kate herself was not in evidence at the moment. From the unseen kitchen came the occasional sound of pan meeting skull.

Spear rested his elbows on the table. "Looks like we might just be working on the same case once again."

"Quite possibly, my boy. And yet again I've left the dirty work to you." Stormfield shook his head. "In my youth, now long fled, I would have been able to outdraw and outshoot friend Angel. Now, alas, such is probably not the case and I was, I must admit, suffering considerable trepidation until you arrived on the scene."

Spear nodded, grinning. "Just happened to be passing by," he told the author. "Now tell me what the U.S. government has you investigating in these parts."

"Several shipments of weapons, destined for various military installations, have been diverted," Stormfield informed him. "These lethal doodads later turn up in Southern climes, down Mexico way, in the hands of bandits and other incorrigible ne'er-do-wells. Are you here to ascertain who in this benighted area is taking a hand in these highjackings?"

"Not exactly," answered Spear. "Although I do have an interest in the problem. Mainly because my client insisted on bringing two wagonloads of arms and ammunition into the Panhandle."

"Yes, Mrs. Cartland mentioned something about that. Is the lad planning to outfit his own little set of soldiers?"

"Something along those lines. Name is Peter Ramsey, over representing an outfit called Horesham Cattle Estates."

"So your primary interest is in the well-being of said cattle and the identity of those who've been rustling same."

"Yep, I want to know where the hell several thousand longhorns originally wearing the Circle BJ brand have gotten themselves to," said Spear. "Ramsey has the idea of going after the rustlers. The guns and ammunition are for the use of whoever he hires to help out on the job. I was hired to get him and his hardware safely here, then lend a hand in finding out why Horesham isn't making a penny."

Nodding, the plump author said, "My predecessor here believed there was a definite link twixt gunrunners and cattle rustlers."

"What's he think now?"

"Perhaps only celestial thoughts, Bradley. I greatly fear we ought to be referring to Elisha Klein as 'the late Secret Service agent.' "

"I knew Klein. He's a good man. What happened?"

"He disappeared a few months ago. It's my task to determine what's become of him. I must also run those responsible for his death, if he is indeed no longer among the living, to ground. I must also put a stop to the theft of United States weaponry."

"That ought to keep you busy for a few days."

Out in the kitchen the crash of a plate was followed by a yowl of pain.

Stormfield inquired, "Where are you based, my boy?"

"Staying at Big Jim Phillips' spread. Horesham has invested around three million dollars in his ranch and so far there haven't been any profits to notice."

"Three million dollars," sighed his friend. "How many more volumes of deathless prose must I pen ere I earn a like sum? And here are these sons of Albion investing such princely sums in cows."

"Any leads on what happened to Klein?"

"Through diligent detective work, and listening to some dreadful piano playing," Stormfield told him, "I found my way to a line shack on the vast estates of my host. Elisha Klein apparently used the place and kept a ledger hidden there." He shook his head forlornly. "It's very likely he was also killed therein. I found evidence of a struggle and some telltale bloodstains. I found as well the burned remains of his notebook. Only a portion of a page escaped the consuming flames. From the surviving words I gleaned his suspicion of a connection between the gun stealers and the cow stealers. I learned as well that Curly was involved with one of the gangs. I was planning on making discreet inquiries there this very evening."

"Where's Molly come in?"

"We met by chance. Since we had similar missions, though I didn't confide mine in her, I decided to accompany her into the fetid atmosphere of the Golden Door. Is she truly the bride of an outlaw?"

"Her husband is riding with the Steve Janson gang, or so she says," replied Spear. "Do you figure the Janson bunch is behind the gun stealing?"

"It is my notion, Bradley, that there is someone higher up pulling the strings, although the Janson louts may well be involved."

"Somebody like Big Jim?"

Stormfield's eyes widened. "I've been led to believe the gentleman in question is only a few steps away from being admitted to sainthood," he answered. "Is such not the case with your host?"

"I got a feeling he's a snake."

"Proof?"

Spear rubbed his fist across his stomach. "Mostly a feeling so far. I don't like the gent at all, so I have to be careful I don't let that sway me." He glanced toward the kitchen. There had been only silence out there for several minutes now.

"Is it your impression, as it is my, that friend Curly has taken off for the high grass?"

"Yep, we won't see him in town for a spell."

"Then I had best return to the Rudd domicile and pursue other threads," decided Stormfield. "And you, my boy?"

"Got an appointment with Rowdy Kate," replied Spear. "Don't know where I'll be going after that. I'll sure keep in touch, though."

"Do that," said the author, chuckling. "Thank you once more for saving my gifted neck."

"Once more, though, and I'm going to have to send you a bill."

Spear pushed back from the table and walked into Rowdy Kate's kitchen.

Chapter 21

Paloma threw his cigarette butt into the campfire. "You *sabe*, Señor Steve?"

Janson was squatting on his heels, an empty tin coffee cup dangling from his forefinger. "I *sabe* my boys and me take all the risks."

The Mexican leaned forward, shifting on the bedroll he was sitting on. His silver spurs jingled and flashed in the firelight. "You don't pay attention so good, amigo," he said, smiling. "When your boys go riding in, that's just only a diversion."

"We gallop in whooping and shooting," Janson returned, running blunt fingertips across his pockmarked cheek. "What's to stop that limey from using them machine guns on us? Like he done before."

"Before, Señor Steve, you didn't have Paloma to do your thinking for you."

"Listen, I don't need no—"

"But Señor Jim believes you do," reminded Paloma. "We both got to take orders from him, don't we?"

"I'd like a whole bunch to see him have to take orders instead of me."

"You got to realize, amigo, that big bosses don't never lay themselves on the line," explained the Mexican. "If you want to save yourself for sure, you got to become a big boss yourself. That's the only sure way."

"You know, Paloma, I get mighty damn tired of you tellin' me what's good for me."

"You just got to listen, amigo, listen good. You and your bunch ride at the barn, shooting, making plenty of noise," continued Paloma, a shade impatient. "That's to distract Señor Ramsey. While he's—"

"What about Señor Spear? He's the one I want."

"He ain't there. I already told you that," said Paloma, as though repeating this to a child. "And while Ramsey is getting ready to fight you off, we break in the back way and overpower him and his crew." He shrugged and spread his hands wide, laughing. "Simple."

"While you're breaking in, he mows us down with a couple of them chatter guns."

"No, no, amigo. I get in there fast, *muy rápido.* Nobody gets killed."

"Having your word on that don't make me feel altogether fine," observed Janson. "What about Big Jim's hands? They all going to keep right on snoozing?"

"Most of them are in the habit of looking the other way, you know that as good as anybody," reminded Paloma. "And to make it look good, I'll have some of my men watching the bunkhouse. Anybody looks out, we shoo him back in with a little friendly gunfire. *Sabe?*"

"He's got a hand name of Tom Curry," Janson mentioned. "I don't like that kid. Got me the feeling he's too damn honest for his own good."

"He won't bother us," promised Paloma. "We will keep all the hired hands penned in."

"The guns and ammunition been unloaded, ain't they?"

"*Sí*, that is so."

"Going to take one hell of a lot of time to load up two goddamn wagons."

"We settle for one wagonful, Señor Steve," said Paloma. "And don't worry. My boys can work quick."

"I never seen that crazy Injun of yours work at all. Pinto's the laziest character, white or red, I ever did see."

"I'm awful quiet, though," a voice came from behind them.

"Jesus!"

Pinto had moved up out of the darkness unheard and was crouching next to the pockmarked outlaw. He held the point of his hunting knife against Janson's neck.

"That's enough kidding around," suggested Paloma.

"Who says I'm kidding?" asked the Indian. "I slice this son of a bitch's throat and things'll be a lot better."

"No, Pinto, Señor Steve is our amigo. We don't knife friends." Paloma stretched up to his feet.

"You making a mistake." Pinto put his knife away, moved back from the campfire.

Rubbing at the spot where the tip of the blade had touched him, Janson said, "I ain't going to forget that."

"I don't want you to."

"We got to be moving out soon." Paloma smiled at them both. "Save your fooling around for afterwards, amigos."

A few dozen yards away from the campfire, Sam Cartland stood beside his saddled horse. He was shivering, keeping his mouth shut tight to kill the sound of his chattering teeth. He'd overheard most of what the two gang leaders had said. He didn't share Paloma's optimism at all. Cartland was convinced there'd be bloodshed tonight. And he had a premonition he was going to get killed.

Well, maybe that was the best thing that could happen. Then he wouldn't have to worry anymore about what to tell Molly.

Peter Ramsey yawned and rose up off the bale of straw he'd been resting on. He began a brisk walk around the barn.

Over in a stall, Seamus Tuck was snoring enthusiastically.

Ramsey kept walking until he felt wide awake again. Halting in the middle of the planked floor, he bent to touch his toes. "Still in whizzer shape," the young Englishman told himself. He proceeded to touch his toes ten more times.

It was a clear night and moonlight was coming in through the small, glassless windows, cutting white stripes across the darkness.

"Don't need Spear at all," he whispered to himself as he swung his arms in wide arcs. Not in the least. Ramsey felt perfectly capable of guarding the artillery on his own. Granted that last evening he'd made something of a fool of himself. Still, he'd had a hell of a time and no real harm had been done.

"Much too somber a chap is Spear." Dour was the word for him. True, he grinned a good bit. Yet there wasn't much warmth to the act.

"Treats me as though I were a blooming idiot."

Yes, patronizing was how you had to characterize the Pinkerton agent's attitude. Deuced patronizing.

And all this pussyfooting around. No need of that. What was called for was a full-scale patrol operation. Yes, by Jove, it had worked in India and it would work equally well here in Texas. Armed men patrolling the borders of the Circle BJ, enough of them to challenge any size attack. After fighting off the rustlers, you pursued them to their lair. All quite simple.

"Bright and early tomorrow I start recruiting," he muttered, breathing the night air in deeply. Should have done that this morning, he mused. But Ramsey had felt decidedly fuzzy in the head. One day wouldn't make much difference.

"Then I'll show Spear what's what. I may be a blooming stranger in this country, but I bloody well know—"

He heard galloping hooves, gunshots ripping through the night. War whoops and curses.

"Tuck, look alive, old boy!" Ramsey ran over to where he'd left a loaded Springfield rifle leaning against the barn wall. "Break out a Gardner gun, Tuck, while I have a bit of a look-see!" He headed for the nearest window.

"What's going on now?" Tuck wanted to know somewhere behind him. "A body can't get a decent night's sleep without some . . . oof!"

"Oof?" Ramsey was easing toward the front window, rifle in hand. "I'm afraid I don't catch your meaning, old man."

"He say 'oof' because I hit him over the head, señor."

"Who the bloody hell—"

A gun butt from behind cut short his question.

*   *   *

Everything was going just fine—up to a point.

Sam Cartland wasn't so nervous now. When they came riding toward the Circle BJ barn he found he was able to holler and fire his Navy Colt up into the black sky. There was still a numb feeling at the center of him, that chill, strong conviction that his life was just about over. But he was able to go through all the motions.

The horses galloped hard over the dark ground. The six-guns blazed, making jagged lines of orange across the black. The noise and the excitement were almost enough to keep Cartland from thinking. And though he hadn't believed it, Paloma had been right after all. There wasn't one single shot fired at them from the barn.

When the big door was shoved open, it was Paloma himself standing there. "Come in, amigos, *muy pronto!*"

Indeed, everything was going fine.

Cartland heard a few scattered rifle shots from over near the bunkhouse as he reined up. That'd be some of Paloma's boys seeing to it nobody got too curious, he thought.

And so the bullet that hit him came as a complete surprise. It was fired from the direction of one of the outhouses.

Hell, he thought as his body filled with pain and he toppled out of his saddle, did I get shot by some son of a bitch who was on the commode?

He tumbled into scrub brush and then the night closed in on him.

Chapter 22

When dawn came on the endless prairie, Spear was already miles from Tascosa, riding from the rendezvous spot Rowdy Kate had told him about.

And maybe riding smack into a trap, he thought.

A faint mist was rising up from the ground and swirling around the hooves of his sorrel mount. Over to the left, about a hundred yards off, a jack rabbit suddenly got scared and went hopping off.

Spear checked his hand from reaching for his six-gun and grinned. That was one of the things that happened to you in this line of work. You were always on guard and you never quite trusted anybody. Such habits kept you alive and kicking, but didn't make for the most relaxed sort of life.

Way up in the brightening morning sky, hawks were circling, five of them. Were they up there wondering if it was okay to come swooping down on their prey? Nope, not likely. They just did it, not having enough brains between them to debate the pros and cons of a thing. You could make out a pretty good case for the advantages of being stupid.

Spear shook his head. "Getting to be quite a philosopher. Pretty soon I'll be taking to a rocking chair and do nothing but whittle and think all day."

Despite all his contemplating, he still wasn't quite sure where Anita Torquay fit into all this. Rowdy Kate swore the girl wasn't an outlaw, but she rode with a gang of men who could sure as hell pass for outlaws. Nita, as Kate called her, had chased off the Janson bunch and kept them from making off with the wagons full of artillery. Or so it seemed. Could be that whole damn raid was staged, thought Spear. Maybe the Torquay gang and the Janson gang were in cahoots. And maybe a third partner was the Mexican gent— Paloma, they called him—who made a try for the guns the other night.

Funny name for an owlhoot. Paloma. Meant "dove" in Spanish. Didn't seem to be anything very peaceful about that gent.

Spear rode on throughout the morning. Just short of midday he sighted the little canyon Rowdy Kate had told him about.

No one had followed him out of Tascosa and he'd spotted no sign that anyone had been riding in front of him along this trail recently. He should have felt safe and secure, but he didn't. He slowed his horse to a trot as he went riding in between the rocky walls of the canyon.

There was mesquite in abundance and a few stands of alder trees. The canyon was maybe two miles long and a half mile across. Just about in the middle of it was the cabin Rowdy Kate had mentioned. He was supposed to go on in there and wait.

Wait until he was contacted. Kate claimed she didn't know whether Nita Torquay would come by herself or just send one of her men to lead him elsewhere.

Spear figured there was no sense sneaking up on the ramshackle cabin. Anybody inside it or hiding anywhere in the canyon would've noticed him by now.

He rode right up into what had been the front yard of the shack and dismounted. The blue-stem grass was knee-high and the weeds were thick. It was very quiet all around. Spear stood, right hand near his holster, watching the doorless entryway to the low log cabin.

He heard absolutely nothing until a voice from behind him said softly, "No need to be shy, Señor Spear. Go on in."

Peter Ramsey groaned. He opened his eyes and saw a concerned, dark-haired young woman watching him. "Sophie?" he murmured, noting that he was lying in an ornate bed under pale blue blankets. "Did I spend yet another night with you? Jove, I know I didn't . . ." Wrinkles spread across his forehead as he tried to remember what had happened. "I'm even fuzzier this morning than I was the other day."

"You got bopped on the coco," explained Sophie.

"Indeed?"

"Gee, I figured you was a goner." She was sitting on the edge of the bed, one hand resting in the gully between her substantial breasts. She was clad in a lacy nightdress and had a shawl thrown over her shoulders. "You've been out like a mackerel for hours."

"The guns!" He remembered now and tried to leap forth from Sophie's bed. His head—bandaged, he now realized—commenced throbbing. He felt dizzy and groaned again.

"You shouldn't get up, Petey," advised the young woman, easing him back under the covers. "You got yourself quite a thwack on the old cabeza. Best you stay put till the sawbones gets here."

"I don't need a doctor." He stayed in bed, though, not quite ready to make another try at arising.

"They didn't fetch the old coot just for you. It's also on account of that man who got himself shot."

"Tuck? Was Tuck shot?"

"We don't know this gent's name, except that old goat Tuck swears he seen him somewheres before," explained Sophie.

"Who shot him and where is he?"

"He got shot by Tom Curry," she continued. "See, Tom was using the commode and he was able, once he pulled his pants up, to get in a few shots. The fellow he dropped seems likely to belong to the Janson gang. They kept Tom pinned down there by the outhouse and he couldn't stop them."

"What's this wounded bloke look like?"

She shrugged. "He's old is all I know, way over forty."

"Jove, I wonder if it could be Sam Cartland."

"He's about halfways dead and in no shape to introduce himself."

Ramsey stretched out his left hand. "Very slowly and carefully, my dear Sophie, I want you to tug me to a standing position," he requested. "I want to have a gander at this chap and then I want to have a word with Big Jim."

"Big Jim was of the opinion it'd be simpler to let him kick off. But your old goat of a driver kept hollering about how he had to be kept alive so as you and that snooty Pinkerton could ask him all kinds of dumb questions."

"Yes, a sound notion on Tuck's part."

Sophie took hold of his hand and pulled. "Easy now."

The floor felt cold under his bare feet. "I say, I don't appear to have a stitch on."

"You was out cold, Petey. So I undressed you and dumped you in bed." She propped him up. "Big Jim said it was okay to use this place of ours for the injured. Made me feel just like a nurse or something."

"I believe I am now capable of standing unaided," he announced. "Leave me, Sophie, and fetch my garments."

"You're as white as a baboon's rump."

"No, actually, child, a baboon's rump is pink."

"No kidding? I never seen one. Just heard the expression."

"Once in India I . . . ah, but I must have my clothes," he said in a thin voice. "I have to get to the barn and determine what was taken."

"About half your guns is gone," Sophie told him, moving clear of him. "Them guys filled a wagon and hauled it off."

Ramsey glanced toward a window. Looking out beyond the lace curtains, he could tell it was approaching midday. "Blighters have quite a head start," he realized. "But no matter, we'll get on their trail and . . . Jove, the floor's behaving in a most . . ."

Sophie lunged and caught him before he fell over completely. "You ain't going to chase nobody."

"Damn, but I believe you're right. I feel as unsteady as a newborn colt." With the young woman's help he returned to bed. "Gad, I dread to think what Spear will say about this calamity."

Stormfield thrust his knife and fork into a stack of

griddlecakes and said, "I appreciate your taking the time to have this chat with me, Dr. Sopkin."

"Taking time to have my breakfast," the wizened old medical man pointed out. "You want to jabber while I'm doing that, go ahead."

"Yes, to be sure. I admire your candor, sir, for in my many and wearisome sojourns about this giddy globe I don't oft meet with such—"

"Get to the point." Dr. Sopkin sliced open his fried egg and watched the yellow yolk spill across his plate.

Out in the kitchen of the restaurant, a frying pan could be heard banging against a wall.

"I'm most anxious about the whereabouts of a young man named Elisha Klein," explained the portly author. "As a physician, you no doubt come in contact with most of the citizens of this fair metropolis."

"Never treated Klein." The wrinkled little doctor opened his mouth just wide enough to insert a forkful of fried egg.

"Oh, so? That is unfortunate, since I hoped perhaps you might have known something about him."

"Klein was hearty as an ox. Didn't need any doctoring."

"Ah, then you did know the gentleman?"

"Saw him around Tascosa." He forked in more egg. "Smallish town, can't keep from seeing most everybody."

"Do you have any idea who he—"

"Doc! Doc Sopkin!" A lanky, freckled cowhand came rushing into Rowdy Kate's.

The doctor continued to eat methodically.

The young man made his way around the tables. "We need you out at the Circle BJ, Doc," he said, breathing hard.

Dr. Sopkin frowned up at him. "Why?"

"Gent got shot pretty bad last night."

"Who?"

"We ain't exactly certain."

The old physician set down his fork. "Slow down a mite, Tom," he advised. "Give me the particulars."

Tom Curry took in a deep breath. "They was a raid last night, Doc. The Janson gang and that Mexican outlaw that calls himself Paloma," he began. "They made off with near half of the Englishman's guns and shells and all. Well sir, I managed to hit one of them. Big Jim'd just as well let him die, 'cause he says an outlaw ain't worth anything anyhow and we'll only have to string him up later on. Old Seamus Tuck, though, and this English gent insist he's got to stay alive on account of they want to talk to him and ask him questions and such. So I was—"

"Okay, Tom, I get the general idea," cut in Sopkin. "How bad's he hurt?"

Curry touched his own side. "Bullet went in about here, Doc," he answered. "Bled quite a bit before I could get to him. That was on account of I was ducked down behind the outhouse and some of the others was shooting at me and I couldn't get over to this hombre until they'd stopped."

"Bullet still in him?"

Curry nodded vigorously. "I got the bleeding more or less stopped, but I didn't want to mess with digging out the damn slug."

"Glad you left something for me to do."

"This gent ain't exactly a kid, and maybe he won't hold up as well as a younger man, so the sooner you can come, Doc, the better."

"Young man," said Stormfield, tugging at his sideburns thoughtfully, "am I correct in assuming the injured man is a member of the Steve Janson congregation?"

"Far as we can tell, unless he belongs to Paloma's bunch. He's been out cold since last night."

"And he's not a youth?"

"Hell, no, he's got to be way over forty."

"Can you describe him?"

"Well sir, he's about medium size, on the lanky side. Got dark hair, but it's going grey over the ears."

Dr. Sopkin wiped his thin old lips with the checkered napkin. "Through with your examination, Mr. Stormfield?"

"Forgive my intruding, Dr. Sopkin," Stormfield apologized. "However, I suspect I may know the identity of the wounded outlaw."

"Who is he?" asked Curry.

"I would prefer to refrain from stating his name until a positive identification can be made. Dr. Sopkin, would it be possible to obtain from you a ride to the Circle BJ when you journey there on your errand of mercy? A ride for myself and a charming young woman with russet tresses?"

"I suppose I can fit you both in my old buggy." The little doctor got up from the table. "Be ready in ten minutes in front of Emerson's Livery Barn." He dabbed a final time at his lips with the napkin. "Be nice if you didn't do much talking on the trip out there."

Stormfield drew himself up to his full height and gave a stiff bow. "I shall be as silent, if you'll forgive the unseemly expression, as the tomb," he promised coolly.

Chapter 23

The man with the Winchester rifle resting across his knees was nearly as big as Spear and a few years younger. He was dark, sported an impressive black mustache, and his head was absolutely bald. He wore dark trousers, a dark shirt and a leather vest. His black sombrero rested beside him on a swaybacked wooden table. He seemed continually amused. "I lost my hair prematurely," he said.

Spear, minus his gunbelt, was seated in a straight-backed chair facing him. "Darn shame."

"No, actually it's a great advantage," his host insisted, absently fingering the gun at his side. "It's been my experience that ladies are greatly aroused by a bald head on a young man. Once, down in Chihuahua, an amazingly endowed señorita expressed it this way. 'Miguelito,' she sighed. . . . Did I introduce myself? Miguelito Chavez, at your service."

"Pleased," said Spear.

" 'Miguelito, light of my life and object of my adoration, I love a man without any hair on his head. It's so smooth. So . . . so erotic!' said she. I accepted that as a glowing compliment."

Spear eyed him. "When do I see Miss Torquay?"

Chavez laughed. "Hombres with a full head of hair do okay, too. No need to take offense, Señor Spear. However, my own illustrious love life would tend to make me believe that—"

"You do work for the Torquay girl, don't you?"

"*Sí*, I am her loyal servitor," answered Chavez. "Only half."

"Hum?"

"You're wondering if I'm a full-blooded Mexican. My answer is, only half," he said. "My mother, my dear departed mother, was Irish and German and possibly a touch Hungarian. When I allude to her as departed I don't mean the dear old girl is dead. She simply up and left my father and me and my two equally handsome brothers several years ago." He paused. "In Philadelphia."

"What's that last the answer to?"

"You were going to inquire where I was educated, since you've been marveling at my command of your own tongue." Chavez grinned broadly. "I attended a religiously oriented high school in the City of Brotherly Love, leaving it shortly before my senior year was completed but conveniently before it was discovered that one of the younger nuns, a quite pretty lass, was going to dabble in maternity before the end of the academic calendar year."

"Could we maybe shift from autobiography to Nita Torquay?"

"You can tell me all about your romantic adventures next if you like," offered Chavez. "I've no objection to becoming an attentive audience. Is it true you once had your way with a fetching young woman while traveling across rough country in the Deadwood stage?"

"Not quite. Now as to—"

"How many other passengers were aboard at the time?"

Spear shook his head. "You're nearly as long-winded as my friend Thomas Alexander Stormfield."

"Do you read his work? A hopeless hack as far as I can see," said Chavez, twisting one side of his luxuriant mustache. "That's what comes from composing too rapidly. I recall spending an evening with a miraculously endowed lady poet in Minnesota once. Minnesota isn't exactly a state you think of as producing many poets, yet there she was. 'Chavez, my own true love,' she moaned as we shared her antique bed, 'you look so erotic without any hair.'" He paused. "Another hour or so."

"That's when Nita arrives?"

Chavez nodded. "Most likely."

Spear asked, "How would you classify the kind of work you're in now?"

"I'm a knight errant."

Grinning, Spear asked him, "You're not an outlaw, huh?"

"None of us who ride with Nita Torquay are criminals, Spear. No more than Robin Hood's merry men were."

"Okay, so you're all riding around the Panhandle doing good deeds and helping the unfortunate."

"We pulled you out of the fire a while back," the baldheaded cowboy reminded him, "when those Janson half-wits tried to wipe you out."

"Appreciate that," said Spear, pushing up the brim of his Stetson with his thumb. "But what I'm curious about is how you make a living."

"For many of the tasks we perform we charge a fee, a commission," explained Chavez. "If we return some missing cattle, for example, we retain a dozen head or so for our own use. The same rule applies to stagecoach robberies we thwart and so on."

"Yep, I see. Funny, though, how you all have the reputation of being crooks and desperadoes."

"Propaganda, bad publicity," Chavez maintained. "People like Big Jim Phillips find it to their advantage to malign us. Keeps him from being scrutinized too closely himself."

"Why'd you join up with Nita?"

"Because I agree with her goals."

"Which are?"

"To help clean up this part of the great state of Texas."

"A sort of vigilante approach," concluded Spear. "Meaning she's not just out for revenge?"

"She has some personal reasons for doing what she's doing," Chavez replied. "Talk to her about that."

"Did you know her before, when she and her grandfather were ranching in these parts?"

"No, I was down in sun-drenched Mexico in those halcyon days. But a friend of mine, who knew her for quite a spell, told me she was looking for trustworthy and resourceful men. So I signed on."

Spear took off his hat and rested it on his knee. "What's she want to talk to me about?"

"That's something you'll have to ask her about."

"Ah, the vastness of it all," sighed Stormfield as their buggy rolled across the hot afternoon prairie.

Dr. Sopkin sneezed, but did not otherwise respond.

Molly Cartland was sitting between the two men.

The fringed canvas roof cast jagged shadow patterns across her face. "It may not be him," she said, not for the first time.

"I think it best, dear lady, to assume your husband is indeed the wounded man. The description matches the one you gave me when first we met."

She ran her fingers over the worn leather of the padded seat. "None of this makes any sense," she murmured. "Sam living like an outlaw, getting gunned down."

"Perhaps he'll be able to explain his actions."

"If he's still alive."

Stormfield put his arm around her shoulder. "Strive to look on the bright side," he advised.

"What bright side?" asked the weather-beaten old doctor.

"Mrs. Cartland has, at long last, located her missing husband. That's something to be thankful for."

"If he doesn't die, they'll likely hang him," said Sopkin. "If he escapes the rope, he'll rot in prison. Nobody takes very kindly to cattle thieves in these parts."

"Sam's not a thief," Molly insisted. "He's a decent, honest man."

"Just like Jesse James and Cole Younger," the doctor returned.

"Have a care," Stormfield warned. "There's no need to upset the lady. Especially since nothing has been proved against her husband as yet."

"Just believe in facing facts."

"At this moment we don't know the facts."

"Know all I need to," said Sopkin.

Up ahead they could see a tall windmill slowly turning. Soon they sighted the collection of buildings that made up the hub of the Circle BJ Ranch.

Seamus Tuck, an immense white bandage around

his grizzled head, came scurrying out of the barn as the buggy pulled up near the main house. "Well, dang it, if it ain't Mrs. Cartland," he exclaimed in surprise.

"The wounded man, is he still—"

"Ain't dead, but still out cold," Tuck interrupted her. "Ain't woke up at all since he got pegged."

Stormfield helped the red-haired woman down. "Mrs. Cartland would like to see the man," he told Tuck, "since she suspects he may be her husband."

"Dang it, me and Wally was speculatin' on the same thing."

Molly leaned against Stormfield for support. "Dr. Sopkin, may I go in with you when you see the patient?"

"That's what I dragged you all this way for, isn't it?" Clutching his black medical bag, he started shuffling toward the main house.

"Whoa, sawbones," called Tuck. "He ain't over there. They got him in the whorehouse over there. Same as Ramsey."

"Was Peter injured as well?"

"Got banged on the skull, same as me," answered the driver. "He decided he needed to stay in bed. Guess I'd feel that way, too, if they'd of put me in with them floozies to recuperate."

"Come along, Mrs. Cartland." Dr. Sopkin started for the Victorian-style private bordello, scowling deeply. "The rest of you remain without."

"I'm always without," muttered Tuck. "Looks like I ain't never goin' to get a gander at the inside of that joint." He spat into the dirt. "Name is Seamus Tuck. What's yours?" He thrust out a gnarled right hand.

"I am Thomas Alexander Stormfield." He shook hands.

"Right pleased to met up with you."

Stormfield asked, "Can you give me some particulars about the raid last night?"

"All I know is I got beaned. When I come around, near half the guns we had stashed in the barn was gone. Ramsey was stretched out on the sod." Tuck glanced at the bordello. "He ain't got a very tough noggin. We also got us a Pinkerton agent along on this trip, but he wasn't here last night due to—"

"Yes, I know. Spear and I are old friends."

"Ain't that somethin'? Like the fat lady said to the—"

"Sam!"

Inside the house Molly had cried out her husband's name.

"Reckon it's him for sure," Tuck declared.

"So it seems," said Stormfield.

Chapter 24

Spear heard neither hoofbeats nor footfalls. The girl was simply all at once in the doorway. "Good afternoon, Mr. Spear."

She was slim, with a boyish figure, dressed in black trousers and a black shirt. She wore a low-crowned black sombrero and her black hair was long and unfettered. The gunbelt around her narrow waist had a silver buckle and her holster held a .44.

"Glad to meet you." He got to his feet, followed by the barrel of Chavez's rifle.

"I appreciate your coming." Her voice was low-pitched, husky. "Hope you didn't mind the wait. We had to make certain you'd come calling alone."

"Chavez and I whiled away the hours."

Nita Torquay nodded at the bald man.

Chavez smiled, put on his sombrero and stood. He tucked the rifle under his arm.

The slim girl stepped into the room and Chavez went out.

Spear remarked, "He's not as talkative with you as he is with me."

"He knows I don't go for useless conversation. Please sit down."

He did and she took the chair Chavez had vacated, sitting very straight and with her knees together.

"Let's neither of us waste any words," said Spear. "What exactly—"

"First I'd be much obliged if you'd show me your identification," Nita requested.

"Surely." He studied her face as he fished out his wallet. She was quite pretty, but there was a guarded quality that made her face seem somewhat masklike.

She went over the papers thoroughly, inspected his photograph. "You look older now than you do in this."

"I am."

"Did you grow the beard originally to make you look older?"

"Grew it mainly because shaving's one of my least favorite pastimes," he answered. "Didn't feel like devoting every morning of my life to it."

Closing his wallet, she rested it on her knee and tapped it with her finger. "You've been a Pinkerton a long time," Nita noted. "Why'd you go into detective work originally?"

"Seemed like it'd be more interesting than lumberjacking."

"Was that the other choice open to you, Mr. Spear?"

He'd been looking at her breasts beneath the dark cloth of her shirt, thinking they were small but provocative, and he missed answering the question right off. "That was what my father did, worked the lumber camps."

"I see." Her finger continued to tap on the wallet.

"Get the feeling you're interviewing me for the

position of bank clerk or new parson," he told her. "Suppose we get down to what you wanted to see me about."

"Why don't you tell me why you came?" With a swift movement of her slim wrist, she flipped his wallet back to him.

He caught it, slid it away. "Curiosity, for one thing," he replied. "But I wouldn't ride way the hell out here just for that. I've been hired to look into the rustling that's going on. I figure you should be able to tell me something about that."

A very faint smile touched her lips. "Meaning that a lady rustler ought to know a good deal?"

"Are you a rustler?"

"No."

"Certain folks say otherwise. Such upright pillars of the community as Big Jim Phillips claim you and Steve Janson are—"

"Big Jim." She said the name as though it were profanity. "If you believe what he says, then you and I have nothing to discuss."

"I was merely pointing out some of the opinions of you that I've come across," he said, grinning. "I've also been told you're Joan of Arc and Robin Hood rolled together. With maybe a dash of Calamity Jane."

"Have you ever met Calamity Jane?"

"Yep."

"What sort of a woman is she?"

"Formidable."

"She has a very colorful reputation over in the Black Hills."

"You're much better looking," Spear informed her.

"The English gentleman you're traveling with has

brought considerable guns and ammunition into the territory. A foolish move."

"I've had similar thoughts." He reached into a pocket for a cigar. "Mind if I smoke?"

"You don't have to ask my permission."

Striking a match, he said, "I can't get over the notion I'm in a schoolroom or a church maybe."

"I was able to keep the Janson gang from highjacking the weapons," the dark-haired girl allowed, "but they'll try again. You're not safe simply because you reached the Circle BJ."

"Another try has been made. By a gent with the peaceable name of Paloma."

"I figured he'd be coming in on this," she remarked.

"How'd you know there was going to be a raid on our wagons that first time?"

"I have various sources of information."

"Would one of those sources have been Elisha Klein?"

She stiffened. "What do you know about him?"

"That's he's missing."

"Elisha's dead."

"For sure?"

"I buried him."

"Kill him, too?"

She stood up, face going pale. "He was my friend," she returned angrily. "I was trying to help him get a line on the gunrunners."

"Who *did* kill him?"

"I'm not sure. I was meeting him now and then at a line shack on the Rudd spread."

"I know about the place."

"Somebody else did, too. The last time I went there to meet Elisha, he was dead."

"Janson or Paloma could've done the job," Spear judged, exhaling smoke.

"Yes, or your friend Big Jim."

"No friend of mine, but folks keep assuring me he's honest."

"A man with his money, lots of people are willing to swear he's most anything he claims he is."

Spear stood and began to pace. "You knew Klein was Secret Service."

"Yes."

"Then why didn't you get in touch with somebody else, contact Washington and report that he was murdered?"

"Oh, yes, they'd have listened to me," she said bitterly. "Even *you* aren't fully convinced I'm not an outlaw."

"The way you live maybe tends to put people off, but—"

"I don't go around in silks and satins and bonnets. You won't see me in church on Sundays," she hissed. "I can outshoot and outride most men in these parts. And, damn it, I'm smarter than a good many of them. Maybe you included, Spear. But none of that makes me an outlaw."

"Why are you doing this?"

"I have a score to settle." She turned away from him. "For something that was done to me."

"Rowdy Kate told me something about that."

"Oh, did she now? My, that must've made for a nice little after-dinner anecdote. Sweet virgin ruined by a gang of drunken, murdering cowhands." She spun to face him, nostrils flaring, fists clenched. "Or aren't you perhaps wondering if it was that way at all? Maybe I'm just like those women your friend Big Jim keeps for pets. Maybe I invited them all to take me. Isn't that what you think about any woman who—"

"Listen," he said evenly, coming closer to her. "I don't think a damn thing one way or the other. I've been in this business a long time and I've seen a lot of women hurt in a lot of different ways. I don't automatically think that they all yearn to jump into bed with me or anyone else. That goes for the whores and the kept women and the back-street ladies, too. Some of them never had much say in the matter." He put a hand on her shoulder. "Just be damn sure you don't get me mixed up with whoever else hurt you once. That's not going to get us anywhere."

Nita shrugged out of his grasp. "I don't like to be touched." She moved nearer the doorway.

He leaned against a wall, watching her slim back. "Now what about our working together?"

"Forgive me for losing my temper. It's only . . . Yes, Chavez?"

"Company approaching," he announced, coming up to the cabin.

"How many?"

"One." He held up his forefinger. "Looks like it might be Tom."

She glanced back over her shoulder. "I'm going to have to trust you," she told Spear. "Not to betray someone to your friend Big Jim."

"Not my friend," he repeated.

"We'll see," she answered.

Tom Curry took a deep swallow out of his canteen. He was squatting near the doorway of the cabin. "I figured as how you better know, Miss Nita."

Nita was sitting on the doorstep, long slim legs

straight out. "Paloma'll run those guns into Mexico soon as he can."

Spear, hunkered on the ground near the girl, said, "He can't move them ten or fifteen miles a day. Catching up with him will be no problem."

"He'll get them to Santa Vergas," the girl responded. "Stash the load there. Then he'll break it up all sorts of ways. In wagons supposedly hauling skins, fruit, grain. In buckboards and covered wagons, in coaches."

"Where's Santa Vergas?" asked Spear while lighting a fresh cigar.

"About thirty miles south of here," answered Chavez. "Wide-open town, no law to speak of."

"You know for a fact Paloma used the town as a base?"

"I've known for several weeks," Nita revealed. "One of the things I wished to discuss with you was how to go after him and put a stop to his activities."

"You best steer clear of Santa Vergas," cautioned Curry.

Spear asked, "Does Paloma control the whole damn town?"

Chavez laughed. "He's but one of several outlaws who compete for that honor."

"Like to take a look at the place." Spear blew smoke at the ground. It drifted out of the shadows and into the bright, hot afternoon.

"I'll take you," offered Nita.

"Wait now, Nita," Chavez warned. "If Paloma sees you in Santa Vergas, he'll come gunnin' for you for sure."

"All sorts of people come and go. I'll make certain he doesn't notice me. And Spear he's barely seen."

"I don't like it." Chavez tugged at both ends of his mustache.

"Me neither, Miss Nita."

"He's going to keep those guns stashed in Santa Vergas for a few days anyway," she told Spear. "I'd like to catch up with him before they start moving across the border into Mexico."

"Okay, sure, that'd be evidence that he's tied in with the gunrunning," Chavez acknowledged. "Having a Pinkerton agent with you might make it almost official. But, damn, Nita, if you don't live long enough to take Paloma out of Santa Vergas, then it's all for nothing."

Spear addressed himself to Curry. "You mentioned a heavyset gent who came along to the Circle BJ with Mrs. Cartland and the doctor."

"Fat was the word he used," corrected Chavez.

"I believe his name is Stormwind or something sort of like that," Curry said.

"His name's Stormfield," said Spear, "and I'd be obliged, Tom, if you'd slip him a message when you get back to the ranch."

Nita frowned at him. "Why? Isn't he the one who writes trashy novels that completely falsify the West?"

"Yep, except that's only a spare time activity with Stormfield. He's also a Secret Service agent."

Curry popped to his feet. "That fat—I mean heavyset old gent is Secret Service?"

"Yep," said Spear, "and I'd like him to know where I'm heading."

The young hand looked at Nita. "Is that okay, Miss Nita?"

After a few seconds she said, "Yes, go ahead."

Chapter 25

Stormfield stood outside in the afternoon shade cast by the private bordello. Hands in pockets, he gazed toward the barn and listened to Dr. Sopkin.

"Cartland ought to pull through," the wrinkled little man was saying. "Still unconscious, but that doesn't worry me much."

"Your ministrations are most appreciated."

"Reason I'm telling you this," said Sopkin, giving his black bag an impatient rattle, "is that because Mrs. Cartland became so hysterical when she saw him, I had to pop her into another spare room and give her a sleeping draft." New wrinkles appeared on his already wrinkle-crowded brow. "Turning a house of ill repute into a hospital isn't my idea of proper, but I'm keeping my feelings on that score to myself."

"A wise course," agreed the author. "Will the prostrated Mrs. Cartland require any further medical attention?"

"If she does, she certainly won't get it from me." Rattling the worn black bag again, he started walking toward the creaking windmill, beside which he'd left his horse and buggy. "I wash my hands of this whole shabby business. I will, however, provide you transportation back to Tascosa. If you are ready to depart at once, Mr. Stormfield."

"While most grateful of your generous-hearted offer, dear Doctor, I believe I will decline it," Stormfield told him as they walked along through the hot, flat afternoon. "I'd best remain at the Circle BJ awhile yet."

"Figuring to take a room in with those tainted women?"

"If duty requires it."

"Duty," sneered the little doctor. He untethered his horse, climbed up into his buggy. "Good day to you, sir."

"Bon voyage to you." Turning his back on the old medic's departure, Stormfield walked rapidly for the barn.

Inside it was a slight bit cooler, and the air smelled of straw and gun oil.

"Oh, I rode into town about sundown. Just me an' my ol' hoss Paint," Seamus Tuck was singing while accompanying himself on his asthmatic concertina. "They tol' me we don't know where your wife is, but we sure do know where she ain't. Oh, I . . . Afternoon to you, Mr. Stormdrain."

"Stormfield," the author corrected. "Feeling worse, are you?"

Tuck patted his bandaged head. "Nope, feel a whole lot better."

"From the way you were wailing, I feared you were at death's door."

"That's singin'," explained the grizzled driver, chuckling and rising off the case of rifles he'd been reclining on. His concertina sighed profoundly as he set it aside.

Hands behind his ample backside, Stormfield began to explore the barn. "Mr. Ramsey most assuredly came well prepared," he observed as he sidestepped along a row of six machine guns.

"A dude," said Tuck, following him when he moved on again. "Got himself the harebrained idea he's goin' to lead an army after rustlers."

"What about the brigands who made off with half your weapons last evening? Does he intend to pursue them?"

Tuck spat into the straw. "Ramsey's still woozy from his bonk on the skonce."

"Yes, I know. I encountered him briefly in the sporting parlor yonder."

"Get a look at them ladies, did you?"

"I briefly viewed two of the residents, yes."

"I hear as how they're better lookin' and as big-breasted as any whores you'll find in a big city like Chicago or New Orleans."

Tugging at his side-whiskers, Stormfield considered. "At least equal to Chicago, yes," he decided finally. "New Orleans, however, has them beat."

"You been in whorehouses all 'round the country, have you?"

"Purely in the interest of research," explained Stormfield. "I am an author and obliged to look life in the eye."

"The eye ain't exactly the spot I'd be lookin' into if I could afford to tomcat from coast to coast."

"Concerning the missing artillery," put in Stormfield. "Am I to understand that Big Jim Phillips does not intend to go after them either?"

Tuck spat again. "He says it ain't exactly his business. 'Sides which he can't spare no hands just now, seein' as how he's got to look after his ranch and his herd."

"You sound as though you don't exactly believe his excuse."

"Don't," admitted Tuck. "Thing is, Mr. Storm-wheels, I just work for Mr. Ramsey. I ain't the boss of nothin'. So I do what I'm told."

"A pity." Stormfield walked out into the bright afternoon.

She had no idea where she was. Not when she awakened at the darkest hour of the night. The room was strange and unfamiliar, smelling strongly of musky perfume. Even the smooth, silky sheets felt odd on her body.

Molly Cartland sat up, blinking, breathing through her open mouth. For several long, blurry moments she sat there in the strange, scented darkness, struggling to awaken fully, to remember where she was.

That horrible little doctor, yes. Sopkin. Dr. Sopkin had forced her to drink half a glass of some awful purplish stuff and she had drifted down into a numbing sleep. That must've been hours ago. When the glaring, hot sun had been out.

Why was she here at all? Why had the doctor put her to sleep?

"Sam," she murmured. "It has something to do with Sam."

Molly struggled out of bed, stumbling, falling to one knee. Someone, she had no idea who, had taken off her clothes and put her into a frilly nightdress. It smelled strongly of perfume.

She reached for the nearest bedpost, pulled herself upright. There was a dark robe draped over the post.

Molly, still feeling unsteady, slipped the robe over her shoulders.

Sam was in this house, she was remembering now. She shook her head from side to side, striving to shake off the lingering effects of the sleeping drug.

Yes, her husband had been wounded. He was in the room next to this one.

"Something's wrong!" Yes, that was why she'd awakened. Her injured husband was in danger and she must go to him.

Molly glanced around the room. She could see more clearly now and she spotted her large purse sprawled in an armchair. Hurrying to it, she thrust in her hand.

They hadn't taken it. Her hand closed around the butt of a Colt .38.

Putting the gun beneath her robe, Molly hurried to the door. The hallway was even darker than the bedroom. She had to feel her way along the wall to the door of Sam's room.

Very slowly and carefully she turned the brass doorknob. The door opened silently, and Molly went across the threshold. Then she gasped.

She could see a dark shape looming beside the bed. The figure had its right arm raised to strike her husband. In the hand was a knife.

"Don't!" Molly pulled out the gun and fired twice.

The dark figure cried out with pain, slumped and tumbled down onto the floor.

Molly stood frozen, shaking, in shock.

Light bloomed behind her. And then a big young blonde woman was pushing by her into the room.

"Sweet Yesus!" the blonde exclaimed. "You done killed Big Yim!"

Chapter 26

Spear awoke with the dawn.

He eased out of his blankets, yawned, rolled them up. He stood, stretched, scratched his beard.

Nita Torquay's camp was in a narrow arroyo some ten miles south of the cabin where he'd met her. There was a trickle of water running across the flat bed of the gulch and Spear walked down to that.

Chavez was stretched out by the campfire, leaning on one elbow. "Top of the morning," he beamed as Spear passed him.

"*Buenos días*," returned Spear.

Squatting by the slim stream, Spear scooped up cold water in his hands and doused his face. Then he opened the small kit he'd brought along and, propping the mirror in the branches of a scruffy bush, he concentrated on trimming his beard.

"I thought you never shaved?"

He looked back over his shoulder and saw the dark-haired girl standing there, slim and pretty. "Once every few weeks I have to trim the beard, otherwise I find myself always tripping over it."

Nita inhaled deeply, hands on hips. "We'll go into Santa Vergas tonight at sundown," she said.

"Paloma ought to be there by then."

"Yes." She moved nearer and sat cross-legged on the ground.

He could see one side of her face reflected in his small oval mirror. "You're sure you want to go ahead?"

"No other way to go," she answered. "Don't let the things Chavez says bother you. He, along with most of the men, tends to act like a big brother to me most of the time."

"When do I meet the rest of this crew?"

"Later on. They're . . . elsewhere."

He ran his fingertips over his beard, gave it a final scrutiny in the mirror and closed up his kit. "Any notion where Paloma'll store the guns?"

"In the church."

"Church? That's an unusual place to cache arms."

"It's called the Church of Our Lady of Sorrows," Nita said. "Quite a large and impressive church for such a low-down town. It was built, as I understand it, by a wealthy rancher some years back. Religion didn't flourish in that town, the priests and the nuns departed and the grand church was put to other more profane uses."

"Paloma hangs out there now?"

"When he's in town he uses it as a storehouse for various goods," Nita replied. "He moves around a lot, has another base down in Mexico."

Spear stood. "He's involved in running cattle across, too?"

"Yes. Most often teaming up with Steve Janson." She rose and when he started walking away from the camp she fell in beside him.

"From what you've seen, in the months you've been playing vigilante, what—"

"I'm not playing at anything, Spear."

"Excuse me." He grinned. "What I'd like to hear is your opinion as to who's behind the whole shebang."

"You already know the answer."

"Big Jim."

"Yes," she attested. "His long-range plan is to take over most of the ranches in this part of Texas, to control all the water and the best trails to the railheads. If you could get a look at the deeds on some of the biggest spreads, you'd see that Big Jim already owns most of them. Secretly. He bought out my grandfather's place, too."

"You tried to stop him?"

The girl shrugged. "Grandfather didn't want to sell, he tried to hold out," she said quietly. "You know what good that did."

"At the time, you said you didn't recognize any of the men involved."

"What I *said* and what I *know* aren't necessarily the same."

"Then why didn't you go to the law?"

"To who? Marshal Beaven?" She laughed. "He's just a toady of Big Jim's!"

"That wasn't the impression I got, talking to Beaven."

"You're an outsider," she reminded him. "You can't expect to ride in here and figure out every blessed thing in a few days."

"True." He pushed up the brim of his Stetson with his thumb. "Going to take me twice that long just to figure you out."

"I thought I was very obvious," Nita said. "Don't

you already have me down in your book as a foolhardy kid?"

"Nope, that's not the category I'd file you under."

"Pigheaded girl?"

"Let's talk about what we're going to do tonight," he suggested.

"Yes, that's a safer topic," Nita decided.

Big Jim growled, "I'm not saying it was attempted murder."

"Most considerate of you," said Stormfield.

The rancher, his left arm in a sling, was sitting up in the most ornate bed in the most ornate bedroom in his private bordello. "After all, the little lady was dazed, doped."

"She vas goofy in da head," added Inga, who sat in a gilded chair close to the bedside.

Stormfield was in a chair somewhat farther from the wounded rancher. "Mrs. Cartland admits to having awakened in a somewhat disoriented condition," he said. "However, she is positive—"

"Disoriented? She vas as nutty as a bedbug. Trying to murder my Yim."

"Hush your lovely mouth for a spell, Inga pet," Big Jim suggested. "Now, Stormfield, if Mrs. Cartland wasn't doped, then why in blue blazes did she take those pot shots at my hide?"

"To protect her husband."

"There's more evidence tending to prove how groggy she was this morning," said Big Jim. "There wasn't a damn thing to protect that son of a bitch from."

"She maintains she saw someone posed over the bed with a knife, about to attack Cartland."

Big Jim boomed with laughter. "Well, that sure as hell wasn't me."

"He neffer killed nobody or tried to."

"I don't have any kindly feelings toward Cartland, that you know," Big Jim went on. "I'd like to see every damned cattle thief in the Panhandle strung up. But I don't go in for murdering folks in their sleep."

"Why exactly were you in his room?"

"I thought I heard the jasper moaning," explained the rancher. "Well sir, I don't like seeing even a low-down skunk suffer, so—"

"You should have let dat yackass moan all night!"

"So I went to take a look in his room." Big Jim gave the blonde a negative shake of his head. "When I got there, he seemed to be sleeping as peaceably as a babe. I was about to steal away when the shooting started."

"Dat bitch."

Stormfield coughed into his hand. "What of that knife she says was about to be plunged into the person of her ailing husband?"

"Hallucination, pure and simple," answered Big Jim. "Brought on by drugs and the fact the room was as black as the inside of a boot." He leaned forward. "You'll recall that no such weapon was found in the room."

"True, yes," acknowledged Stormfield. "I myself, of course, did not reach the room until several long minutes after the unfortunate shooting incident."

"I vas in dere yust after she shoot poor Yim," Inga put in. "Dey vasn't no knife. Except in her goofy imagination."

"Fortunately the wound was superficial," Big Jim said. "I don't believe I'll even have to send for that sourpuss Sopkin. No, a day or so in bed and I'll be as good as new."

"I don't like it vhen you is in bed, but can't fool around, Yimmy."

"You may tell Mrs. Cartland that I have no hard feelings, Stormfield," the rancher said. "Her actions were, I know, those of an overwrought woman."

"No vunder she vas overwrought, married to dat dirty crook."

"I don't intend to call in the law or make any trouble for Mrs. Cartland."

"Most magnanimous."

"Her damn husband, however, is another story. He must be delivered over to the law as soon as he's mended," said Big Jim, scowling deeply. "Is the man conscious yet?"

"Not yet, no." Stormfield rose from his chair. "Thus far he hasn't spoken a word. Interesting to speculate on what he'll have to say when he does finally awaken."

"Isn't it, though," agreed Big Jim.

Sam Cartland opened his eyes and there was his red-haired wife smiling hopefully at him. He closed his eyes and opened them again. Molly was still there.

"Guess I didn't die," he said weakly.

She moved her chair even closer, taking hold of his hand. "You're only wounded, Sam, and the doctor is pretty sure you'll pull through."

"I knew I was going to get shot, had a premonition. Except I figured I'd die from it."

"You're not going to die." She held tight to his hand.

"How come you're here?" He moved his head

slowly from side to side, taking in the room. "Hell, I'm not even sure where I am."

"We're at the Circle BJ."

"Then they just dragged me in here after they shot me."

"You've lost a lot of blood. No one wanted to risk moving you."

"You know what I've been up to, Molly?" Sam asked.

"Yes. But I don't know why."

He closed his eyes, but kept talking. "Hell, Molly, just another one of my fool notions. I figured as how I could make some quick money, buy us a new ranch somehow."

"What happened to the one we had?"

"I . . . well, I lost it."

"How, Sam?"

He opened his eyes, met hers. "Same old way. Playing cards."

Her hand tightened on his. "You were going to give that up. We'd been so lucky in getting that land, this was our dream come true."

"Molly, I don't think I'm ever going to be really lucky," Sam confessed. "I just can't seem to hold onto anything good. You and the ranch and—"

"You should've written, told me what happened."

"I just couldn't," he admitted. "Just couldn't tell you I'd screwed up another time, Molly."

She took a deep breath. "Well, now we'll just have to get out of this mess."

"How? I've been running with a gang of outlaws. I never killed anybody, or even much hurt anybody. Around here, though, they hang you for stealing even one damn cow. And with a powerful rancher like Big Jim, anything could happen."

"He came in here last night and tried to kill you," she told him.

"What? Big Jim himself? Why in blazes would he want to do that?"

"Why do *you* think he wants you dead?"

"I reckon he hates cattle thieves."

"Could he have another reason for wanting you dead and quiet?"

"Never even met the man," her husband replied. "He'd have no reason to . . . except, well . . ."

Molly urged, "Go on, Sam."

"Well, I was just remembering the last time we stole cattle from the Circle BJ, few nights ago," he said, sitting up a little. "Everything went real smooth, you know. Too damn smooth. When we were cutting through the barbed wire, I swear there was two of Big Jim's hands close enough to've seen us plain. They didn't pay any damn attention at all, just kept riding on."

"What did Steve Janson say about things like that?"

"Told me it was none of my business."

"Janson never told you he'd made some kind of a deal with Big Jim?"

"Even if he had, Janson would never have confided anything like that."

"But maybe Big Jim is afraid he did," she said.

Stormfield was ensconced in a wicker chair near the window of the room he'd been provided in the main house. His plump knees were raised and he had a large leather-bound book open across them. "I have been sadly neglectful of my literary career," he murmured, rubbing the tail end of his wooden pencil across his chin. "Let me see. Where did I leave off in this latest adventure of Sweetwater Sid, the Masked Texas Avenger?"

> . . . a vision of absolute feminine loveliness stood before him in the mysterious cavern into whose dark and fetid bowels he had sojourned in his relentless quest for the strange secret of the Ruby Ring of Montezuma. Her alabaster upper limbs, each of a perfection to make the most casual admirer of female pulchritude gasp and exclaim in abject wonder, ended in hands of exquisite and breathtaking beauty. Alas, this vision of almost magical beauty was marred by the twin six-guns the titian-haired goddess held pointed, with awesome accuracy, at vital portions of young and handsome Sweetwater Sid, often alluded to by friend and foe alike as the Masked Texas Avenger.
>
> "Grab yurself some sky, varmint!" this mysterious female trilled.
>
> "Fair lady," responded Sweetwater Sid, noblest gunfighter in all the vast sun-blazed Panhandle of wild and wooly Texas, an amused grimace stealing across his sun-bronze and handsome visage, "my quarrel is not with you. Nay, were I not dedicated to seeking the fabled Ruby Ring of Montezuma, vilely purloined from the stately mansion of Count Maurice deHorn by the villainous Johnson Brothers, I should . . .

Stormfield tugged at his left sideburn, then at his right. "What should this whelp do?" He chewed at the

end of his pencil for a moment, then commenced to
write.

> . . . sweep you off your dainty feet and ride
> like the wind with you thrown across my
> unique and specially crafted silver-trimmed
> saddle. Aye, upon my trusty black as night
> stallion, Primrose, sometimes dubbed the Su-
> per Horse of the Wild West, I should carry
> you across the vast and awesome plains of
> Texas to some distant bower, whereat I
> should, I vow, shower you with hot kisses
> upon those . . .

The wicker chair creaked as Stormfield paused in
his labors to lean back and reflect.

> . . . luxuriant ruby lips. Yes, kisses that
> would . . .

Someone was standing on the other side of Stormfield's closed door. He'd heard a floorboard creak.

He poked his pencil into the breast pocket of his
frock coat, closed his notebook and stood up.

When he was only halfway to the door, an envelope came sliding under it. The author's full name was
written across the face in a bold and familiar hand.

Stooping, not the easiest of tasks anymore, Stormfield plucked up the missive. After the fluttering in his
ears and the slight dizziness brought on by the bend
had subsided, he tore the envelope open.

The letter within was, as he had deduced from the
inscription, from Brad Spear.

Thomas, seems possible Paloma and the stolen guns may be in a wide-open town named Santa Vergas. I am operating on that assumption. Case you don't hear from me in a reasonable time, act accordingly. **B.S.**

"Very terse style the lad possesses," said Stormfield half aloud, while rubbing the folded letter across his plump chin. "He'll never be able to pen novels of sufficient length to satisfy a public that cries for glut and prolixity."

Depositing the letter in an inner pocket, he left his temporary quarters.

Chapter 27

They rode into the town at sunset, Spear and Nita. Spear looked much the same as usual in his comfortable working clothes, but the girl was dressed in a bright scarlet skirt, an off-the-shoulder white blouse and a bright shawl. Her lips and cheeks were rouged, and her dark hair was piled high and held with a silver comb.

Santa Vergas was about seven blocks long and three blocks wide, a gaudy, brightly lit, noisy splotch on the plains. Music, on key and off, spilled out of the cantinas and saloons. Every sound a human voice could make, from rough laughter to frightened screaming, could be heard. Dogs barked and howled, pistols went off, guitars plunked.

A fat Mexican, clad only in sombrero and serape, came crashing out through the second-floor window of an adobe bordello.

"Bastard! *Cabrón!*" cried the naked girl who watched him plummet from her window to the dusty street below.

"Quite a lively town," observed Spear.

From out of the Black Bull Saloon a white-bearded cowhand came hopping. His left foot was on fire.

"That's rich!" shouted a younger cowpoke, who stood in the saloon doorway laughing and hugging himself.

"Full of fun," added Spear.

"There's the church." Nita nodded to her left from the saddle of her black mare.

"Noticed it."

The church didn't fit the town at all. It rose majestically amidst the false-front and adobe buildings. It was made of stone, and had a great metal cross topping its spire. Three of its original six stained-glass windows were still intact, depicting Christ working various miracles. A drunken man was sprawled on the marble steps with a dog sniffing at his bare feet.

"Guards in the alleys on the left and right," mentioned Nita as they rode by.

"Noted them, too."

A thin youth in the loose white clothes of a peon leaned against a wall in one alley. A thickset man in dark clothes was in the other. They were trying so hard to look casual that they gave themselves away.

"Likely to be at least two more in back," the girl said.

"Meaning Paloma is definitely in town."

"I'd say so." She tugged on the reins and headed into a narrow side street.

The noise and light were considerably less down this way. The only music came from a lone guitar. Near the entrance of an adobe building labeled Las Flores Cantina, a fat woman in a dusty black dress was retching, one hand spread wide against the white-washed wall to keep her from falling.

"We want the next place down," Nita told him.

This saloon was housed in a two-story adobe building painted a bright yellow and bearing a signboard designating it as English Freddie's.

Nita reined up, dismounted and hitched her mount to the rail, which was painted red and white like a barber pole.

Spear followed suit. "Did I mention how authentic you look?"

She nodded faintly at him in the dusk. "Just remember you're a notorious gambler, if anyone asks."

"Can't stand card games," he said, pushing the lopsided green door open for her.

She walked into the place, laughing loudly. She took hold of his arm, kissed him roughly on the cheek. "We can always have a good time here!" she roared.

English Freddie's had a dirt floor, a dozen small tables and a serving bar that consisted of two wooden doors propped atop barrels. English Freddie himself was stationed behind this rude bar. He was a squat man with blond hair the color of dusty sunlight. He also had a very impressive glass eye.

There were five other patrons in the saloon, three of whom were stupefied at three separate tables. The other two, one an extremely youthful cowhand and the other a whore with shoulders twice as wide as his, were sharing a pint of what looked like kerosene at a table in the dimmest corner of the room. Everything smelled of raw liquor, bad tobacco and, quite possibly, a dead cat.

"Evenin', folks," welcomed Freddie. He had a whetstone in one speckled hand and was honing a wicked-looking carving knife. "Allow me ter welcome yer to me establishment. What'll it be, gov?"

Nita leaned toward him. "We'd like a room for a few hours, Freddie," she said, winking broadly.

"I surely hope you ain't meanin' ter use it fer immoral purposes, lass."

"We're looking for a card game that Buck here can sit in on," the girl explained loudly. "But we'd like to . . . rest up a bit first."

Freddie had been scrutinizing her face. "Lor' blimey. I didn't recognize yer at first . . . That is ter say, I got just the bloomin' room fer yer." He set the knife and the stone aside. Glancing off to his left, he called, "Martha! You old slut, drag your ancient carcass in here on the bloody double!" When he looked at Nita again, he winked. "Me old woman's gettin' more feeble every year."

"Keep that bloomin' guff to yerself, Freddie." A massive woman with a head of improbable blonde hair emerged from a back room and stood glaring at the proprietor. "What the bloody hell do yer want?"

"You watch the bar whilst I escort this happy couple up ter the royal suite, will yer, love?"

"You called me in here just so a couple of lowlifes can knock off a quick—"

"Now, now, woman, there ain't no need for improper lingo." He scooted out from behind the bar after moving the sharpened knife farther out of his mate's reach, then hurried to a green door at the far side of the room. He beckoned Nita and Spear to follow.

Martha made a snarling sound, then went lumbering behind the doors and barrels to fill in for her husband.

The staircase leading up to the dark second floor of English Freddie's was narrow and greasy. Throwing open a door halfway along the upper corridor, Freddie exclaimed, "This is it, folks. Me pride and joy, the best blinkin' room in the whole house." He snatched up a hurricane lamp and lit it.

The room was the size of a jail cell, though not quite as lavishly furnished. There was a stained, grey mattress on the bare plank floor and a three-legged chair leaning against the cracked plaster wall for support.

When all three were inside, Freddie shut the door softly and placed the smoky lamp on the floor near the ancient mattress. "Lor', I fairly didn't know yer right off, Nita," he explained, chuckling. "You looks like a whore fer sure." He held out his hand to Spear. "Pleased ter meet yer . . . Buck, was it?"

Spear shook hands. "So it seems."

"Now then, what can I do fer yer, Nita love?"

She took a position against the wall, near the room's single window. "Is Paloma in town?"

Freddie became interested in his fingernails. "He might be."

Nita nodded. "Brought something in with him, too, I'd guess."

Freddie bit at a hangnail. "So I hear."

"We'd like to stay here for a few hours," she told him.

"I wouldn't exactly want the likes of Paloma mad with me, lass."

"He'll never even know we were your guests, Freddie," she assured him, reaching into her blouse.

"Well, seein' as we're old friends, it'll be twenty dollars for the room."

"We're better friends than that." She gave him ten.

Freddie's freckled hand closed over the money. "Fer yer, love, it's ten." The money disappeared into a pocket of his checkered trousers. "Now let me bid yer good night. Nice ter have met yer, Buck."

"Yep, same here, Freddie."

As soon as he was gone, Nita moved to the lamp and doused it. Then she crossed to the window and drew back the stiff, yellowed curtain. "We can see the backside of the church from here," she noted. "Later on, we'll wander over for a closer look."

Spear joined her at the window. "Two more guards," he said, watching the darkening street through narrowed eyes. "By the way, next time you christen me with a fake name, don't make it Buck."

"Oh? It seems to suit you."

"You've dealt with Freddie before," he said. "You trust him?"

"Yes, he's okay. He's never betrayed me or let me down."

"So far," said Spear.

The moonlight seemed to bring a pale chill into the room. It was a few minutes past two in the morning and Santa Vergas had quieted down some. Less shouting, less shooting. Down in the dark street a guitar player picked out a sad tune, a Mexican song about lost love and dying young.

Spear was squatting near the window, guardedly watching the grey shape that was the church. "Only one guard on duty now, and he's nodding."

"We'll move soon," Nita answered.

"Is Paloma likely to be inside the church?"

"No, he's probably elsewhere. Once we make sure the guns are stashed over there, then we'll see about finding him." She was sitting on the ruin of a mattress, her long legs tucked under her.

Spear moved away from the vicinity of the window and carefully lit a cigar. The flare of the match gave him a fleeting picture of her pretty, sad face. "What happens once you bring down Big Jim?" he asked.

"What do you mean?"

"When the gent is behind stone walls or decorating the end of a rope, then what will be left for you?"

"So now you believe me, about his being the boss of what's going on?"

"He's a damn good candidate," conceded Spear, blowing out a wisp of smoke that went spinning down toward the seated girl.

"You're implying that all that keeps me going is a desire to get even with him," she murmured. "Once he's caught and brought to justice I won't have anything to live for. Is that it?"

"Something along those lines."

She shook her head. "Big Jim's just one crook. There'll be a lot of them left in Texas when he's gone."

"Meaning you'll go on forever?"

Nita looked up at him. "I've heard a few stories about you."

"Lot of 'em floating around." He puffed on the cigar. "A few true, most not."

"They say you're quite a womanizer."

"I never let it interfere with my work." He sat back near her against the rough plaster wall.

"I must be annoying," she sighed. "A woman you can't make love to."

Spear said slowly, "Maybe I haven't accepted that fact or . . ."

"Or maybe you're just not interested."

"Tell you what," he responded, dropping the cigar to the floor and grinding it under the heel of his boot. "When I was back in New York City recently, I saw a play that they called a drawing room drama. For three solid acts a bunch of very well-dressed ladies and gents sat around on some expensive furniture and talked at each other. Sort of boring." He got up. "When, and if, I decide to make a move, Nita, we won't talk about it beforehand. Things'll just happen."

She rose to her feet, stood facing him. "I wouldn't advise you to try anything like that."

"You'd shoot me in order to discourage me?"

"If I had to, sure."

She couldn't see his grin in the darkness of the room. "What say we amble over for a look at that church?"

After a long pause, she said quietly, "There were six of them."

Spear said nothing.

"Two of them held me while . . . while they killed my grandfather," she whispered. The darkness of the room seemed to close in around her. "They didn't just kill him . . . they mutilated him. Laughing. Even when he screamed and pleaded, they laughed. He was a strong man, not a coward . . . but what they did. . . . He cried and begged them to stop. All but one of them laughed . . . five of them. They took turns with me. They made me take off my clothes myself . . . undress for them. And if I didn't do exactly what they wanted, they cut me, using the same knives they'd used to. . . . It went on and on and I . . . had to keep . . . pleasing them. It's funny, what you'll do to stay alive sometimes. I wish I'd just let them kill me. They made love to me—only love isn't the word for what they did—for hours . . . hours. . . . And our house burned away to ashes. I passed out and they woke me up . . . I fainted again and they awakened me and made me do it all over again. . . . Then finally I passed out, and when I came to, it was just ashes and my dead grandfather. They were gone."

Reaching into the dark, he found her hand and took hold of it. "Easy, Nita. It's all over."

She pulled free of him. "It'll never be over."

Spear should have realized something because it was all so easy, so damn smooth. He should have suspected they'd been sold out, but he didn't.

Maybe it was because his mind was preoccupied, going over the story Nita had just told him. Seeing in his mind the young girl being raped by the five men. Men, it was fairly obvious, who'd come from the Circle BJ. And maybe he was thinking, too, about how much he wanted this slim dark girl himself and yet might never have her.

The guard at the rear of the church never even turned around. Spear came stalking out of the deep shadows that spilled around the tall stone church. He got an armlock around the man, clapped a hand over his mouth. The guard was not young, and he was too fat and he smelled of wine. Spear knocked him out with ease, dragged him back into the shadows. Nita was waiting there and she tied and gagged him.

Spear picked up the .44 that had fallen from the man's clothes during their brief, silent struggle, and he thrust it into his waistband. "C'mon, let's take a look inside."

He turned the knob on the dark wooden door, nudged it a few inches open. After several seconds, he stepped into the near darkness on the other side.

Two small windows let in enough moonlight for him to make out the sacristy, the room where the long-gone priests had put on their robes and where the various sacred vessels had been stored. That had been some time ago.

Nita came in and quietly shut the door after her. "I was right," she whispered, nodding across the dirty floor.

Stacked against the far wall were four cases of Springfield rifles.

Spear had already seen them and was opening the heavy door that led out to the center of the church.

Moonlight slanting down through the stained-glass windows threw pale, multicolored patterns across the floor of the high, vaulted room. Only half the pews remained. The rest had been taken away or chopped up and left strewn about the church. Straw was scattered all over the marbled floor and there was evidence that horses had been stabled here recently.

"This is most of the rest of it," whispered Nita at his side.

"Yep, sure is."

There were cases of rifles, cartons of pistols, boxes of shells and dynamite. Seven Gardner guns were lined up along the broken altar rail.

Something moved in the deep blackness beside the altar.

Spear's hand swung down to his holster.

"Not smart, señor."

A gun barrel pressed into the back of Spear's neck.

"I kill him, señorita, unless you remain still."

Nita had been tensing to run.

Sparks crackled near the altar, a match flared and a kerosene lantern was lit. It was held by one of the guards Spear had seen earlier out in front of Santa Vergas' imposing church.

"I'm disappointed." Paloma moved around in

front of them with his gun still in his hand. "I hoped for more of a struggle." He shrugged, laughing.

"Holster that six-gun," offered Spear, "and I'll give you a struggle."

"No need now," said the pleased outlaw. "I have the rifles and guns, I have you and the señorita. The guns will bring a fine price in my own country and this *muy bonita* young lady I think I will also be able to sell. *Sí,* because I have been given to understand she likes very much to satisfy more than one man at once. There is a great demand for so eager a whore."

"What about me?" asked Spear, noting that there were two more men—each toting a rifle—at the back of the church near the font. "Who do I get sold to?"

Paloma laughed again. "Maybe I don't sell you to nobody," he smiled. "No, maybe I got something else in mind for you." With his gun aimed at Spear, he reached out with his free hand and pulled at the edge of Nita's blouse.

"Damn you," said Spear, "don't touch her."

"Ah, such small breasts." Paloma closed one big hand over one of the bare breasts he'd exposed. "I don't know now if I can get as much for this one as I thought. What do you think, Nacio?"

The man with the lantern chuckled. "Better check out the rest of her, boss."

"*Sí,* that's a very good idea." He let go of Nita's breast and thrust his hand into the waist of her skirt. "Maybe her—"

"Leave her alone!" Spear lunged, reaching for the Mexican's gun hand.

Paloma swung that hand up suddenly, dodging Spear's grasp. The barrel whacked Spear hard in the chin.

He went staggering to one side.

Paloma shifted his grip on the gun, using it as a hammer, and cracked Spear across the temple with the butt.

Spear dropped to his knees. The colored moonlight melted swiftly into black as he fell to the floor of the church.

Chapter 28

A monotonous creaking sounded again and again.

Spear coughed, nearly choking. He was lying facedown in a bundle of dirty rags. His hands were tied behind his back. His head pounded with each creak and pain went zigzagging through his skull.

"Brad?" whispered Nita.

Out of the corner of his left eye he saw the crimson cloth of the girl's skirt. The material was torn now, spattered with dried blood.

"What'd they do to you?" he asked, his voice sounding rusty and in need of oil.

"Nothing dire," she answered.

"That blood on your dress. . . ."

"It's Nacio's. I managed to give him a bloody nose before they tied me up."

Using his elbow, Spear managed to raise up on his side. The creaking sound was being made by wagon wheels. He and Nita had been dumped on the floor, amid cases of guns and ammunition.

"I'm getting mighty tired of traveling with Ramsey's hardware," he said. "Do you know whereabouts in Mexico we're heading for?"

"Probably Tijeras," she answered. "It's a border town with even less law than Santa Vergas."

Over the tailboard of the wagon he saw the hot yellow morning outside. "How long we been on the move?"

"Roughly two hours."

He tried to move his hands, but they were bound tight. The leather thongs dug into his flesh. "You trussed up tight as I am?"

"Hand and foot. I've been trying to work free ever since they tossed us in here."

He discovered his legs were tightly bound just below the knees. Tilting his head, he looked toward the front end of the wagon. "Who's our driver?"

"Nacio."

"Where's Paloma?"

"Riding on horseback. There are two other wagons like this one in our little procession."

"Well sir," said Spear, "I got to admit things don't look as bright as they might. Hate to wait until we get to Tijeras to try to escape."

"Brad, I don't think he intends to take you all the way there."

"That's right. He mentioned having something special planned for me. Any notion what?"

"Whoa! Stop!" Nacio shouted at the horses.

The wheels screeched. The heavy wagon shivered and shook and it came thumping and rattling to a stop. Hoofbeats sounded right outside. Spurs jingled.

"*Buenos días,* Señor Spear." Paloma was letting down the tailboard of their wagon. "This, I fear, is as far as you go."

"Didn't know this was my station." Spear could

see only flat, dry desert country beyond the halted wagon.

"What you're going to find out about this spot is two things, amigo." Paloma reached in and grabbed Spear by the collar of his shirt. "In the daytime it is *muy caliente*. But at night, *muy frío*. You *sabe*?"

"I'm going to be spending some time here, huh?"

Paloma laughed. "The rest of your life." He tugged, jerked Spear clean out of the wagon and let him fall to the hard, gritty ground.

Spear bit his tongue when he hit. "Going to shoot me in the front or the back?" he asked, spitting blood.

"I'm not going to shoot you. Don't you know that shooting a Pinkerton agent is a serious offense?"

"We got the stuff, Paloma." Nacio had joined them. Clutched in one hand were four sharp wooden stakes and several lengths of leather cord.

Smiling, Paloma bent and took hold of Spear by the armpits. He dragged him across the rough ground until he was about fifty feet from the wagons. There was a scattering of saltbush nearby and that was about all.

The dragging had buffed a raw spot into Spear's right shoulder, allowing blood to ooze out and stick to the torn cloth of his shirt.

Another Mexican appeared, carrying a mallet. "This where you want him?"

Paloma was circling the spot where he'd left Spear, rubbing thoughtfully at his chin. "What do you think, Señor Spear?" he asked, squatting beside him. "Is it going to be hot enough for you here? *Sí*, I think probably so. And maybe you'll meet some sidewinders or coral snakes pretty soon." He rose up, laughing. "You're going to have yourself one hell of a good time."

With one fancy boot Paloma kicked Spear in his side and rolled him over onto his face. He slit the cords that tied his hands and legs. "Don't try to run."

Nacio chuckled. "Hell, he can't even walk after being tied that long. He's helpless as a *niño*."

Bending again, Paloma slit Spear's shirt up the back. "You don't look presentable with this dirty shirt on. Besides, it's really too warm for that."

The other man, Francisco, ripped the shirt off Spear's torso. "He's pretty dark for a *gringo*, ain't he?"

"He sure is." Paloma caught one of Spear's arms and flipped him over onto his back.

Francisco took a stake and drove it deep into the hard ground. Then he took a leather cord and tied Spear's wrist to it tightly. He did the same to the other wrist. Then he and Nacio, after tugging off Spear's boots and flinging them aside, staked his feet to the desert ground.

When Spear was spread-eagled, Paloma said, "Francisco, I got something for him over on my saddle. You fetch it, *por favor*."

Francisco strolled off.

Nacio stood frowning down at Spear. "How come she likes him better than you, Paloma?"

"Because she knows him better," explained the outlaw. "Wait, amigo, and by the time she's been with me in Mexico a few days she'll change. Especially when she sees how I live like a king."

"Like a king?" Nacio considered that, then laughed. "Hey, that's so, ain't it."

Francisco came back, toting Spear's gunbelt.

"In case any rattlesnakes come along or maybe a buzzard," said Paloma as he took it, "this will come in handy." He dropped the gun and holster about ten feet away from Spear. "All you got to do is get up and take it."

"You sure are nice to him," Francisco smiled.

Paloma crouched again beside Spear. "I give you some advice," he said softly. "Don't wear yourself out calling for help, because nobody is going to be passing this way. You see, for the past hour or more we've been off any trail. Hardly anybody is likely to come by here." He stood up. "Adios, Señor Spear."

"Not adios, Paloma," said Spear. "Just *hasta luego.*"

Laughing, the three of them walked away and left him there.

He could close his eyes, but that didn't help much. The glare of the hot noon sun seemed to burn right through his eyelids. Sweat poured down his forehead and across his face, but in spite of all that wetness, his lips were cracked and dry.

Taking a deep breath, he went to work again with his left hand. Francisco hadn't driven that stake in quite as deep. Working at it, tugging at it, Spear was certain he'd loosened the damn thing some. Not much, but some.

Three damn hours he'd been tugging. His wrist was raw and bloody, caked with crimson-stained sand.

"The stake's loosening, though," he told himself.

Maybe it wasn't. Maybe he was just kidding himself. Going slowly loco out here in the desert.

Nope, he wasn't crazy. He was going to get free of this, going to catch up with Paloma.

He tried not to go over in his mind what they'd do to Nita Torquay. Funny, he'd slept with three women since heading out here from New York City. But right now the only woman he was thinking about was the one he hadn't made love to, had barely even touched.

Gritting his teeth against the pain, he kept at it with his left hand, pulling, jerking, over and over, struggling to work the stake loose.

Another hour dragged by. Maybe it was even longer. Spear was losing track of time. The sun had seemed to make a sudden jump across the dazzling blue of the sky. Must have dozed off, he thought.

The pain from his bleeding wrist was flowing down his arm, spilling into his body. His ribs were starting to ache. He was running out of energy fast. Slowly he readied himself once more to give a hard, painful tug at the long wooden peg.

He pulled at the stake and it came free of the earth, shedding dirt.

He held his bloody wrist up, staring at the dangling stake. He didn't realize for a few seconds what he'd managed to accomplish at last. After a few more seconds he used his newly freed hand to frisk himself. They hadn't taken his penknife in his trouser pocket.

After prying it open with his teeth, Spear sawed away at the cords binding his other wrist to the desert ground. When both hands were free, he tried to sit up. That wasn't as easy a task as he'd expected. He had to push down with both palms against the sandy ground, and that sent sharp, sizzling pains across his midsection. Sitting up at last, he went to work on the thongs holding his feet.

Standing up was the next problem. After kneeling for a couple of minutes, he made a very wobbly attempt and got up. But once he was on his feet, he fell immediately. Another try, another fall. The third time he stayed up.

Retrieving his gunbelt and getting it strapped back

on nearly toppled him again. He stayed standing, though, and after that he managed to get his boots tugged back on. He also found his Stetson a few yards away, flung out of the wagon, apparently.

They hadn't bothered to take his watch. That told him it was a few minutes past three in the afternoon.

"So here I am. Without a spot of food or a drop of water, and shirtless on top of it, about fifty miles from nowhere."

What was that spiritual he'd heard once outside a church down in New Orleans? Something about having fifty miles of elbowroom when you got to heaven.

He had that right now. He had this whole hot, hazy stretch of desert country to himself, miles from any established trail, miles, far as he knew, from another single human being.

"Well, no use giving in. Might as well . . ."

Spear frowned, wondering if there were mirages that you just heard and didn't see. Because from far behind him he was damn sure he'd just heard the mournful wheeze of a concertina.

Chapter 29

The wagon came rolling into sight. It was a bright, gaudy contraption. The body was painted gold, sky blue and fiery red, the canvas topping emblazoned with slogans, testimonials and the name, in letters nearly a foot high, of Professor William Emerson Pepper. Beneath this, in letters half the size, were the words *Inventor Of The Bioptiscope! Tamer Of The Lightning! Bringer Of Blessed Rain!*

Sitting beside the driver of this wheeled eyesore was none other than Seamus Tuck, his concertina on his lap. "Oh, I am a lonesome cowboy," he was singing.

Driving the quack wagon was not the frazzle-headed Professor Pepper, but Thomas Alexander Stormfield. "Halt, you forlorn creatures! Whoa!"

The two ancient horses stumbled and staggered to a stop, bringing the gaudy wagon to a shuddering halt a few feet from the amazed Spear.

"Good afternoon, my boy," said Stormfield, setting the brake and climbing down. "What a fortuitous meeting."

"What in the hell are you doing out here?"

The author walked over to him. "We encountered the esteemed Professor Pepper while en route to Santa Vergas," he explained. "It occurred to me, in one of my typical flashes of brilliance with which I am frequently visited, that this vehicle would make an excellent disguise for us. A veritable Trojan horse as it were, within which we might enter unsuspected into various and sundry enemy camps. For while citizens always suspect a quack, they usually suspect him of nothing more than quackery. The prompt payment of seventy-five dollars in cash of the realm convinced our eminent authority of the heavens and the moisture contained therein to lease us his flamboyant vehicle for a few days."

"Where does Tuck fit in?"

"I felt the need of an assistant on this venture of following in your footsteps, Bradley. His honesty and his feistiness impressed me. Although his singing I could give up with nary a twinge of regret."

"Howdy, Spear," called Tuck. "Looks like you been collectin' a sunburn for yourself."

"That's what I get for going out in the sun without a shirt," said Spear. "Listen, Thomas, how did you find me? I was informed only snakes and wild beasts ever came this way."

The portly author coughed into his hand. "Certain judicious queries in that pest hole known as Santa Vergas resulted in my learning that Paloma had set out for Tijeras with wagons containing arms, ammunition, and you and a young lady."

"I got me an eagle eye for followin' a trail," put in Tuck, spitting into the desert. "Wasn't hard followin' you."

"We didn't expect to find you so soon," Stormfield

admitted, putting a hand on Spear's shoulder. "Paloma jettisoned you far short of his goal, it seems."

"Had me staked out for the buzzards," answered Spear. "He and I just didn't hit it off. This'll sure teach me to be more likable in the future."

"Get into the wagon and I'll treat those injuries of yours," said Stormfield. "Pepper actually has a real medical kit within."

"You figuring to keep on after Paloma?"

"Such was my intent. Unless you have some alternate plan."

"Nope," said Spear. "That's exactly what I mean to do."

"The Torquay girl, I take it, is still with him."

"He's taking her to Tijeras." Spear walked over to the wagon. Glancing up into the glare of the afternoon, he sighted three large birds—probably buzzards—circling high above. "Not this time, gents."

Spear hadn't intended to sleep. But he did. Inside the wagon, slouched down amidst Professor Pepper's props and paraphernalia and the machine gun and six rifles Stormfield had added to the contents, Spear fell into a deep slumber.

When he woke, the wagon was halted and there was darkness all around. He'd been sleeping with his left arm under him and his bandaged wrist ached and throbbed. At least his gun hand was in pretty good shape.

"When it's nighttime on the prairie and the doggies go to sleep," Tuck was singing out in the night, "then I unpack my bedroll and get set for to creep . . ."

Spear yawned and let himself out over the tailboard. The night world seemed to be all sky. A clear, intense blackness rich with stars. Up near the front of

the medicine show wagon a small campfire was burning. Stormfield was seated close beside it, his notebook
open across his knees and his pencil moving rapidly
across a page.

"Ah, good evening, my boy," he said to the approaching Spear. "Feeling better, I trust?"

"Maybe we ought to keep moving."

"I think it best to rest for a few hours," Stormfield
advised. "Especially for the sake of the good professor's steeds. You see them yonder, tethered and looking most weary."

"It's just that—"

"Paloma has to stop, too. Especially weighed
down with guns and ammunition as he is."

"Whenever he halts, he's going to turn his attention to Nita."

"Bradley, there's no use fretting over something
you can do absolutely nothing about," the author told
him. "From what you've told me of Miss Torquay, she
can survive whatever happens. She's a very tough
young lady."

"Yeah, but the idea of her with him doesn't exactly sit well with me."

"That's what causes so much trouble and strife in
the world today. Imagination," said Stormfield. "Now,
sit down and have a cup of absolutely vile coffee, concocted by our own Mr. Tuck. His beverage is as
wretched as his singing voice, but it may warm you up
some."

Spear poured himself a tin cup of coffee and took
a sip. "Yep, that's God-awful."

"Thank you kindly," Tuck put in, then went back
to singing.

Spear settled on the ground near Stormfield,

watching the crackling logs. "What's the situation back at the Circle BJ?"

"Big Jim Phillips is laid up," he said as he put his pencil into his breast pocket and shut the notebook. "I fear I'll never meet the deadline on this latest opus. Big Jim was shot by Molly Cartland."

"No kidding?"

"She claims she caught him on the verge of murdering her ailing spouse."

"What's Big Jim say?"

"He was merely paying a humanitarian visit to his ailing guest in the wee hours of the morning. Molly swears she saw him about to sink a knife into her husband, but Big Jim points out that no such weapon was found. Mrs. C, in his version of the yarn, was simply an overwrought lady given to hallucinations."

"He didn't want Cartland to talk," Spear said. "Afraid he could tie him in with the rustling."

"That is my conclusion as well." Stormfield sighed. "Unfortunately, when Cartland did get around to speaking, it became evident he is but a very small cog in this business. He knows he works for Steve Janson and little else. Although he *has* noticed that rustling the Circle BJ herds was never very difficult or hazardous."

"All that proves is that some of Big Jim's hands look the other way," Spear told him. "Big Jim can still claim he knows nothing about that."

"Precisely, my boy."

Spear tried a little more of the vile coffee. "What about Molly's husband? What's his personal story?"

Stormfield spread his hands wide. "Alas, we have here yet another example of human frailty. Cartland lost the ranch in a poker game. Thereafter he fell in with the Janson bunch in the foolish hope of earning quick money. His silence in regards to his wife was because of shame."

"Molly ought to think about getting a new husband."

"She professes to love this one."

"Not exclusively."

"Be that as it may. The only stumbling block to a fully happy reunion is the fact that Sam Cartland is a cattle thief. Around here the followers of that particular trade most often end up on the gallows. Especially those who get caught."

"Think Big Jim'll try to kill him again?"

"He must be aware by now that Cartland simply doesn't know enough to harm him," Stormfield replied. "He will, however, keep agitating to have the poor fellow lynched as a cow thief."

"What sort of shape is Ramsey in?"

"He received a nasty blow on the head. When I took my leave of the Circle BJ, he was on his feet again and spouting chivalrous talk about looking after Mrs. Cartland and her fallen spouse. There isn't likely, therefore, to be a hanging for a while."

"Ramsey," said Spear. "Him and his damn guns have caused me one hell of a lot of trouble."

"Ah, but look on the bright side," suggested Stormfield.

"Which is?"

The author poked his tongue into his cheek, thinking. "Let me ponder for a bit," he said at last. "I'm certain to come up with something."

Chapter 30

Spear spotted the castle first.

They were parked in the small plaza of the town, midday sun shining down on the borrowed wagon and the scattering of mostly white-clad citizens of Tijeras who had gathered to listen, somewhat listlessly, to Stormfield extol the virtues of Pepper's Lightning Water.

The author was perched on the open tailboard, legs wide and in a salesman's crouch, holding a bottle of Professor Pepper's wonderful elixir toward the heavens. "My friends," he was saying in relatively flawless Spanish, "no one can exaggerate the virtues of Pepper's Lightning Water! Nay, for it is the most wondrous liquid ever concocted and is purer than both the driven snow, which you possibly are not overly familiar with in this torrid clime, and the innocent tears of a newborn babe!" He tapped the black-and-yellow label with a plump forefinger. "You will note, when you have wisely purchased at least one wondrous bottle of Pepper's Lightning Water to take to your place of residence for the benefit of you and your loved ones, that imprinted upon this handsomely engraved label, a work of art in its own right and nearly worth the paltry price of purchase, are testimonials from the great and near great who inhabit this vast globe. Yes, testimonials testifying to the blessed relief to be found within this blessed glass container!" He somewhat reverently brought the label closer to his eyes. "Here, for instance, my dear friends, we see the solemn, sworn statement of no less a world luminary than the heir apparent to the throne of candelabra. 'Threw away my truss after only one swig,' he attests. And here we find Baby Princess Elana of . . ."

Spear, wearing a patched white medical smock found in a costume trunk, was stationed beside the wagon and was holding a carton containing twelve bright bottles of Pepper's Lightning Water. Beside him was Seamus Tuck, wrapped in an imitation Indian blanket, holding his concertina at the ready.

The plaza was ringed with a dozen stunted trees and then adobe buildings of various sizes and shapes, whitewashed and tile-roofed. Across the way a husky woman vending freshly made tortillas was playing to a bigger audience than they were.

The town of Tijeras had been built on the foothills of a low mountain range. From its town square one could see a good deal of the town climbing up the hillsides. One large building in particular interested Spear. It was at least a mile off, a pale ocher in color, sporting an impressive stone tower and a high brick wall around it.

Leaning toward a thin adolescent boy who was, with evident skepticism, taking in Stormfield's spiel, Spear inquired, "That building up there with the tower, what do they call it?" His Spanish was not as good as Stormfield's, but passable.

The youth glanced briefly in the direction Spear had pointed. "Everybody knows that."

"Except me."

"That's the Castle." He returned his attention to Stormfield.

Spear nodded. "Thought so."

Tuck eased over to him. "What you jawin' about with the natives?"

"Architecture."

"I bet you're asking about where you can get a little—"

"My associate, who lived ten years among the fierce Apache and is now their blood brother of that fierce clan, will now play you a stirring ditty," Stormfield was announcing. "Meanwhile, my other associate, Major Buck, will pass among you and allow you, for the insanely low, low price of a mere two pesos a bottle, to purchase as much as you want of this miracle fluid." With some huffing, he climbed down from the tailboard.

Spear stepped out into the sun, his case of bottles rattling.

"Step right up," invited Stormfield, arms held high. "Who will be the first fortunate sufferer to change his life radically for the better? Who will banish ill health, dull hair and sundry . . ."

Their audience was fragmenting, drifting away across the bright plaza.

Stormfield popped off his high hat, mopped his brow with a crisp white handkerchief. "No wonder Pepper was so eager to unload this rig on us," he said, coming over to Spear. "My pitch is infinitely better than his, yet we've sold not a single dollop of Pepper's Lightning Water."

"That'll make it easier to live with your conscience."

"True, I won't feel guilt over selling colored bilge to gullible invalids," admitted Stormfield, donning his hat again. "Yet, Bradley, I have a strong salesman's urge, as must all true free-lancers, and it galls me to fail this way."

"Tell him about the arky-texture," said Tuck, who'd never gotten to play his ditty.

"Eh?" said Stormfield, wiping his upper lip.

"That handsome edifice up in the hills over there, the one with the tower and all," said Spear. "It's known locally as El Castillo."

"The Castle," murmured Stormfield.

"Occurs to me that Paloma's joke about living like a king might have been a reference to that place."

"Yes, that is quite possible." The author became aware of the unsold bottle of Pepper's Lightning Water in his hand and deposited it in Spear's carton. "A few discreet questions at the local cantinas ought to provide us with further intelligence."

"You'll have to handle that," said Spear, "since you're the only one of us that Paloma and his boys have never laid eyes on."

"I shall gather news in my guise of wandering charlatan and mountebank," Stormfield offered. "If your surmise is correct, my boy, then when night falls on Tijeras, we'll see about laying siege to yon castle."

Molly Cartland slowed in the hall, then stopped. "What are you doing here?"

A thickset cowhand was leaning back in a kitchen chair next to the door of her husband's room. His Navy Colt was out of its holster and resting on his knee. "Howdy do, Mrs. Cartland," he greeted the red-haired woman in a gritty voice. "I'm Zeke Bensen and I'm on guard duty."

Her fingers went to the lace at the bodice of her frock. "You're guarding my husband's sickroom to keep people out?"

"Keep 'em out, keep him in." He jerked a thumb at the door.

"He's ill, hardly able to move."

"Hope you won't get riled up at me, ma'am," Bensen said. "See, I just take orders. I was told not to let anybody in to murder him and not to let him escape. So that's why I'm sitting here like this." He chuckled. "I appreciate the job, since Big Jim don't usually allow the likes of me inside his little whore . . . um . . . little place here, ma'am."

She took hold of the doorknob. "I'm not to be kept out, am I?"

"Heck no, ma'am," he assured her. "You can come and go as much as you like."

"Will you be on duty day and night?"

"I'm here till sundown, Mrs. Cartland, then Loco Ed Hunsberger takes over," replied Bensen. "In a way he might just have the best shift, 'cause I got a feeling there's more to be seen here come nightfall."

"You're probably right." She smiled at Bensen and then went on into Sam's room.

Her husband was awake, propped up in bed and not quite as pale as he had been the previous day.

"You look better," she told him.

"I suppose I am," he said as she took his hand. "Don't know as how that's going to do me much good. Sooner I'm mended, the sooner they turn me over to the law."

Molly glanced back at the closed door of the room. "You won't go to jail, Sam."

"I don't see where else I can go."

"Just let me worry about the details. I'll get you out of here and safely away."

"How the hell can I escape from this fortress?"

"Big Jim's posted a guard outside your door. But I don't think they'll be patrolling the outside of this place. Especially at night. That means we can use the window and—"

"A guard? You sure it isn't somebody who's going to sneak in and try to kill me again?"

"Big Jim's not going to attempt anything like that for a while," she soothed. "For now he's pretty much convinced you don't know much about who's backing the Janson gang."

"I really don't, Molly. Honest, I don't. You know, I wasn't very high up on the chain of command. In fact, I was at the bottom. They didn't tell me nothin'."

"How soon do you think you can move well enough to make a break?" she asked, leaning close to him.

Cartland shook his head. "I'm still pretty weak."

"Another day or two?"

"Well, maybe two."

"I want to make our move before Spear's back," she said. "Ramsey is being a bit secretive about where Spear's gone to, but I don't think he'll be back too soon. Stormfield is gone, too, along with that old goat Seamus Tuck."

"I'll try to be ready as soon as I can," Cartland sighed, not sounding very hopeful. "But, Molly, I know my luck's run out."

"You don't need luck," she said firmly. "You've got me."

* * *

To English Freddie's way of thinking, what his old woman didn't know wouldn't hurt her. If she believed he attended a friendly card game twice a week with a group of his cronies, that was just fine. He always made sure he returned home promptly at eleven p.m. And he never seemed to lose very much money. So the old sow didn't give him too bad a time.

Whistling, hands in the pockets of his checkered trousers, a touch of lilac water dabbed on his neck and under his chin, Freddie was strolling along a twilight street and wending his way across Santa Vergas.

His destination was a small and somewhat exclusive establishment on the outskirts of town. A bit more expensive than many of the other bordellos, it provided a much better class of girl. One in particular—her name was Pearl—had taken his fancy, and English Freddie had arranged to reserve her services for two full hours twice a week. Martha knew nothing about his modest little savings he'd earned from being a stooge, so he never had to account for the cost of his twice-a-week pleasures.

An incredible lass was Pearl. Not more than seventeen and half Mexican. Her father couldn't have been Mexican, though, because she had golden blonde hair. It reminded him of a girl he'd loved long ago back home in Surrey. Ah, what breasts that girl had, and what hips! he thought.

"Señor Freddie, a moment of your valuable time."

The saloonkeeper hesitated, breaking his jaunty stride. Someone had hailed him from an alley on his right.

"What?"

"This is important, Freddie. Big money involved."

More money might allow him to attend to Pearl three nights a week instead of two. "Who is it?" He couldn't quite make out the figure in the patch of darkness between the two vacant adobe buildings. He took a few tentative steps toward it. "Do I know yer?"

"But of course, old friend." A strong hand caught the front of his pink dress shirt and yanked him right into the alley. "It's your dear chum, Miguelito Chavez."

Freddie tried to break free, but couldn't. "Nice ter see yer, Chavez, m'lad. I got an urgent appointment over—"

"But Freddie, I'd be offended if we didn't have a chat." His fingers had fastened around the smaller man's throat.

"Right, Chavez, we can have a real talk. You just drop into the saloon in about three hours."

"No. We talk now." Chavez was smiling. Freddie could see his teeth.

"I swear now, Chavez, I ain't seen hide nor hair of Nita in . . . oh, blimey, it must be a month. Closer to two, in fact. How's she gettin' on, that sweet lass?"

Chavez tightened his grip. "Can you make out what I hold in my other hand?"

"Looks sort of like a knife."

"Very perceptive, Freddie. A knife it is." Chavez smiled wider. "If you were to arrive for your clandestine rendezvous with the fair Pearl, say, minus a vital part of your lovemaking equipment, it might well cause you embarrassment, eh?"

"How'd yer know about her?"

Chavez shrugged. "I had a great-grandmother who was a Spanish Gypsy, Freddie, and I just seem to know things," he said. He moved the knife until the tip of it was under the saloonkeeper's bulb of a nose. "Where is Nita?"

"Blimey, Chavez, I haven't the foggiest notion!"

"Let's cut it out," the big, mustached man suggested. "I know she was going to check in with you."

"Well now, it must have been somethin' happened to the poor lass afore she ever got ter town."

"Going through life without your lovemaking gear, Freddie, is a real social handicap. For a horse, perhaps no. But for a fellow like you—"

"Listen now, Chavez, you put me in an awkward position."

"I can make your life a lot more awkward."

"See, mate, the thing of it is this. Paloma, if he ever gets wind I talked to you, will—"

"He'll never hear," promised Chavez. "Because dead men, from what the latest medical evidence seems to indicate, are deaf."

"Paloma ain't dead."

"He's as good as," said Chavez, "if he's done a damn thing to Nita."

Freddie found himself shivering, something he seldom did on balmy nights such as this. "Okay, Chavez, I'll tell yer," he said through chattering teeth. "See, I had to tell him. It wasn't just fer me own sake, yer understand, but fer me dear wife. I wouldn't want him to harm a hair on her dear head, yer see. So I—"

"Where's Nita?"

"Her and some gent she called Buck, lad about yer size and sportin' a neat beard, they went pokin' around in the church."

"Where Paloma had the guns hidden."

It was difficult for English Freddie to shrug, dangling from Chavez's hand as he was. He attempted it nevertheless. "Don't know what he had in the bloody place," he insisted. "But I knew he wouldn't want them two snoopin' 'round inside, so I went over. That is, when he came ter me place, I felt I had to tell him.

Especially when he made threats against me and me loved ones, don't yer know."

"He caught them?"

Freddie nodded as best he could. "Both of 'em."

"What did he do with them?"

"Now here's a bit of bright news, Chavez," said Freddie, laughing very unconvincingly. "Paloma didn't kill either one. No, he just tossed them inter one of his bloomin' wagons and took off."

"Going where?"

"Lor', bless me if I have the faintest idea."

"You better come up with an idea in under sixty seconds."

"Well now, I'd guess, and this is just a guess, mind yer, I guess he's haulin' them guns . . . that is, he's takin' whatever it is was in them wagons inter Mexico. The town'd most likely be Tijeras."

"He's got a hide-out there?"

"Right fancy place from what I hear. Calls it El Castillo, which means—"

"I know what it means."

"Oh, that's right, you're Mexican," said Freddie, attempting to swallow. "You're such a toff, I keep forgettin' yer ancestry."

Chavez let go of him. "Freddie, you've talked to Paloma and you've talked to me. Don't talk to anyone else."

"Mum's the bloomin' word from now on." He made a shaky cross over his pink shirt with his hand. "You have me solemn word on . . . Chavez?"

Freddie realized he was talking to darkness and that his inquisitor had departed down the narrow alley.

He stood there shaking, trying to decide whether or not he was at all in the mood for a visit to Pearl.

Chapter 31

Through the barred window Nita saw the sun set behind the hills of Tijeras. Darkness spread down through the houses that dotted the hillside. Light appeared at a distant window. It seemed to be floating there, giving her a glimpse of a young girl combing her hair. The darkness grew thicker and thicker, smothering what was left of the daylight.

Nita was sitting in an upholstered chair in a high-ceilinged white bedroom. They had carried her here and untied her after the wagons had arrived at Paloma's castle that morning. Francisco had slid his hand beneath her dress, but Paloma had warned him to leave her alone. And they all had.

She'd spent the whole long day alone in this white-walled room. No one had come near her, not even to bring her food. Thick wrought-iron bars masked both the windows. The heavy wooden door was locked from the outside. She had finally had to use the earthenware chamber pot she'd found beneath the big four-poster bed.

There was a single oil lamp on the marble-topped

table next to the bed. But there were no matches, not even a tinderbox. The drawers of the bureau that stood between the two barred windows were empty and smelled faintly of spices and mouse droppings.

The dark-haired girl had, however, been able to fashion a weapon for herself. Just a few moments before, when she was certain no one in the rear courtyard below could make out what she was doing up in her second-floor prison, Nita had taken a pillowcase from the bed and wrapped it around her right hand. Then, carefully, she'd smashed a panel in one of the windows. She'd managed to save most of the sharp jagged pieces that resulted. Selecting the one most closely resembling a knife blade, she wound a strip of the pillowcase around its base. It was primitive and likely to break, but it gave her something to fight with.

She stood now, slipping the improvised weapon into the waist of her skirt. She knew the odds were against her, since Paloma had something like eight or ten men in his castle. She'd seen most of them this morning when they'd arrived. Seen some of the crew unloading the weapons and ammunition and storing it in two of the big outbuildings below.

Well, she'd do the best she could. Fight them off, try to get away when they came for her.

Nita wasn't like the heroines of some of those novels she'd read as a girl. Her motto wasn't death before dishonor. She had no intention of killing herself to keep Paloma and the others from making love to her. She'd been raped before and it had been the worst thing in her life so far. It was something she could never completely get rid of or forget. It was like a disease you carried with you all your life.

Even so, Nita was certain she wanted to stay alive and that if she couldn't fight her way free, then she was tough enough to endure whatever happened. The chance of anyone coming to her aid seemed remote. Chavez would probably try to track her down, but whether he'd ever find his way to Tijeras she didn't know.

And Spear . . .

She found herself shivering at the thought of him. Nita hadn't expected to like Spear at all. She'd imagined he'd be a grim, coarse man, a braggart, probably, not that much different from Paloma.

But he wasn't like that at all. She'd been attracted to him, and if she weren't Nita Torquay and that night at her grandfather's burning ranch hadn't happened. . . .

Too late now.

Always was too late in her life. She was a jinx. Men who tried to look after her, like her grandfather and Spear, ended up dead. And they didn't die easy.

But is Spear dead? she wondered.

They hadn't killed him, she was certain of that. From what Nita had been able to see, sprawled out in the wagon, Paloma and his men had staked him in the desert, leaving him there to die of thirst and hunger or worse. Still she didn't think Spear was that easy to kill.

A key grated in the lock.

Nita moved quickly across the darkness and positioned herself so she'd be behind the door when it opened.

The knob rattled, the door swung inward and a swatch of yellow light fell across the floor from the hallway.

"Did you think we forgot all about you, señorita?"

Nacio came into the room, a tray of food in his left hand and a six-gun in his right.

Nita kicked the door shut, the light from the hall died. She leaped, got an arm around Nacio's neck.

He hollered, dropping the tray.

She brought the jagged sliver of glass up against his unshaven cheek.

As the two struggled, a plate cracked underfoot.

"Drop the gun," she ordered, "or I'll slice your goddamn throat!"

"Puta!" He kicked back at her, but didn't try to swing the gun up and around.

"Drop it!"

Nacio didn't comply.

She slashed the splinter of glass across his face, gouging deep.

He cried out in pain, struggled to aim the gun back over his shoulder.

Nita could see well enough in the darkness now to slash him again. This time she cut into his gun hand. As Nacio whipped around, she kicked him in the groin and gave him a shove back. Nacio dropped the six-gun, doubled over and stumbled to the side, clutching his groin and swearing.

The girl swiftly caught up the gun and brought it down over his head. Nacio fell flat, mashing down the beans and tortillas he'd brought for her dinner.

She hit him again with the butt of the gun for good measure. He groaned, shuddered and passed out.

The door started to open.

She spun, bringing the six-gun up into firing position.

"Hey, you wasn't supposed to hurt her yet," said Francisco, stepping in. "What you—Jesus!"

The light from the hall showed the dark-haired girl facing him with a six-gun and Nacio sprawled on the floor in a mess of blood and chili sauce.

"Come on in," she told him.

He came in, but made the mistake of lunging at her and going for her gun.

Nita fired. The slug tore into Francisco's face, shattered the cheekbone, sliced through his tongue and came exploding out his jaw. He brought both hands up to his face, like a child who had just come upon something he didn't want to look at.

Nita kicked at his leg and that was enough to send him over on top of Nacio.

"Too much noise, damn it," Nita grumbled, going to the doorway. There was no sign of anyone else out there yet.

She took only three steps out of the room before Paloma came at her from where he had been pressed against the corridor wall. One strong hand closed around her gun wrist, the other gave her a brutal slap across the side of her head.

She let go the weapon, went staggering across the hall and smashed into the wall.

He came after her and grabbed her arm while she was flat against the stucco wall. He twisted her arm up behind her, making the girl gasp with pain.

"Come downstairs, señorita," he said cordially. "There is someone here I wish you to meet."

Seamus Tuck ignored the rifles. He flicked his whip and urged the venerable horses to pull the Lightning Water wagon through the open gates at the rear of the castle. They were following a vintner's cart onto the grounds.

"Hey, you crazy *gringo!* Where you going?" shouted one of the large guards as he pointed his rifle up at the driver's seat.

Tuck didn't stop until their wagon was in the

middle of the flagstone courtyard at the rear of Paloma's castle. "Eh?" he inquired, cupping his hand to his ear.

"*Tonto!*" yelled another guard. "We only were letting in Señor Novello and his wine. You got no business coming in here!"

"I know nothing about this," lied the wine seller. He was a small, bent man and it had required twenty pesos for him to allow them to tag along on his weekly delivery of wine. "Their misbegotten wagon fell in behind me when I departed from my humble shop, wherein my wife of many years lies at this moment suffering from a most awful attack of gout."

"We don't want to hear what you don't know, old man." A third guard had emerged from the shadows near the rear entry to the huge house. He ran for the wagon, a six-gun in each hand. "You hombres get off the grounds at once!"

"Gentlemen, gentlemen." Stormfield appeared from the wagon and took a seat next to Tuck. He had the Bioptiscope in his hands. "Allow me to introduce myself. I am no less a personage than Professor William Emerson Pepper, and I can explain exactly why I am here."

"What you doing here?" the two-gunned guard demanded to know.

"Precisely what I am in the process of explaining, my good man," continued Stormfield unruffled. "I am an eminent man of science, and your master—a gentleman known as Señor Paloma—has retained me, and my gifted, European-educated, staff to journey here tonight to demonstrate the many wonders of my inventions."

Back inside the wagon Spear had been making use of the various small peepholes in the canvas. He'd shed the smock and replaced it with a dark shirt. There were four guards to worry about right off—the three who were paying attention to Stormfield, Tuck and the bribed Novello, plus the old gent who opened and shut the gate.

This last fellow was shuffling up across the flagstones now to get a better look at the fracas. A moment later he passed close to the rear of Professor Pepper's wagon. Too close.

Spear reached out, grabbed him and pulled him up inside the wagon. He made sure the gatekeeper passed out before getting any opportunity to speak or otherwise make noise.

After relieving him of his gun, Spear trussed him up, gagged him and left him on the wagon floor. Then he dropped quietly over the tailboard onto the courtyard stones. He stayed in the shadows beside their wagon and moved toward its front.

"Paloma don't want no rain!" one of the guards was insisting.

"I cannot accept that, gentlemen, for only today he professes keen interest in my Bioptiscope."

"Your what?" asked the one with two guns.

Stormfield closed his finger around the trigger of the contraption he was holding across his lap. "This, sir, is the scientific instrument of which I speak."

"What the hell does it do?"

"It does this." Stormfield squeezed the trigger.

An impressive bolt of lightning leaped forth from the tip of the gadget and hit the two-gunned guard square in his fat chest.

He shrieked, jumped back, let both his guns go flying from his slack fingers. Next he fell over backwards into a border of decorative cacti.

Spear moved then. He ran for the closest of the

other guards, who was still gazing open-mouthed at his fallen colleague.

Tuck had come flying from his driver's seat and had fallen on the remaining guard.

After knocking out his man, Spear lent Tuck a hand.

"This will spoil my business," Novello complained as he watched the events unfold.

Straightening up, Spear moved to Stormfield's side. "Supposed to be, according to what we found out in town, a few more men inside," he noted. "Suppose you two stay out here while I make use of the back entrance."

The author consulted his watch. "We'll follow in ten minutes should you not reappear."

"I'll reappear," Spear assured him.

Paloma had shoved her hard, his hand in the small of her slim back, and Nita had gone staggering into the drawing room of the castle. The floor was hardwood, and shocks went up through her arms when she fell and braced herself with the heels of her hands. The room had a high, beamed ceiling and had once been lavishly furnished. These furnishings had not been treated with too much respect of late. There were wine stains on the thick carpet, rips and burns in the satin coverings of the sofas and chairs, tears in the purple drapes and, over the deep, empty stone fireplace, three recently made bullet holes. On the grand piano in the far corner a sooty white rooster was preening.

"Ah, *muy bonita*," commented a dry old voice that sounded like claws scraping across stone.

Nita got to her feet, brushed at her torn skirt and found herself being stared at by a wreck of a man in a white suit which seemed to glow faintly blue against the dark satin of the tufted chair he sat in.

He was either very old or very ill, or possibly both. His flesh was stretched drum-tight across his facial bones, making him look like a mummy that had been processed by some long-forgotten magical technique. He had his gnarled, spotted hands folded over the golden head of a heavy black cane. There were huge gold rings decorating most of his lumpy fingers. They were kept from sliding off by wads of white silk. He couldn't have weighed more than ninety-five pounds.

"So young, so pretty," he rasped, his thin purplish lips pulling back off his yellowed teeth.

"Señorita Torquay," said Paloma, who was leaning with his broad back against the shut door of the room, "allow me to present Señor Cadella, a very important man in Mexico."

She said not a word.

Cadella scratched at his parched chin with the gold head of his cane. "Proceed, if you please, Paloma."

Paloma crossed to the girl. "Señor Cadella operates a very famous establishment," he explained to her. "His clients travel from all parts of Mexico as well as from your own United States. They seek the special and the unusual. Naturally many of them will be interested in a famous lady desperado such as yourself. Señor Cadella is, therefore, most anxious for you to enter into his employ."

Nita said, "I pass."

Cadella said, "Enough talk."

"To be sure." Paloma reached out and pulled down the girl's blouse so that her breasts fell free.

The old panderer made a dusty rattling noise that

might have been a chuckle of appreciation. "Small," he observed, "yet exquisitely formed. Squeeze one, Paloma."

Paloma clamped his strong fingers over the girl's exposed right breast. "Very pleasant to the touch."

"Ah," said Cadella. He lifted one gnarled hand to make a shaky get-on-with-it gesture.

"He would like to see you perform," said Paloma, smiling. "Since you've incapacitated Nacio and, from what I was told by the man I sent to look into it, sent poor Francisco off to a better world, I find myself short-handed. Yet I fear I won't be able to take you unless someone holds you down."

"You'll need a half dozen," she said coldly.

"Or perhaps only one." He reached toward his holstered six-gun.

That was when the door was booted open and Spear came across the threshold. "Party's over, Paloma," he said matter-of-factly.

"Santa Maria!" The outlaw shook his head. "I should have killed you for certain in the desert."

"Yep, that was a tactical error on your part."

"I regret it now. But still I hope . . ." He went for his gun. So did Spear.

Spear was faster. His first slug drove into Paloma's chest. Paloma, still smiling, started tumbling backwards. The smile froze and turned bloody, and he fell over into the great empty fireplace. Still, he made a final try for his gun.

Spear's next bullet went driving in an inch to the left of the first one.

Paloma never felt that one. He'd died a second before it hit.

"Look out!" warned Nita, picking up a brass candlestick and throwing it at Cadella.

He had been able to tug a derringer out of his breast pocket and was aiming it at Spear.

The candlestick whacked Cadella across his face and he slumped and let go of the gun.

The rooster, who'd long since jumped off the piano, went squawking angrily up to the chandelier.

Cadella, making a hollow bellowing sound, slid all the way off his chair and crumpled to the floor.

Nita pulled up her blouse and then held out her hand to Spear. "Thank you."

He holstered his six-gun, crossed and took her hand. "Hope you won't think me forward, miss." He pulled her to him, slipped his arms around her and kissed her firmly on the mouth.

Chapter 32

Steve Janson lit his cigarette and scowled. "Who the hell is this?" he grunted. He got up from beside the dying campfire and peered into the distance. He saw one of his men escorting a rider into the gulch where they were camped.

"Looks like a Mexican," said a scrawny youth who was pouring himself a cup of coffee.

Janson said, "Maybe that son of a bitch Paloma has sent him to tell me why I ain't got my share of the dough yet."

"We ought to get extra, seeing as how Doc got killed."

"To hell with Doc. I just want what's coming to me for helping steal the guns." He took a quick drag on the cigarette as the two riders approached through the early morning.

The Mexican's face was thick with stubble and had a nasty inflamed scab angling down one cheek. He looked pale and ailing. "You know me, Señor Janson," he said while climbing gingerly down off his saddle. "I am Nacio."

"All look the same to me. Did Paloma send you?"

Nacio sighed and wiped at his perspiring forehead. "He's dead."

Janson dropped his cigarette. "What kind of bull is this?" he demanded. "If that guy's trying to get out of splitting the dough—"

"It is true," swore Nacio. "I saw him. He was all shot up. Dead."

"Goddamnit. Who gunned him down?"

"I think it was the Pinkerton. Or maybe it was Nita Torquay."

"Don't you know?" he asked incredulously.

"I was hurt," explained Nacio. "I only got a quick look at Paloma and then I had to get the hell out of there. I know they got the guns back."

"Who, Spear and that bitch?"

"*Sí*, them and a couple of old men. They were in a wagon painted like a circus and they put our guns and ammunition in that and one of Paloma's wagons."

"Why do you keep rubbing your crotch?" asked Janson, annoyed.

"Because that's where I got hurt. That *puta* kicked me."

Janson laughed. "Jesus, what a bunch of jackasses I tied up with! You let some scrawny wench beat you up and Paloma gets knocked off by some Pinkerton agent." He shook his head. "That's what I get for working with goddamn Mexicans."

"You been doing okay," Nacio growled. "You made plenty of money off the cattle before now."

"That's all over. Paloma's dead and I got to set me up a new deal down in Mexico."

"I can do that," Nacio declared.

"You? You trying to be funny or somethin'?"

"Go easy, señor," Nacio warned. "You need

friends in Mexico. You don't want no enemies down there."

"Listen, you ugly bastard—"

"No, you listen, hombre," Nacio cut him short. "I didn't come all this way so you could call me names. I know which way they're taking them guns back. We can stop them and take over again. Then I can set up a deal with the same damn people Paloma was planning to work with. We can still sell that stuff."

Janson rubbed his hand across his pockmarked cheek. "I get it, you want to be the next boss, huh?"

"That's right, señor. And you won't find the guns without me."

Nodding begrudgingly, Janson said, "Okay, we got a deal."

Seamus Tuck dropped his concertina back into the medicine show wagon. "This trip has been most illuminatin'," he said to Stormfield.

The portly author was at the reins of their wagon, which was following Spear's across the plains. The sun had nearly set and there was a purplish tint to everything.

"In what way?" he inquired.

"Well sir, I been listenin' to myself sing," said the grizzled muleskinner, "and I have come to the conclusion that I ain't all that good. I may just give up."

"Nonsense, my boy. You have a great natural talent," Stormfield told him. "You are what I would term a true folk artist."

"No kiddin'?"

"Exactly, and as a folk artist, you don't have to worry about being good or bad. Your only concern is to be true and honest."

Tuck chuckled. "So all the people who tell me I is God-awful, they're wrong?"

"Misguided."

"Doggone." He reached around, retrieved his instrument and set it beside him. "Just goes to show what talkin' to an educated gent such as you can do."

"We're both artists, Seamus, and thus must stick together."

"Right you are," Tuck smiled. He leaned on his knees with his elbows, squinting through the fading light at the other wagon ahead of them. "Seems like in this world the artists bring up the rear and the other gents get to ride with the ladies."

"In his own way Bradley is an artist."

"He sure killed that Paloma nice and artful."

Up in the lead wagon, borrowed from the late Paloma, Nita was at the reins.

Spear, Stetson tilted low, was sitting beside her.

"I wonder," the girl murmured.

"About what?"

"If I met someone like you about a year ago it might have helped me get over . . . well, get over what was bothering me."

"Seems to me you usually meet folks about the time you're ready to meet 'em," he said. "We'd have probably passed each other by on opposite sides of the street a year ago without so much as a look."

She laughed. "Oh, you would've looked, Brad," she assured him. "Especially if I had these clothes on, red skirt and flimsy blouse. And with my hair up and a lot of rouge dabbed on, you'd have crossed that street."

"Nope, because I crave a little subtlety in a woman."

Nita was silent for a moment. "This business is not over yet," she said finally.

"Few loose ends to tie up."

"Funny thing about time. It seems to me I was in that castle for days and yet . . . Brad?"

He'd heard it, too. "Somebody coming." He reached back into the wagon for a rifle.

The hoofbeats of a galloping horse could be heard, drumming across the dying day.

"Whoa!" Nita said to the horses, tugging on the reins. "We might as well stop and face them."

Spear leaned out and saw the rider, coming from behind them fast. "Just one lone gent."

Nita could see the rider now, too. "Only one man I know rides with that sort of swagger." She stood up and waved. "Chavez!"

The mustached man drew up beside their wagon, doffed his sombrero and revealed his hairless head. "I have been following in your wake for untold hours," he said. "Good evening, Señor Spear."

"Evening, Chavez. What brings you this way?"

"Dedication," he replied. "I came looking for you two when you didn't return in a reasonable time."

"We got sidetracked some," Nita imparted.

"I found that out," replied Chavez with a smile. "Tijeras is still talking about the massacre you staged at Paloma's hide-out. And a respected resident named Cadella threatened to write a scathing note to Rutherford B. Hayes, esteemed President of all the United States."

"I'd love to read a copy," said Nita.

"You know it was English Freddie who sold you out to Paloma?" Chavez asked.

"I figured that out about the time Paloma was tossing me in his wagon," said Spear.

"Well, after many tribulations we are reunited once again."

"We're just about ready to halt for the night," said Spear. "You might as well join us for chow, Chavez."

"I'd have to look at the menu first," Chavez replied.

Spear swung his right hand from under his blanket. His holster was draped over his nearby saddle and he reached for it.

"You're not in any danger," said Nita. "At least I don't think so."

He saw her kneeling beside him in the predawn darkness. "Something wrong?"

"Nothing, no."

Spear had bunked down on the far side of their wagon. Stormfield and Tuck were camped off beside theirs and Chavez was sitting up by the campfire out of sight.

"Thought it was your turn to sleep," Spear told the girl.

"Restless." She glanced around. "None of the others can see us here."

"Nope, it's about as private as you can get sleeping out-of-doors with several other folks around."

"My bed up in the wagon was fairly comfortable."

"Glad to hear it."

"I decided I don't want to sleep by myself anymore."

He took her hand and guided her under his blanket with him. He was in his long johns and she was still wearing the skirt and blouse. Spear put one arm around her, stroking her long dark hair with his other hand.

"Just hold me for a while," Nita whispered.

He eased both arms around her, pressing her slim body close to him.

"You won't ever settle down, will you?" she asked.

"Doesn't seem likely," he admitted. "If I was going to do that, I'd have accomplished it by now. Maybe when I'm a codger I'll get a job as a sheriff or a marshal someplace, might even become a house detective in a fancy hotel. Sit around in a big leather armchair, smoke fat cigars and tell tall tales about how I used to chase lady rustlers and all kinds of wild characters."

She smiled. "So if I were to fall in love with you, I couldn't expect much."

"You're a very special woman," he said. "And one of the few who . . . But nope, I won't be lingering in Texas and you can't tag along when I leave."

She nodded, as though his answer was exactly what she had expected. Her silky hair brushed his cheek. "Then we'd just better make love while we can."

"That's always the best way."

Nita very carefully removed her blouse. The nipples on her small breasts were already erect.

Spear cupped one with his hand and petted it. Then he twisted and ran his tongue around the stiff nipple.

The girl began to run her hands along his sides, making soft and pleased sounds.

He took her skirt off for her and the lacy underthings beneath it. Taking his time, treating her gently, he rubbed his palm along her inner thighs and spread her legs. Then he touched the soft lips hidden beneath the triangle of hair below her belly.

Nita sighed, held him tighter, locked her slim warm legs around his probing hand.

Spear worked his finger around and in and out, producing a warm, moist response.

Then he eased her over onto her back. Nita caught hold of his staff and guided it into her.

He went in slowly, with tender care, reassuring her as he pushed deeper. He stayed there, quiet, not stroking for a moment. He kissed her, ran a hand through her hair, nuzzled her neck.

Then he began to drive into her. Slowly he increased the pace, and she thrust forward in time with him. He prolonged the act, building her passion and delight, stretching out their pleasure. Then he found release and a vast satisfaction spread through his body.

A moment later he could feel the spasms of satisfaction that she was experiencing. She hugged him hard, kissing him eagerly, never wanting to let him go. Slowly he subsided and then withdrew, keeping her in his arms.

"I think I'm going to be in love with you anyway," Nita told him, her breath warm on his face. "At least for now."

Chapter 33

When the outlaw who had crawled across the dawn prairie made a grab for him and lunged with his hunting knife, Stormfield rolled away and managed to yell. He'd awakened a few seconds before and he went spinning over the ground, shouting, "We're under attack!"

"Son of a bitch!" said the man with the knife as he made another try.

Then there was a strange, wheezing thunk.

"Good thing I was sleepin' with my squeeze-box handy!"

Untangling himself, Stormfield stood and saw Tuck standing beside the unconscious outlaw with his concertina dangling in his hand.

"Bradley! Chavez! It's a raid!" Stormfield shouted, scrambling up into the wagon.

"*Sí*, I know," replied Chavez, who was wrestling by the dying campfire with the outlaw who'd sneaked in and tried to incapacitate him.

Spear was on his feet beside the other wagon, strapping on his gunbelt over his long johns. "Damn,

I've been doing more business in my underwear lately than I care to."

Nita, naked, was climbing up into their wagon. "Five of 'em coming at us yonder on horseback!" she warned.

The rest of the Janson gang was riding in, galloping hard through the new morning with guns blazing.

Spear joined the girl in the wagon, started getting one of the machine guns ready for action.

A bullet came tearing through the canvas a foot or so over his head.

"Stay low," he advised Nita.

"Can't shoot that way." She came up, bare breasts quivering, and fired at the approaching raiders with a rifle.

One of the outlaws screamed and went flying straight up out of his saddle.

Spear got the machine gun chattering and felled two more. "Think I just shot our old pal Nacio."

"Good."

The remaining two outlaws were having second thoughts. They reined up, turned tail.

"One of those gents looks an awful lot like a wanted poster of Steve Janson I once saw." Spear went leaping from the wagon and ran, still wearing only his underwear, for his horse. There was no time to saddle it. He unhitched it, climbed aboard and kneed it into action.

Janson, on a grey mare, was nearly a quarter of a mile ahead of him.

Spear urged his sorrel on and began to cut down the distance. After five minutes of hard riding he was only a hundred yards from the outlaw.

The fleeing Janson made no attempt to fire back

at Spear, knowing it was next to impossible to hit anyone that way.

Spear wasn't at all sure he could wing Janson either. So he shot his horse, which was a much larger target.

The animal collapsed and threw Janson free of the saddle. When the groggy outlaw got to his knees, Spear was standing over him with his six-gun aimed at his head.

"You ain't even got any clothes on," noticed Janson.

"This isn't a formal occasion," said Spear, grinning. "You and me are just going to have a little talk."

Molly Cartland quietly crossed the dark bedroom.

Her husband awoke with a start. "I didn't mean to— Oh, it's you, Molly," he realized, sitting up. "Scared me some."

She lit the lamp on his bedside table. "How are you feeling?"

"Well, I'm a little better, but still in no shape to do any riding."

"Sam, we're leaving," she told him quietly.

He looked beyond her, toward the door. "Right now?"

"I've made all the arrangements," Molly confided. "You'll go out that window at exactly midnight and I'll be there waiting. I'll take you where two horses are tied up."

"Tonight?"

"It has to be tonight, Sam. We can't wait any longer."

"Sure, I can see that," he said, running his tongue over his upper lip. "Thing is, I really don't think I'm in good enough shape yet to ride."

She took hold of his hand, held it tight, as though she were trying to transfer some of her own strength to him. "You can do it."

"I don't even have any clothes. How can I get out of here with no clothes?"

"I'll bring you clothes later on, when the man on the door is a little drowsier," she told him. "I'll smuggle them in under my cloak."

"A gun," he mentioned. "I ought to have a gun, too, Molly."

"I only have mine. I couldn't arrange for another one."

"They might come after us and we'd have to shoot our way—"

"Nobody's coming after us," she soothed. "By the time they notice you aren't in your bed, we'll be long gone."

"You could give me your gun when you bring the clothes," he suggested.

"No, I'm going to keep it."

"But Molly, you act like you don't even trust me to take care of you."

"Listen to me, Sam. At exactly midnight I'll be outside your window. You get dressed and climb out. Then—"

"I know, you already told me."

"You're more than strong enough for this."

Cartland nodded absently. "How'd you get us horses?"

"I arranged it."

"How?"

"Somebody's doing us a favor, that's all. There's nothing to worry about."

"Us? Or just you? Who is he and why is he doing this favor?"

"Sam, I have to go now."

"Wait." He took hold of her wrist. "What did you have to do to get those horses? Did you and some man—"

"He's simply doing me a favor," she said evenly. "I didn't sleep with anyone to get this favor, if that's what you mean."

"I wouldn't blame you if you did." Letting go of her, he brought both hands up to his face and began crying. "I'm no damn good to you anymore, in bed or out. There's no reason why you should even stay with me."

"For God's sake, Sam, stop blubbering!" Molly turned her back on him. "We have to get out of here tonight and you can't be acting like a baby. I'll see you in an hour or so with the clothes."

He let her take three steps in the direction of the door. "Molly?"

"What?" She stopped, faced him.

His face was streaked with tears. "It's no use, you know," he said, shaking his head sadly. "I can't go with you tonight."

"You can," she maintained, moving back to his bedside. "You aren't sick anymore!"

"It's not because I'm sick," Cartland explained. "It's because I'm afraid."

Chapter 34

Spear came in with the sunrise. He walked right on into Big Jim's private bordello by way of the front door, unannounced and uninvited.

Stopping in the ornate hallway, he brushed at the trail dust on his boots. Then he cupped his hands to call out, "Big Jim Phillips! Time to rise and shine!"

About ten seconds later a girl squealed behind one of the closed bedroom doors.

Spear whacked the wall with his fist. "Hey, Big Jim! We've got business!"

The door to Inga's room opened. The big blonde peered out, sleepy-eyed, her hair unkempt, one ample breast about to escape from her satin wrapper. "Vhat you vant?"

"Big Jim," replied Spear, grinning.

"Vhy?"

"Business."

"It could vait."

"Nope, this is important. Tell him we've caught the rustlers. Killed might be a better word in some cases."

There was a rumbling from within the bedroom. Then Big Jim bellowed, "Tell the son of a bitch to come in!"

"Big Yim says you—"

"I heard." Spear brushed by her and entered the dim bedroom.

"Inga, go brew some coffee," called out the rancher. "Don't bring it in, though, till I holler for you." He was propped up in bed, covers up nearly to his chin, hands not showing. He wore a candy-striped nightshirt and a nightcap to match. The tassel hung close to his prominent nose. "This better be goddamn important, Spear. Because even a Pinkerton can't just come barging into my personal bedroom."

"It's important, Big Jim." He grabbed up a gilded chair, dropped it down a few feet from the rumpled bed and straddled it. "Mighty important."

"Well then, go ahead," said the rancher. "Where the hell you been anyway?"

"Here and there," Spear answered. "By the way, you'll be happy to know we got the guns back. They're coming here in wagons. I rode on ahead."

"Say now, that is good news," said Big Jim with a chuckle. "Yep, that'll make Ramsey happy and keep him from chewing my rump about 'em. Did that Mexican have the stuff?"

Spear nodded. "Yep."

"I imagine he put up a fight."

"Not much of one. We sort of took him by surprise."

"Where is he now?"

"Hard to tell. He's dead, but beyond that your guess is as good as mine."

"This is all very gratifying, Spear. That son of a bitch has been making off with my cattle for months."

"That's not all the good news I have for you."

"Oh?"

Grinning, Spear pushed up the brim of his Stetson with his thumb. "We also managed to put most of the Steve Janson gang out of commission."

The rancher blinked. "Is that a fact? Kill most of 'em, did you?"

"A few," confirmed Spear. "But I managed to take Janson alive."

"Really?"

"Yep. And after a bit of persuading, he decided to confess everything." Spear tapped his shirt pocket. "Got the document, a signed confession, right here. Plan to turn it and Janson over to the marshal in Tascosa."

"You're smart, Spear," said Big Jim. "But not quite smart enough." He pulled his right hand out from under the covers. There was a .44 in it.

"Figuring to kill me?"

"You got it."

"Be sort of embarrassing to explain."

"Not at all." He had the gun leveled at Spear. "See, it's not going to be me that kills you. I mean, as far as that idiot marshal ever knows. What's going to happen is this. Sam Cartland is going to go a little goofy and gun you down with a gun he managed to steal from me somehow. He's going to be so riled about you rounding up the Janson gang that he's going to kill you dead. Well sir, I'm not going to be able to stop the loco bastard in time. I'll shoot him down afterwards, but you'll be dead by then. Great shame."

"Might work," admitted Spear. "And that'd keep most folks from ever learning your being behind all the cattle rustling and gunrunning in these parts. That you and Janson and Paloma were partners and that you bilked the Horesham crowd out of millions of bucks."

"It'll work, don't fret."

"Don't think so," Spear disagreed. "First off, Stormfield and Tuck still have Janson, and they heard him confessing before he got around to writing it all down."

"Those old geezers can have all sorts of accidents before they ever get to Tascosa."

"Possibly," said Spear. "The second snag, though, is going to be harder to overcome."

"What's that?"

"Me," said Nita Torquay from the open bedroom window just behind him.

The big rancher paled. "Who's that?"

Deftly, the dark-haired girl climbed over the sill and into the room. She held a six-gun and stopped a few feet from the bed. "You haven't seen me for a couple of years, Big Jim," she told him. "Not since the night you burned down my grandfather's ranch and killed him."

"I wasn't anywhere near—"

"You kept your bandanna up over your damn face," she fumed, gun aimed directly at him. "I knew it was you."

"I never touched you."

"No. But you watched while your five hired hands raped me!"

"There's no reason to—"

"Real careful now," she instructed him, "put the gun down." Her gun was pointed straight at him. His was pointed at Spear.

"I can still shoot Spear," Big Jim snickered.

Nita shook her head. "I've been waiting for nearly

two years for an opportunity to kill you. If you don't shed that gun in the next ten seconds I'm going to blast you to glory."

"Jesus, Anita, you don't have to go—"

"The gun!"

He inhaled, then dropped the weapon on the quilt.

Spear reached over and picked the gun up. "Much obliged."

The beaten rancher was eyeing the girl. "I put it down, for Christ's sake."

She still held her gun pointed at his chest. Her face was filled with anger.

"Nita," said Spear. "We've got enough on him to get him hanged legal."

"He just watched and laughed," she responded in a flat voice. "Told them new things to try when they ran out of ways to hurt me."

"It wasn't really you my quarrel was with," insisted Big Jim. "Your grandfather was—"

"You killed him, damned near killed me, too."

Spear left his chair and moved to her side. "All over now."

The girl hesitated. After a few seconds she lowered her gun. "You're right. It is."

Ramsey shifted in his saddle. "You've done a smashing job, old chap," he told Spear.

The two men were riding through the afternoon, checking out the miles of barbed wire that fenced in the Circle BJ.

"Things worked out pretty well," said Spear.

The young Englishman nodded. "We've cleaned up rustling hereabouts once and for all."

"There'll be other rustlers."

"In time, yes," admitted Ramsey. "For now,

though, I'm wagering the blokes'll stay damn well clear of us. The fate of Steve Janson will be a dread warning to them."

"Along with the fate of Big Jim Phillips," added Spear.

"I imagine you think me somewhat of a dupe," Ramsey sighed, glancing up into the clear sky. "Being taken in by Big Jim for a time."

"Got to admit he was a hospitable cuss."

Ramsey blushed. "I don't want you getting the wrong impression of me, old man. I mean to say, I've known many a woman in my time."

"What there's been of it."

"Eh? Oh, come now. I'm not exactly a beardless youth," protested Ramsey. "Out in India, Spear, I had some experiences with . . . well, the young ladies here at the Circle BJ are most assuredly not the first such I've . . . er . . . encountered."

"What do you figure on doing now?"

Ramsey cleared his throat. "You won't have to escort me from here on. Nor, from what I gathered from Marshal Beaven when I visited him yesterday, will you be needed at either the trial of Janson or of Big Jim."

"Then I'll be heading out in a day or so," he replied. "You're aiming to stay on for a spell?"

"As a matter of fact, old man, I've written to my Horesham colleagues," he said, smiling, "informing them, don't you know, that I shall be remaining in Texas for a while."

"How long?"

"Well, I dare say it might be indefinitely. I have in mind trying my hand at managing the blooming Circle BJ. With Big Jim headed for prison or the scaffold, there's no one else to take things in hand."

"You're going to need a lot of new men," Spear pointed out. "Since a few of the present hands were, if only passively, tied in with the rustling."

"I am fully aware of that. I've hired Tom Curry, an honest and upright lad, to be my new foreman. He's already at work enlisting new men and dismissing the bad apples."

"It's a big spread," observed Spear as they rode across the vast grasslands.

"India's a big country, yet I managed quite well there."

"Well, since Big Jim didn't show any profit at all, you ought to be able to do better than him right off."

"Ah, I'm glad you reminded me of that," said Ramsey, brightening. "I've retrieved nearly a million dollars."

"Really?"

"Yes, it seems Big Jim had it stashed away in a hidden safe, to fall back on in an emergency."

"Safe was hidden in his private whorehouse maybe?"

"It was, yes." Ramsey nodded his blond head. "Inga was most helpful in pointing it out to me. I have something of a knack for cracking safes of this sort and it was no trouble."

"Where's the rest of the money?"

"Spent, scattered to the winds," he answered. "I do believe, when the Horesham Cattle Estates, Ltd. receives the bank draft for $750,000 I sent them, they'll be more than willing to allow me to continue in command here. I'm retaining $250,000 for operating expenses."

Spear grinned. "Such as Inga and her associates?"

"Well, dash it all, Spear, one can't simply throw those poor creatures out into the world. I do hope, however, you won't mention to anyone that I am operating—"

"A house of ill repute?"

"Good heavens, no! I will simply allow them to continue to reside in that eyesore of a house," explained the young Englishman. "But they shan't be obliged to . . . er . . . practice their trade."

"Even with you?"

"See here, Spear, there are certain aspects of one's private life which one wishes to keep private."

"Looks like you'll be having an interesting time of it, all things considered," Spear said. "What have you decided about Sam Cartland?"

"Don't think me sentimental, but I'd quite made up my mind to let the chap go free. He seems a bit of a weak sister, but Molly apparently is deuced fond of him and it would serve no useful purpose to prosecute him."

"So that's what you're going to do?"

"It was, except your chum Stormfield was also in a generous mood," answered Ramsey. "He'd already informed the marshal that Cartland was actually working for him, don't you know, as an undercover agent. Quite impressed Beaven by flashing his Secret Service credentials. A complete fabrication, of course, yet it gets Cartland off the hook."

"Fiction is Thomas' strong suit."

Ramsey was frowning thoughtfully. "I say, Spear, what do you think of their chances, Molly and that husband of hers? I mean to say, is she being foolish to stick with him?"

"Probably."

"She says he's learned his lesson, won't gamble ever again and won't fall in with rogues." He shook his head. "One would like to hope that good things lie in store for them both."

"Either Cartland'll change or he won't," said Spear. "I'm inclined to bet he won't."

They rode on for a few moments before Ramsey spoke again. "I thought originally, old man, that you and Molly didn't hit it off. Yet, from certain hints she's dropped in recent conversations, I have the notion such may not be the case. What exactly is the nature of your relationship?"

"We're just good friends," answered Spear.

Chapter 35

The grass had grown up high around the blackened ruins of the ranch house. Nita Torquay stood in what had once been the front yard, dressed in trousers and a checkered shirt, her long dark hair held back with a scarlet ribbon. "We still have a chimney," she noted.

Spear took a look toward the red brick chimney which had survived the raid two years ago. "All you got to do now is build a new house around it."

Nita hugged herself, smiling. "Don't suppose you'd care to help out on that?"

"Nope, I'm leaving first thing tomorrow," he replied. "Thomas and I both are going to Dodge City."

"I didn't really think you'd be interested," Nita said, "but thought I'd ask. I do, anyway, appreciate your getting Peter Ramsey to turn this place back to me."

"Was fairly sure you wanted it, and it was the right thing for Ramsey to do," he said. "He's got considerable cash, in case you need anything to get started up on."

"He already gave me something, when he returned the deed to my grandfather's land." She walked to where the front porch had once been. "He explained this was a reward for my help in fetching back the guns from Mexico. So I'm in pretty good shape."

"Those damn guns," Spear grumbled. "He's got 'em storehoused in the Circle BJ barn again. Some other owlhoot's going to get the notion to steal 'em before long."

She kicked at a clump of weeds. "Chavez and some of my men are going to help out, be the hands here, I mean. Chavez will be foreman."

"He's a good man."

"Oh, and I hired Seamus Tuck."

Spear laughed. "To do what?"

"Well, besides playing the concertina and singing, he's going to be my cook."

"Didn't know he could rustle grub."

"I'm not at all sure he can, but he claims to be a crackerjack cook," the girl said. "And besides, I like him."

Spear nodded toward a tent that sat just beyond the ruins of the house. "You camping here?"

"We figure to get going on building the new house by next week. Chavez pitched that and he and the boys are bunking on the ground for now."

"I wish you well, Nita."

"Oh, hell!" She ran up to him and threw her arms around him. "I've been trying to be calm and ladylike, but . . . I'm going to miss you like the devil, Brad."

"I know, Nita." He stroked her hair. "Thing is, I'm just not the ranching sort, no use pretending I am."

"No use pretending." She was crying against his chest. "You know, everything has been going so well since you came along that I—"

"Whoa, now. Going well?" He pushed her out to arm's length, his hands on her slim shoulders. "Since I came along you got yourself kidnapped, hauled to hell and gone in a wagon, and mighty near sold to a Mexican whorehouse! Don't see how you can call that going well."

"But it was fun," she insisted. "Especially when you were around."

"Matter of fact," he agreed, "it sort of was."

"We're both really . . ."

Hoofbeats sounded in the distance. Chavez could be seen riding across the prairie, his broad smile discernible to Nita and Spear.

Nita moved close to Spear again, kissed him once very slowly and deliberately. "Until we meet again," she murmured.

Stormfield ceased contemplating the plains rolling by beyond the train window. "Buffalo remains," he sighed. "What an enormous *momento mori* a buffalo skull makes."

Spear occupied the aisle seat next to him. He had his Stetson tilted low and was apparently slumbering.

Returning his vagrant attention to the open notebook upon his broad lap, the portly author put pencil to paper, writing:

> . . . the mighty orb of the sun sank below the horizon, bathing the amber fields of waving grass in an unearthly golden hue. Sweetwater Sid, sometimes referred to as none other than the Masked Texas Avenger, stood beside his faithful milk-white steed, his orbs drinking in the refined beauty of the lovely young gentlewoman he had but scant

moments before rescued and extricated from the vile clutches of the unsavory Johnson Brothers.

"Ah, fair maid," he intoned in full manly tones, "yon sinking ball of fire tints your glorious tresses a most wondrous shade of gold. Thus making your beauty all the more ravishing."

"Your words, brave Sweetwater Sid, quite touch my heart," she most graciously replied. "Like the fabled arrows of swift Cupid's bow."

He doffed his milk-white headgear and executed a graceful bow. "I must ride on now, dear lady," he declared. "For new deeds call, other rights must be wronged, other maidens set free. Should you ever again need a protector, you have but to call for Sweetwater Sid, also known as the Masked Texas Avenger, and he will rush to your fair side like Mercury himself."

"Before you go, my stalwart champion," the beautiful lass requested demurely, "would you grant me one favor?"

"Whatever boon you desire, my fair one, shall be thine," the dashing cowboy promised from the heart.

"I would like, therefore, to see the face that lies beneath your famous crimson mask. For I know full well you must needs resemble a god or—"

"Nay, nay, no." He put a hand in front of his masked visage to thwart her attempts to unveil him. "None may ever view my countenance, because . . ."

Stormfield sat back, rubbing the tail of his pencil across one chubby cheek. "Why the devil not?"

"Finished?" asked Spear, taking off his hat and sitting up.

"I've reached an impasse," the author told him. "I can't seem to recall just exactly why Sweetwater Sid won't let anyone see under his blessed mask."

"A scar?"

"No, I used that with the Two Gun Avenger," said his friend. "And Dakota Dan had the Lazy W brand emblazoned on his forehead."

"He's really a famous person and wants to do his good deeds anonymously," suggested Spear.

"Used that gimmick in *The Phantom Vice President; or, The Masked Politician of the Wild West.*"

"Could be the gent is just shy."

"Ah, I remember at last. He has a tiny birthmark over his left eye, which links him to a disgraced old European family." Stormfield scribbled a few more lines. "How's this final sentence sound to you, Bradley, my boy? 'He rode toward the setting sun and out of her young life forever.'"

"Brings tears to the eyes."

Stormfield shut the notebook, put away his pencil. "Well, be that as it may, the line finishes off another opus."

"When's your next novel due?"

"Ah, not for a full three weeks." Stormfield gazed again out the window of their rattling, chuffing train. "I can pen it at my leisure."

"I admire your energy, Thomas."

"I am but a weary old hack."

"A weary old hack and a Secret Service agent. That's an accomplishment."

"Mayhap," he said. "At any rate, I am glad you and I had yet another opportunity to work together, and that you're journeying eastward on the same train." He fluffed his sideburns. "I don't believe you've yet mentioned why you are returning to the East Coast of our great and wondrous land."

"I haven't?"

"New assignment for the Pinkerton Agency, perhaps?"

"Nope, I have a few weeks off," answered Spear. "Decided to visit Boston."

"A shrine of culture. 'Twill do you good."

"There's a young lady who lives there. I want to visit her, I decided."

"Would this be the young lady we met a few months back in the fabled Black Hills?"

"It would," said Spear. "She's somewhat special."

" 'Twas my impression that Nita Torquay struck you as being special as well."

"She did," admitted Spear, "but she's got a lot of things to do right now, rebuilding her ranch and starting a new sort of life. In a year or two I'll maybe drop in on her."

"By then friend Chavez may have supplanted you."

Spear shrugged. "Even so, I . . . Yes?"

The conductor had halted beside him in the swaying aisle. He was a small man and his dark uniform was three—possibly four—sizes too large. "Mr. Spear, I presume?"

"Yep."

The conductor smiled and winked, reaching into

his mammoth coat. "I have been entrusted with a message for you, sir," he explained. "Now where the dickens did I . . . oh, yes, here she is." After pausing to sniff at it, he handed over a pale blue envelope. "Haven't smelled anything that pretty since my youth."

"Thank you for delivering it."

"Oh, to be sure." He moved away, swaying in time with the train.

Opening the envelope, Spear extracted the note that was inside.

"This can't be business, scented thusly?" queried Stormfield.

"Nope, it isn't." Spear read the note.

> Brad dearest,
>
> I was absolutely overjoyed when I learned you were aboard the same train as I. I had the most wretched of times on my singing tour and have curtailed it drastically. I am now en route back to New York City, which is at least partially civilized. Would you think me too awfully forward if I were to invite you to visit me in my private car? You'll find it attached to the rear of this very train.
>
> Eagerly yours, Nelly Quill

Folding up the note, Spear returned it to its scented envelope and tucked it into his pocket. "Thomas, you'll have to excuse me."

"Oh, so?"

"Turns out I have a social engagement." He stood up and stretched.

"Shall I expect you at dinner this evening?"

Spear shook his head. "Nope, but you might figure on breakfast," he said. "A late breakfast."

He adjusted his hat and went strolling off toward the rear of the train.

MISSED ANY?

Look for these best-selling titles in the
popular AGENT BRAD SPEAR SERIES

Order NOW by mail!

#1
The Cheyenne Payoff
by Chet Cunningham

Sent to Cheyenne to look for a missing Pinkerton agent, Brad
Spear encounters the enticing dance hall singer Lily and the
beautiful Lady Jane. Trouble starts the moment Spear steps
off the train, when two men try to bushwhack the agent—but
only one lives to tell the story. A mysterious saloon fire, an
extortion ring and the defrocked priest Pierre Dufond provide
the clues that lead Brad Spear on the trail of the missing
agent.

#2
The Silver Mistress
by Chet Cunningham

The setting is Silver City, Nevada, in the heart of the precious
Comstock Lode, during the era when men fought and died for
the wealth of silver that came from the depths of the mines.
When Brad Spear begins to investigate a scandal in Land
Grant certificates, a chance encounter with the mysterious
"Silver Mistress" helps him uncover a diabolical scheme. A
man-hating woman named Bunny uses poison to kill her
prey, and delights in their suffering, while a ruthless doctor
threatens her with the horrors of Fetterman's Asylum. Brad
Spear fights with fists, guns and dynamite to rescue a town
and save a mine from destruction.

#3
The Tucson Temptress
by Chet Cunningham

Beautiful and independent, the jewel thief Louisa Wentworth
is looking for three million dollars' worth of diamonds when

she comes to Tucson—but she gives up her secret in the arms of Brad Spear. Leaders of Tucson plan to massacre an entire Indian village to win the diamonds. Brad Spear and a fierce Indian girl make a courageous attempt to save the village, and a mad ride through the sagebrush ends in an astounding discovery for the agent.

#4

The Frisco Lady

by Chad Calhoun

Plunging into the sinister, crime-ridden world of San Francisco, Brad Spear discovers the vicious practices of the Chinese gangs and learns the truth about the beautiful, mysterious woman who comes to his aid. A ruthless ship's captain, a wealthy heiress and a hated Chinese gang leader all try to prevent Brad Spear from discovering their greedy hold on illicit opium traffic. But the irresistible Annabelle Rigg lures the Pinkerton agent to her hideaway and unwittingly gives away the clue to a hideous crime, unveiling the secret of her own bizarre past.